HARD ROW

MARGARET MARON

GRAND CENTRAL PUBLISHING

NEW YORK BOSTON

This book is a work of fiction. Names, characters, places, and incidents are the product of the author's imagination or are used fictitiously. Any resemblance to actual events, locales, or persons, living or dead, is coincidental.

All chapter epigraphs are from *Profitable Farming in the Southern States* by J.W. Fitz, "Assisted by a Large Corps of Prominent and Successful Agricultural Writers," 1890. Franklin Publishing Company, Richmond, Virginia.

Grand Central Publishing
Hachette Book Group USA
237 Park Avenue
New York, NY 10017
Visit our Web site at www.HachetteBookGroupUSA.com

Grand Central Publishing is a division of Hachette Book Group USA, Inc. The Grand Central Publishing name and logo is a trademark of Hachette Book Group USA, Inc.

Printed in the United States of America

Original published in hardcover by Hachette Book Group USA
First Mass Market Edition: August 2008

10 9 8 7 6 5 4 3 2 1

ACKNOWLEDGMENTS

Special thanks to Jay Stephenson, my friend and neighbor, for sharing his practical knowledge and farming expertise; to Margaret Ruley for insights into stepmothering; and to my cousin Judy Johnson for giving me tuberoses. As always, I am indebted to District Court Judges Shelly S. Holt and Rebecca W. Blackmore, of the 5th Judicial District Court (New Hanover and Pender Counties, North Carolina), and Special Superior Court Judge John Smith, who keep a watching brief on Deborah's grasp of the law.

That most farmers have had "a hard row to hoe" during the last few years is a fact which admits of no argument.

The famous poets who never plowed a furrow in their lives go into raptures over rural life.

—*Profitable Farming in the Southern States,* 1890

HARD ROW

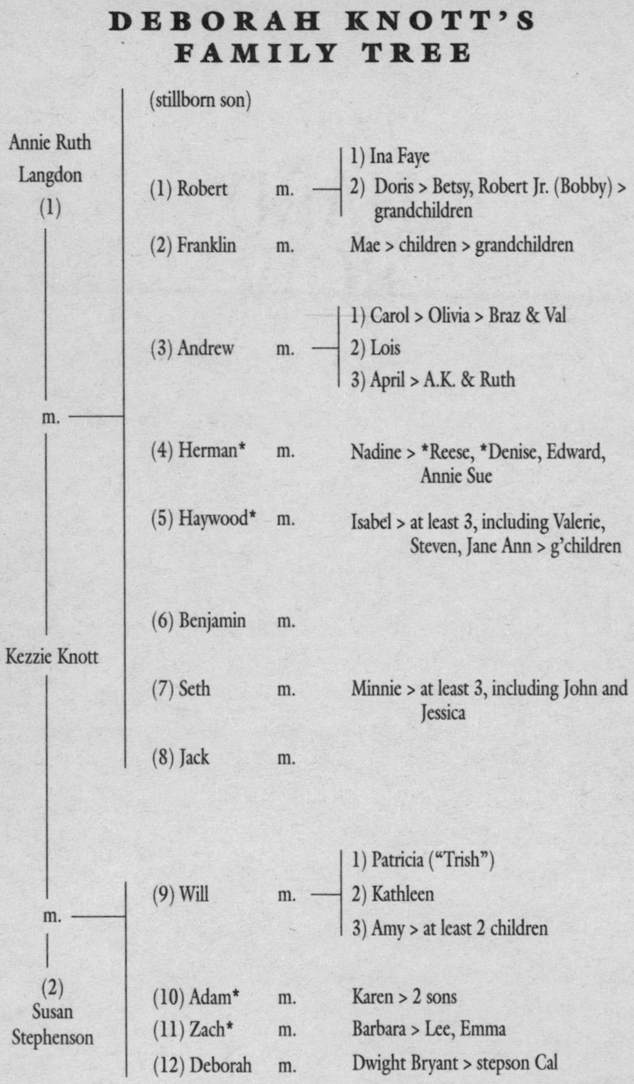
DEBORAH KNOTT'S FAMILY TREE
Annie Ruth Langdon (1)
m.
Kezzie Knott
m.
(2) Susan Stephenson
(stillborn son)
(1) Robert m. 1) Ina Faye
2) Doris > Betsy, Robert Jr. (Bobby) > grandchildren
(2) Franklin m. Mae > children > grandchildren
(3) Andrew m. 1) Carol > Olivia > Braz & Val
2) Lois
3) April > A.K. & Ruth
(4) Herman* m. Nadine > *Reese, *Denise, Edward, Annie Sue
(5) Haywood* m. Isabel > at least 3, including Valerie, Steven, Jane Ann > g'children
(6) Benjamin m.
(7) Seth m. Minnie > at least 3, including John and Jessica
(8) Jack m.
(9) Will m. 1) Patricia ("Trish")
2) Kathleen
3) Amy > at least 2 children
(10) Adam* m. Karen > 2 sons
(11) Zach* m. Barbara > Lee, Emma
(12) Deborah m. Dwight Bryant > stepson Cal
*Twins

JANUARY

El Toro Negro sits next to an abandoned tobacco warehouse a few feet inside the Dobbs city limits. Back when the club catered to the country-western crowd, a mechanical bull used to be one of the attractions; but after a disgruntled customer took a sledgehammer to its motor, the bull was left behind when the club changed hands. Now it stands atop the flat roof and someone with more verve than talent has painted a picture of it on the windowless front wall. As visibly masculine as his three-dimensional counterpart overhead, the painted bull is additionally endowed with long sharp horns. He seems to snort and paw at hot desert sands although it is a frigid night and more than a thousand miles north of the border. Two weeks into January, yet a white plastic banner that reads *FELIZ NAVIDAD Y PRÓSPERO AÑO NUEVO* still hangs over the entrance. A chill wind sweeps across the gravel parking lot and sends beer cups and empty cigarette packs scudding like tumbleweeds until they catch in the bushes that line the sidewalk.

Every Saturday night, the parking lot is jammed with work vehicles of all descriptions and tonight is no exception. Pickup trucks with extended crew cabs predominate. Pulled up close to the club's side entrance is a refurbished schoolbus, its windows and body both painted a dark purple that looks black under the lone security light. A rainbow of racing stripes surrounds the elaborate lettering of the band's name. Los Cuatro Reyes del Hidalgo are playing here tonight and whenever the door opens, live music with a strong Tejano beat swirls out on gusts of warm air.

Like most of the Latinos clustered beneath the colored lights around the doorway, the muscular Anglo who passes them is without a woman on his arm. He has clearly been drinking and the bouncers at the door glance at each other, silently conferring if they should let him in; but he has already handed over his fifteen-dollar cover charge. They sweep him thoroughly with their metal detector and make him empty his pockets when the wand beeps for a handful of coins, then stamp the back of his hand and let him pass.

Inside, he heads straight to the far end of the long bar that stretches down the whole length of one wall. Even though dark faces beneath wide cowboy hats line the bar three and four deep, they move aside to let him prop a foot on the wooden rail and order a Corona. In addition to the hats, most of the other men are wearing tooled cowboy boots, fleece-lined jackets, and belt buckles as big as tamales. The Anglo is tall enough to see over the hats and when his beer comes, he takes a deep swig and scans the further room.

On a low stage at the back, the Hidalgo Kings are belting it out on keyboard, drum, and guitars to an enthusiastic audience. Colored lights play across the dancers as their bodies keep time to the pulsating rhythm. Between songs, the click of balls can be heard from the pool tables in a side room.

The bouncers keep an eye on the Anglo, but the sprawling club is crowded, men outnumber women at least four to one, and tempers can flare with little provocation. A Colombian accuses a Salvadoran of taking his drink when his back was turned and the bouncers move in to break it up.

At the bar, the Anglo orders another *cerveza*, and after a while, the bouncers relax their surveillance of him.

Shortly before midnight, he leaves his third beer on the counter and moves through the crowd toward the restroom just as a woman bundled in a bulky jacket and knitted hat urgently approaches a knot of men still nursing their beers.

"*¿Dónde está Ernesto?*" she asks.

With a tilt of his head, one of the men gestures toward one of the side rooms and the woman hurries over to the pool table. "*¡Ernesto! ¡Date prisa!*" she says to the man who looks up when she speaks. "*Es María. Ya viene el bebe.*"

He immediately throws down his cue and follows her through the crowd. His friends call after him, "*¡Felicitaciones, amigo!*"

Inside the bathroom at the far end of the club, the big Anglo quickly grabs a man waiting his turn at a urinal.

The man is smaller and shorter, and before he can defend himself, his white hat goes flying and the Anglo has his bolo tie in a stranglehold with his left hand while his right fist delivers a punishing blow to the victim's chin.

A second blow opens a gash over his eye. Gasping for breath as his bolo tightens around his neck, the Latino fumbles frantically for a beer bottle lying atop others in the trash bin and in one sweeping motion smashes the end against the sink.

Several men reach to pull the two apart. Others open the door and cry out to the bouncers as the bottle gleams in the dull light.

Blood suddenly spurts across the white cowboy hat now trampled beneath their feet and the big Anglo crashes to the floor, writhing in pain.

CHAPTER 1

If a man goes at his work with his fists he is not so successful as if he goes at it with his head.

—Profitable Farming in the Southern States, 1890

Deborah Knott
Friday, February 24

A cold February morning and the first thing on my calendar was the State of North Carolina versus James Braswell and Hector Macedo.

Misdemeanor assault inflicting serious bodily injury.

I vaguely remembered doing first appearances on them both two or three weeks earlier although I would have heard only enough facts to set an appropriate bond and appoint attorneys if they couldn't afford their own. According to the papers now before me, Braswell was a lineman for the local power company and could not only afford an attorney, but had also made bail immediately. His co-defendant, here on a legal visa, had needed an appointed lawyer and he had sat in the Colleton County jail for eleven days till someone went his bail. Each was charged with assaulting the other, and while it might have been better to try them separately, Doug Woodall's office had decided to join the two cases and prosecute them together since the charges rose out of the same brawl. Despite a broken bottle, our DA had not gone for the more serious charge of felony assault because keeping them both misdemeanors would save his office time and the county money, something he was more conscious of now that he'd decided to run for governor.

Neither attorney had objected even though it meant they had to put themselves between the two men scowling at each other from opposite ends of the defendants' table.

Braswell's left hand and wrist had been bandaged last month. Today, a scabby red line ran diagonally across the back of his hand and continued down along the outer edge of his wrist till it disappeared under the cuff of his jacket. The stitches had been removed, but the puncture marks on either side were still visible. I'm no doctor, but it looked as if the jagged glass had barely missed the veins on the underside of Braswell's wrist.

The cut over Macedo's right eye was mostly hidden by his thick dark eyebrow.

I listened as Julie Walsh finished reading the charges. Doug's newest ADA was a recent graduate of Campbell University's law school over in Buies Creek. Small-boned, with light brown hair and blue-green eyes, she dressed like the perfectly conservative product of a conservative school except that a delicate tracery of tattooed flowers circled one thin white wrist and was almost unnoticeable beneath the leather band of her watch. Rumor said there was a Japanese symbol for trust at the nape of her neck but because she favored turtleneck sweaters and wore her long hair down, I couldn't swear to that.

"How do you plead?" I asked the defendants.

"Not guilty," said Braswell.

"Guilty with extenuating circumstances," said Macedo through his attorney.

While Walsh laid out the State's case, I thought about the club where the incident took place.

El Toro Negro. The name brought back a rush of mental images. I had been there twice myself. Last spring, back when I still thought of Sheriff Bo Poole's chief deputy as a sort of twelfth brother and a handy escort if both of us were at loose ends, a couple of court interpreters had invited me to a Cinco de Mayo fiesta at the club. My latest romance had gone sour the month before so I'd asked Dwight if he wanted to join us.

"Yeah, wouldn't hurt for me to take a look at that place," he'd said. "Maybe keep you out of trouble while I'm at it."

Knowing that he likes to dance just as much as I do, I didn't rise to the bait.

The club was so jammed that the party had spilled out into the cordoned-off parking lot. It felt as if every Hispanic in Colleton County had turned out. I hadn't realized till then just how many there were—all those mostly ignored people who had filtered in around the fringes of our lives. Normally, they wear faded shirts and mud-stained jeans while working long hours in our fields or on construction jobs. That night they sported big white cowboy hats with silver conchos and shiny belt buckles. The women who stake our tomatoes or pick up our sweet potatoes alongside their men in the fields or who wear the drab uniforms of fast-food chains as they wipe down tables or take our orders? They came in colorful swirling skirts and white scoop-neck blouses bright with embroidery.

We danced to the infectious music, drank Mexican beer from longnecked bottles, danced some more, then stuffed ourselves at the fast-food *taquerías* that lined the parking lot. I bought piñatas for an upcoming family birthday party, and Dwight bought a hammered silver belt buckle for his young son.

It was such a festive, fun evening that he and I went back again after we were engaged. The club was crowded and the music was okay, but it felt like ten men for every woman and when they began to hit on me, I had to get Dwight out of there before he arrested somebody.

So I could picture the club's interior as Walsh called her first witness to the stand.

"*¿Habla inglés?*" she asked.

Despite his prompt *Sí,* Macedo's attorney asked that I allow an interpreter because his own client's English was shaky.

I agreed and Elena Smith took a seat directly behind Macedo, where she kept up a low-pitched, steady obligato to all that was said.

"State your name and address."

The middle-aged witness twisted a billed cap in his callused hands as he gave his name and an address on the outskirts of Cotton Grove. His nails were as ragged and stained as his jeans. In English that was adequate, if heavily accented, he described how he'd entered the restroom immediately after Hector Macedo.

"Then that man"—here he pointed at Braswell—"he push me away and grab him—"

"Mr. Macedo?" the ADA prompted.

"*Sí*. And he hit him and hit him. Many times."

"Did Mr. Macedo hit him back?"

"He try to get away, but that one too big. Too strong."

"Then what happened?"

"Hector, he break a bottle and cut that one. Then he let go and there is much blood. Then the bouncers come. And *la policía*."

"No further questions, Your Honor," said the ADA.

Braswell's attorney declined to cross-examine the witness, but Macedo's had him flesh out the narrative so as to make it clear to me that the smaller man had acted in self-defense when Braswell left him with no other options.

A second witness took the stand and his account echoed the first. When Walsh started to call a third witness, Braswell's attorney stood up. "We're willing to stipulate as to the sequence of events, Your Honor," whereupon the State rested.

Macedo, a subcontractor for a drywall service, went first for the defense. Speaking through the interpreter, he swore to tell the truth, the whole truth, and nothing but the truth. According to his testimony, he had been minding his own business when Braswell attacked him for no good reason. He did not even know who Braswell was until after they were both arrested.

Under questioning by Braswell's lawyer, he admitted that he was at the club that night with one Karen Braswell.

Yes, that would be the other defendant's ex-wife although he had not known it at the time. Besides, it wasn't a real date. She worked with his sister at the Bojangles in Dobbs and the two women had made up a casual foursome with himself and a friend. He'd had no clue that she had a husband who was still in the picture till the man began choking and pounding him. Macedo's attorney called the sister, who sat in the first row behind her brother and strained to hear the interpreter, but Braswell's attorney objected and I sustained.

"Defense rests."

"Call your first witness," I told Braswell's attorney.

"No witnesses, Your Honor."

"Mr. Braswell," I said as his attorney nudged him to stand. "I find you guilty as charged."

"Your Honor," said his attorney, "I would ask you to take into consideration my client's natural distress at seeing his wife out with another man while he was still trying to save their marriage."

"I thought they were divorced," I said.

"In his mind they're still married, Your Honor."

"Ms. Walsh?"

"Your Honor, I think it's relevant that you should know Mr. Braswell was under a restraining order not to contact Mrs. Braswell or go near her."

"Is this true?" I asked the man, who was now standing with his attorney.

He gave a noncommittal shrug and there was a faint sneer on his lips.

"Was a warrant issued for this violation?"

"Yes, Your Honor, but he made bail. He's due in court next week. Judge Parker."

"What was the bail?"

"Five thousand."

I could have increased the bail, but it was moot. He wasn't going to have an opportunity to hassle his ex before Luther Parker saw him next week. Not if I had anything to say about it.

"Ten days active time," I told Braswell. "Bailiff, you will take the prisoner in custody."

"Now, wait just a damn minute here!" he cried; but before he could resist, the bailiff and a uniformed officer had him in a strong-arm grip and marched him out the door that would lead to the jail.

Macedo stood beside his attorney and his face was impassive as he waited for me to pass judgment. I found him guilty of misdemeanor assault and because he'd already sat in jail for eleven days, I reduced his sentence to time served and no fine, just court costs.

He showed no emotion as the interpreter repeated my remarks in Spanish, but his sister's smile was radiant. "*Gracias*," she whispered to me as they headed out to the back hall to pay the clerk.

"*De nada*," I told her.

"State versus Rasheed King," said Julie Walsh, calling her next case. "Misdemeanor assault with a vehicle."

A pugnacious young black man came to stand next to his lawyer at the defendant's table.

"How do you plead?"

"Hey, his truck bumped me first, Judge."

"Sorry, Your Honor," said his attorney.

"You'll get a chance to tell your story, Mr. King," I said, "but for our records, are you pleading guilty or not guilty?"

"Not guilty, ma'am."

It was going to be one of those days.

CHAPTER 2

It should be borne in mind that "home" is not merely a place of shelter from the storms and cold of winter and the heat of summer—a place in which to sleep securely at night and labor by day. It is a place where the children receive their first and most lasting impressions, those that go far in molding and forming the character of the man and woman in after life.

—*Profitable Farming in the Southern States*, 1890

The year had turned and days were supposed to be getting longer. Nevertheless, it was full dark before I got home.

When things are normal, Dwight's work day begins an hour earlier than mine and ends an hour sooner, which means he often starts supper. I half expected to see him at the stove and to smell food. Instead, the kitchen was empty and the stove bare of any pots or pans as I let myself in through the garage door. The television was on mute in the living room though and Cal looked up from some school papers spread across the coffee table. A brown-eyed towhead, he's tall for his age and as awkward as a young colt. In his haste to neaten up, several sheets of paper slid to the floor. His dog Bandit, a smooth-haired terrier with a brown eye mask, sidestepped the papers and trotted over to greet me.

Cal wore a red sweatshirt emblazoned with a big white 12 and he gave me a guilty smile as he gathered up his third-grade homework and tried to make a single tidy pile. A Friday night, he was already on his homework, yet he was worried about messing up the living room?

I'm no neat freak and a little clutter doesn't bother me. Dwight either. But Cal was still walking on eggs with us, almost as if he was afraid that if he stepped an inch out of line, someone would yell at him.

Neither Dwight nor I are much for yelling, but when you're eight years old and your whole world turns upside down overnight, I guess it makes you cautious.

Six months ago he was living with his mother up in Virginia and I had been footloose and fancy free. I lived alone and came and went as I chose, accountable to no one except the state of North Carolina, which did expect me to show up in court on a regular basis. Then in blurred succession came an October engagement, followed by a Christmas wedding, followed by the murder of Dwight's first wife before the ink was completely dry on our marriage certificate. Now my no-strings life suddenly included two guys and a dog with their own individual needs and obligations.

As soon as I saw Cal's shirt though, I remembered why I was on my own for supper tonight, and a quick glance at the calendar hanging on the refrigerator confirmed it. Pencilled there in today's square was *HURRICANES—7 PM.*

Dwight came down the hall from our bedroom, zipping his heavy jacket and carrying Cal's hockey stick under his arm.

"Oh, hey!" A smile warmed his brown eyes. "I was afraid we'd have to leave before you got home. You 'bout ready, buddy?"

Cal nodded. "Just have to get my jacket and a Sharpie. I'm gonna try to get Rod Brind'Amour's autograph tonight."

As he picked up his books and scurried off to his room, Dwight hooked me with the hockey stick and drew me close. I've kissed my share of men in my time, but his slow kisses are blue-ribbon-best-in-show. "Wish you were coming with us," he said, nuzzling my neck.

"No, you don't," I assured him. "I promised to honor and love. There was nothing in the vows about hockey."

"You sure you read the fine print?"

"That's the first thing an attorney does read, my friend."

I adore ACC basketball, I pull for the Atlanta Braves, and I can follow a football game without asking too many dumb questions, but ice hockey leaves me cold in more ways than one. When you grow up in the south on a dirt road, you don't even learn to roller skate. Yes, we have ponds and yes, they do occasionally freeze over, but the ice is seldom thick enough to trust and the closest I ever got to live ice-skating was once when the Ice Capades came to Raleigh and Mother and Aunt Zell took me and some of the younger boys to see them. We all agreed the circus was a better show. My preadolescent brothers preferred hot trapeze artists to cool ice goddesses and I kept waiting for the elephants.

But Cal had played street hockey on skates up in Shaysville and had become hooked on the Canes when he spent Christmas with us and watched four televised games.

Four.

In one week.

He and Dwight didn't miss a single one. I'd wanted to bond (not to mention snuggle in next to my new husband), so I joined them on the extra-long leather couch Dwight had brought over from his bachelor apartment. I honestly tried to follow along, but the terminology was indecipherable and I never knew where the puck was nor why someone had been sent to the penalty box or why they would abruptly stop play for no discernible reason to have a jump ball.

That made Cal laugh. "Not jump ball," he had told me kindly. "It's a face-off."

Two grown men fighting for possession of a small round object, right? Same thing in my book.

But now that Cal was living with us permanently, it had become their thing. I went off and puttered happily by myself when they were watching a game, and I had scored a couple of decent seats for the last half of the season with the help of Karen Prince, a former client who now worked in the Hurricanes ticket office.

"The drive back and forth to Raleigh will give you and Cal a chance to be alone together and talk. Kids open up in a car," I told Dwight when he questioned why I hadn't badgered Karen for three seats.

I really did think they needed the time and space to help Cal cope with all the changes in his young life, but it wasn't unadulterated altruism. Put myself where I couldn't read a book or catch up on paperwork? Get real.

Dwight laughed and gave me another quick kiss as Cal came back ready to go.

"Have fun," I said and when the door had closed behind them, I happily contemplated the evening's sybaritic possibilities.

"So what do you think, Bandit?" I asked the dog. "Popcorn and a chick flick video, or a long soak in the tub followed by a manicure?"

Or I could bake a cake to take for Sunday dinner at Minnie and Seth's house. Seth is five brothers up from me, the one I've always felt closest to, and his wife has acted as my political advisor from the day I first decided to run for a seat on the district court bench.

I unzipped my high heel boots and had just kicked one off when the door opened again. Dwight had the phone pressed to his ear and there was a glum look on Cal's face.

"Tell Denning and Richards I'll meet them there in ten minutes." Dwight flipped the phone shut. "Sorry, Cal, but I have to go. It's my job."

He headed for our bedroom where he keeps his handgun locked up when he's off duty and I followed.

"What's happened?" I asked as he holstered the gun on his belt.

"They've found two legs in a ditch near Bethel Baptist," he said grimly.

Bethel Baptist Church is on a back road about halfway between our house and Dobbs, Colleton's county seat.

My mind fought with the grisly image of severed limbs. "*Human* legs?"

"White male's all I know for now."

And it was clear that he didn't want to say any more. Not with Cal standing disconsolately in the doorway.

Dwight sighed and laid the hockey tickets on the dresser. "I really am sorry, son."

"It's okay," Cal said gamely. "Brind'Amour might not even be playing tonight."

"Don't wait supper," Dwight told me as he started back down the hall. "This could take a while."

"That's all right," I said. "And if you get home first, you don't have to wait up for *us*."

That stopped them both in their tracks and Cal looked at me in sudden hope as he saw the tickets in my hand.

I smiled back at him. "Well, I've got a driver's license, too, you know. And I know how to get to the RBC Center. You just have to promise not to get embarrassed if I yell 'High sticking!' at the wrong time, okay?"

"O*kay*!"

Home court for NC State's basketball team and home ice for the Carolina Hurricanes, the RBC Center is named for the Royal Bank of Canada—part of the global economy we keep hearing about. It's less than ten years old and sits on eighty acres that used to be farms and woodlands, just west of Raleigh and easily accessible by I-40. It was supposed to cost $66 million and seat 23,000. It wound up costing $158 million and seats only 20,000. Was there ever a public project that didn't cost at least twice as much as originally estimated?

When Dwight and Seth and I were figuring how much it'd cost to add on a new master bedroom, we actually overestimated by a thousand. Either we're smarter than those professional consultants who get paid big money out of the state's budget or else those consultants maybe fudge the figures so that legislators won't panic and refuse to fund a project until it's too late to back out.

Even though I'm a Carolina fan, I don't begrudge the Wolfpack their new arena. I just wish it could've been named for something a little less commercial than a Canadian bank.

On the drive in, Cal tried to bring me up to speed on the rules and logic of the game and I really did try to concentrate, but it was so much gobbledygook.

When we got to the entrance, orange-colored plastic cones divided the various lanes and he knew which lane would get us to the parking lot closest to our seats. Inside, we bought pizza and soft drinks, then found our seats in the club section, which was sort of like first balcony in a regular theater. Up above us, the retired jerseys of various NCSU basketball players hung from the rafters. Down below us, red-garbed hockey players warmed up on the gleaming white ice.

Don't ask me who the Hurricanes played that night. I don't have a clue. But a couple of minutes into play, the Canes scored the first goal and the whole building went crazy. Cal and every other kid in the place jumped to their feet and waved their hockey sticks. Men high-fived, women hugged and screamed, horns blared, and the near-capacity crowd roared maniacal cheers of triumph, while flashing colored lights chased themselves around the rim of our section in eye-dazzling brilliance.

Wow!

CHAPTER 3

Shall we ask, Am I my brother's keeper? Or say in the language of a former cabinet officer, "Gentlemen, this is not my funeral."

—*Profitable Farming in the Southern States,* 1890

Dwight Bryant
Friday Night, February 24

Even before he turned onto Ward Dairy Road, Dwight could see flashing lights in the distance. When he got there, state troopers were directing homeward-bound commuter traffic through a single lane around the scene, so he turned on his own flashers behind the grille of his truck, slowed to a crawl as he approached, and flipped down the sun visor to show the card that identified him as an officer of the Colleton County Sheriff's Department. Activity seemed to be centered directly in front of Bethel Baptist, between the entrance and exit driveways that circled the churchyard. He started to power down his window, but the troopers recognized him and immediately shunted him into the first drive. He parked and pulled on the new wool gloves Deborah had given him for Christmas, grabbed his flashlight, and walked over toward the others.

Most of the county roads had wide shoulders and this one was no exception. Even with the yellow tape that delineated the crime scene, there would have been enough room for two cars to pass had there not been so many official vehicles gathered around like a flock of buzzards there for the kill, as his father-in-law would say.

Trooper Ollie Harrold gave him an informal two finger salute. "Over here, Major Bryant," he said, illuminating a path for Dwight with his torch.

Yellow tape had been looped across a shallow ditch and was secured to the low illuminated church sign a few feet away. Inside the tape's perimeter, the focus of all their attention, two brawny legs lay side by side—male, to judge by their muscular hairiness. Even in the fitful play of flashlights, Dwight could see that they were a ghastly white, drained of all blood. He aimed his own flash at the upper thighs. The bones that protruded were mangled and splintered as if hacked from the victim's torso with an axe or heavy cleaver. No clean-sawn cut. No apparent blood on the wintry brown grass beneath them either, which indicated that the butchery had taken place elsewhere.

The pasty-faced man who had reported them was a thoroughly shaken local who worked at a nearby auto repair shop and who now stood shivering in a thin jacket that did not offer much protection against the sharp February wind.

"I was riding home," he said, "when I saw 'em a-laying there in the ditch. Almost fell in the ditch myself a-looking so hard 'cause I couldn't believe what I was a-seeing. I went straight home and called y'all, then came back here to wait."

Dwight glanced at the rusty beat-up bicycle propped against one of the patrol cars behind them. "Bit chilly to be riding a bike."

"Yeah, well . . ." The words trailed off in a shamefaced shrug.

"Lost your license?"

"Used to be, you had to blow a ten to have 'em take it." The man sounded aggrieved. "I only blew a eight-five, but the judge still took it. I'm due to get it back next month."

"There's no light on your bike," Dwight said, looking from the bicycle to the grisly limbs in the shallow ditch.

"I know, but I got reflecting tape on the pedals and fenders and on my jacket, too. See?" He turned around to show them. "Didn't need my own light to see that, though. People don't dim their high beams for bicycles."

"You ride past here on your way to work?"

The man nodded. "And 'fore you ask, no, they won't here this morning. I'm certain sure I'd've seen 'em."

The officer assigned to patrol this area was already on the scene and others of Dwight's people started to arrive. Detective Mayleen Richards was first, followed by Jamison and Denning on the crime scene van. As they set up floodlights so that Percy Denning could photograph the remains from all angles, Richards took down the witness's name and address and the few pertinent facts he could tell them, then Dwight thanked him for his help and told him he was free to go.

"I can get someone to run you home."

"Naw, that's all right. Like I say, I just live around the curve yonder." He seemed reluctant to leave.

An EMT truck was called to transport the legs over to Chapel Hill to see what the ME could tell them from a medical viewpoint.

"We already checked with the county hospitals," Detective Jack Jamison reported. "No double amputees so far. McLamb's calling Raleigh, Smithfield, Fuquay, and Fayetteville."

"We have any missing persons at the moment?" Dwight asked.

"Just that old man with Alzheimer's that walked away from that nursing home down in Black Creek around Christmas. His daughter's still on the phone to us almost every day."

Despite an intensive search with a helicopter and dogs, the old man had never been found.

"I hear the family's suing the place for a half a million dollars," said Mayleen Richards.

"A half-million dollars for an eighty-year-old man?" Jamison was incredulous.

"Well, a nursing home in Dobbs wound up paying fifty thousand for the woman they lost and she was in her nineties. And think if it was your granddaddy," said Richards, a touch of cynicism in her voice. "Wouldn't it take a half-million to wipe out your pain and mental anguish?"

Jamison took another look at those sturdy legs. In the glare of Denning's floodlight, they looked whiter than ever. "That old guy was black, though, and they said he didn't weigh but about a hundred pounds."

"Too bad we don't have even some shoes and socks to

give us a lead on who he was or what he did," said Richards. "You reckon he's workboots or loafers?"

She leaned in for a closer look. "No corns or calluses and the toenails are clean. Trimmed, too. I doubt if they gave him a pedicure first."

It was another half hour before the EMT truck arrived. While they waited, Denning carefully searched the grass inside the perimeter. "Not even a cigarette butt," he said morosely.

The patrol officer was equally empty-handed. "I drove down this road a little after four," he reported. "It was still light then. I can't swear they weren't there then, but shallow as that ditch is, I do believe I'd've noticed."

A reporter from the *Dobbs Ledger* stood chatting with someone from a local TV station. Because neither was bumping up against an early deadline, they had waited unobtrusively until Dwight could walk over and give them as much as he had.

The television reporter repositioned her photogenic scarf, removed her unphotogenic woolly hat, and fluffed up her hair before the tape began to roll. "Talking with us here is Major Dwight Bryant from the Colleton County Sheriff's Department. Major Bryant, can you give us the victim's approximate age?"

Dwight shook his head. "He could be anything from a highschool football player to a vigorous sixty-year-old. It's too soon to say." Looking straight into the camera, he added, "The main thing is that if you know of any white male that might be missing, you should contact the Sheriff's Department as soon as possible."

Both reporters promised they would run the department's phone numbers with their stories.

Eventually, the emergency medical techs arrived, drew on latex gloves, bagged the legs separately, then left for Chapel Hill. The yellow tape was taken down and the reporters and patrol cars dispersed, along with their witness, who pedaled off into the night.

"We probably won't hear much from the ME till we find the rest of him," Mayleen Richards said.

"Well-nourished white male," Denning agreed. "They'll give us his blood type, but what good's that without a face or fingerprints?"

"We're bound to hear something soon," Dwight said. He grinned at Richards. "Men with clean toenails usually have a woman around. Sooner or later, she'll start wondering where he is."

As he turned toward his truck, he paused beside the dimly lit church sign. Beneath the church name, the pastor's name, and the hours of service was a quotation from Matthew that entreated mercy and brotherhood and reminded passersby that "*With what measure you mete, it shall be measured to you again.*"

Not for the last time, he was to wonder what measure their victim had meted to provoke such violence against him.

Back at the house, Dwight let Bandit out of his crate, put a couple of logs on the fire, then switched on the television. End of the second period and the Canes were behind 3 to 2. He went back to the kitchen and rummaged around in the refrigerator until he found a bowl of chili that one of Deborah's sisters-in-law had brought by the day before. While it heated in the microwave, he drew himself a glass of homemade lager from the refrigerated tap, a wedding present from his father-in-law.

Every time he used the tap or held his glass up to the light to admire the color and clarity he had achieved with his home brew, he thought again of the potent crystal clear liquid Kezzie Knott used to produce.

He hoped that "used to produce" was an accurate assessment. Deborah would not be happy with either one of them if he had to arrest her daddy for the illegal production of untaxed moonshine, but with that old reprobate, anything was possible.

The microwave dinged and he carried his supper into the living room to watch the game. Bandit jumped up on the leather couch beside him and curled in along his thigh as if prepared to cheer the Canes on to victory. Going into the third period, they tied it 3-all. Cal was probably swinging from the rafters about now, Dwight thought. He hoped Deborah was not too bored.

He finished eating, then stretched out on the couch and stuffed a pillow behind his head. Tie games can be exciting, but it had been a long day. The chili was hearty, the beer relaxing, the room comfortably warm. The fire gently crackled and popped as flames danced up from the oak logs.

The next thing he knew, the kitchen door banged open and Cal erupted through the door from the garage, his brown eyes shining, his arms full of Hurricanes paraphernalia. Deborah followed, a Canes' cap on her light brown hair.

"It was awesome, Dad! We won! Tie game, overtime, *and* a shootout! Did you watch it?"

They both glanced at the television screen just in time for Dwight to see himself on the late newscast. He hit the mute button.

Talking more excitedly than Dwight had seen him since he came to live with them, Cal unloaded a souvenir book, a flag for the car window, a couple of Canes Go Cups, and a long-sleeved red T-shirt with a number 6 on it onto the coffee table.

"Who's number six?" Dwight asked.

"Bret Hedican. He signed it for me. Well, not for me. It's Deborah's. And I got Rod Brind'Amour to sign my stick, too. Look!"

"New cap?"

"Yeah, and she got you one, too."

He laughed. "So I see."

Deborah's face was flushed and her blue eyes sparkled with an excitement that matched Cal's.

"That was absolutely amazing, Dwight! It's so different seeing a live game. Did you know that Hedican's married to Kristi Yamaguchi?"

"I knew it. I'm surprised that you do."

"He scored the tying goal at the beginning of the third period," she told him.

"Yeah, Dad," Cal chimed in. "He was awesome. Just drove down the ice and slapped it in."

"So we had a tie game—"

"—then the tie-breaker—"

"—but no one scored so we had to have a shootout."

"Ward blocked their shot, then Williams put it in!"

"Yes!" Deborah exclaimed and they high-fived.

Dwight shook his head at the pair of them. "Did I just lose my seat here?"

"Deborah says that next year we're getting three seats," Cal told him. "For the whole season."

CHAPTER 4

There are few things that have so important a bearing upon the success or failure of the farmer's business as the choice of crops to be produced.

—*Profitable Farming in the Southern States,* 1890

DEBORAH KNOTT
FRIDAY NIGHT, FEBRUARY 24

Cal called to Bandit and went to bed soon after we got home, totally worn out and nearly hoarse from cheering the Canes to victory, but it took me till almost midnight to come back down from the high of my first live hockey game, and it wasn't till Dwight and I were in bed ourselves that I remembered the reason I had gone instead of him.

Lying beside him with my head on his chest in the soft darkness of our bedroom, I asked about the legs that had been found in front of Bethel Baptist and he described the scene, right down to the bare feet.

"None of your friends are missing a man, are they?" he asked.

"Not like that," I said. "Although K.C. was grumbling about Terry being gone all week to teach some training seminar up in Chicago."

Terry Wilson's an SBI agent, a man who could make me laugh so hard that I seriously considered hooking up with him a few years ago. He was between wives at the time, still working undercover. While I was almost willing to take second place to his son, no way was I going to take third behind the job. These days, though, he's a field supervisor working from a desk and K.C.'s come in off the streets, too. She used to work undercover narcotics, one of the most successful agents the State Bureau of Investigation ever had. She was absolutely fearless and so blonde and beautiful that dealers fell all over themselves to give her drugs. Somewhat to my surprise, they had gotten together late last summer and he had moved into her lake house.

"She keeps swearing it's just for laughs," I told Dwight, "but this may be fourth time lucky for Terry."

"That would be nice," said Dwight, who likes Terry as much as I do.

I smiled in the darkness. "Now that you're an old married man, you want everybody else to settle down?"

"Beats sleeping single in a double bed," he said as his arms tightened around me.

Next morning, after breakfast, our kitchen filled up with short people. During the week, Cal goes home on the schoolbus with Mary Pat, the young orphaned ward of Dwight's sister-in-law Kate, who keeps him for the hour or so till Dwight or I get home. In return, we usually take Mary Pat and Kate's four-year-old son Jake for a few hours on Saturday so that Kate can have some time alone with Rob and their new baby boy.

It was raining that morning, a cold chill rain that threatened to turn to sleet, so I kept them indoors and let them help me make cookies. I'm no gourmet chef, my biscuits aren't as tender and flaky as some, and my piecrusts come out so soggy and tough that I long ago gave up and now buy the frozen ones, but I'll put my chocolate chip cookies up against anybody's. (The secret is to add a little extra sweet butter and then take them out of the oven before the center's fully set. Black walnuts don't hurt either, but pecans will do in a pinch.)

We had a great assembly line going. I did the mixing and got them in and out of the oven, Mary Pat and Cal spooned little blobs of dough onto the foil-lined cookie sheets, while Jake stood on a stool and used a spatula to carefully transfer the baked cookies from the foil to the wire cooling racks. Of course, they nibbled on the raw dough as they worked and their sticky little fingers went from mouth to bowl whenever they thought I wasn't looking.

I pretended not to notice. Didn't bother me. If there were any germs those three hadn't already shared, the heat of the oven would probably take care of them and I knew the eggs were safe.

Once Daddy's housekeeper Maidie heard about the dangers of raw eggs, she kept threatening to stop baking altogether until Daddy and her husband Cletus rebuilt the old chicken house and started raising Rhode Island Reds again. The flock was now big enough to keep the whole family in eggs, and when the wind's right, I can hear their rooster crowing in the morning. Every once in a while, another rooster answers and it's a comforting signal that there are still some other farms in the community that haven't yet given way to a developer's checkbook.

Whenever I make cookies, I quadruple the recipe, so it was almost noon before we finished filling two large cake boxes to the brim. I planned to take one box to Seth and Minnie's the next day, I'd send some home with Mary Pat and Jake, and I figured the rest should last us at least a week if Dwight and Cal didn't get into them too heavily.

"Ummm. Something in here smells good enough to eat," said Dwight, who was back from helping Haywood and Robert pull a mired tractor out of a soggy bottom.

"Why was Haywood even down there on a tractor this time of year? It's way too wet."

"He wants to plant an acre of garden peas." Dwight had left his muddy boots and wet jacket in the garage and was in his stocking feet, making hungry noises as he lifted the lid on a pot of vegetable soup. I cut him off a wedge of the hoop cheese I was using to make grilled cheese sandwiches to go with the soup and it disappeared in two bites.

"Garden peas? A whole acre? What's he going to do with that many peas?"

"Well you know how your brothers are trying to come up with ideas for cash crops in case tobacco goes downhill?"

I nodded.

"So Haywood's thinking he might try his hand at a little truck farming. He even said something about raising leeks for the upscale Cary and Clayton crowds."

"Leeks?" I had to laugh. "Haywood's heard of leeks?"

"He's decided they're just fancy onions and he's already taken a dislike to Vidalias. Says they're nothing but onions for people who don't really like onions."

Privately, I agreed with my brother. What's the point of an onion with so little zest that you could peel a dozen without shedding a tear? Give me an onion that stands up for itself.

After so much cookie dough, the children weren't very hungry and asked to be excused to go play in Cal's room. When we were alone, Dwight told me that he'd heard from Chapel Hill. The ME could not give them a specific time. Depending on whether or not those legs were outdoors and exposed to the freezing night temperatures or inside, the hacking had been done as recent as forty-eight hours or as long ago as a full week. The dismemberment had been accomplished with a heavy blade that was consistent with an axe or hatchet. And yes, the legs did indeed come from a well-nourished white male, probably between forty and sixty, a male with blood type O.

"The most common type in the world," he sighed, reaching for the untouched half of Cal's grilled cheese.

"Maybe someone will call in by Monday," I said and slid the rest of my own sandwich onto his plate.

After lunch, Dwight volunteered to take the children to a new multiplex that recently opened about ten miles from us. I grumble about all the changes that growth has brought, but I have to admit that sometimes it's nice not to have to drive thirty miles for a movie. With the house quiet and empty, I finally got to do some personal weekend pampering. I put Bandit in his crate out in the utility room, gave him a new strip of rawhide to chew on, then took a lazy bubblebath, followed by a manicure. And as long as I had clippers and polish out, I decided to paint my toenails as well.

The phone rang when I was about halfway through. Portland Brewer. My best friend since forever and, most recently, my matron of honor.

"Why are you putting me on speaker phone?" she immediately asked. "Who else is with you?"

"No one," I assured her. "But I'm giving myself a pedicure and I need both hands. What's up?"

"Nothing much. I'm just sitting here nursing the deduction while Avery works on our income tax. You know how anal he is about getting it done early."

The deduction, little Carolyn Deborah, is about eighteen hours younger than my marriage. Back in December, my brothers were making book on whether or not Port land would deliver during the ceremony.

"How'd it go this week?" I asked.

After the baby's birth, she'd taken off for two months and this was her first week of easing back into the practice she and Avery shared. He did civil cases and a little tax work; she did whatever else came along, although she was particularly good in juried criminal cases.

"It's okay. I hate leaving the baby, but she doesn't seem to mind one bottle feeding a day as long as I'm here for the others. And let's face it, after working fifty- and sixty-hour weeks, thirty hours is a piece of cake."

She told me about the new nanny ("a jewel"), how her diet was coming if she expected to get into a decent bathing suit by the summer ("I'm an absolute cow and if anybody gives me one more 'got milk?' joke, I'm gonna stomp him"), and whether or not Reid Stephenson, my cousin and former law partner, was having an affair with that new courthouse clerk ("I saw them going into one of the conference rooms at lunch yesterday").

I told her about my newfound hockey enthusiasm ("Did you know Bret Hedican's married to Kristi Yamaguchi?"), how Cal was settling in ("He still acts like a long-tailed cat in a room full of rocking chairs, but I think we really connected last night"), and what my docket had looked like yesterday ("Doesn't anybody just talk anymore? Why does it always have to be knives or fists or baseball bats?").

"That reminds me," said Portland. "I have a new client. Karen Braswell. Was her ex one of your cases yesterday? A James Braswell? Assault?"

"Assault?"

"A Mexican took a broken beer bottle to his arm out at that Latino club. El Toro Negro."

"Oh, yes." The details were coming back to me. "Your client's his ex-wife? That's right. He violated a restraining order she took out against him? He's supposed to come up before Luther Parker the first of the week, but I've got him cooling his heels in jail till then."

"Good. She's really scared of him, Deborah. That's why she's retained me to speak for her when his case comes up. I just hope Judge Parker will put the fear of the law in him."

Our talk moved on to other subjects till the baby started fussing. "Lunch sometime this week?" Portland asked before hanging up.

I agreed and put the finishing dab of polish on my toenails. It was a fiery red with just a hint of orange. Later that evening, I wiggled my bare toes at Dwight. "It's called *Hot, Hot, Hot*," I told him. "What do you think?"

He patted the couch beside him. "Come over here and let me show you."

Cool!

CHAPTER 5

If farmers wish their sons to be attached to the farm home and farm life they must make that farm home and farm life sufficiently attractive to induce some of their boys to stay.

—*Profitable Farming in the Southern States,* 1890

"What's wrong with garden peas?" my brother Haywood asked belligerently as he reached for another of my chocolate chip cookies next day. "Everybody I know likes 'em, they don't have no pests and they're easy to grow."

"Which is why they wholesale for less than a dollar a pound in season," Zach said patiently. "And picking them is labor intensive. After we pay for help, what sort of return would we get on our investment?"

"Messicans work cheap," Haywood said, "and they can pick a hell of a lot of peas in a hour."

His wife Isabel rolled her eyes at the use of profanity on a Sunday, but it was Daddy who frowned and murmured, "Watch your mouth, boy." Not because it was Sunday but because there were "ladies" present and the older he gets, the more he holds with old-fashioned beliefs about the delicacy of our ladylike ears. (For Daddy, all respectable women, whatever our race or color, are ladies. The only time he huffs and mutters "You women!" is when we try his patience to total exasperation.)

Seth and Minnie had called this meeting for those of us who still live out here on the farm. Even though Dwight and I are not directly involved with crops, what's grown here is certainly of interest to us since we're surrounded by the family fields and woodlands. Both of us grew up working in tobacco—hard, physical, dirty work. From picking up dropped leaves at the barn when we were toddlers, to driving the tractors that ferried the leaves from field to barn as preteens, to actually pulling the leaves (Dwight) or racking them (me), we each did our part to help get the family's money crop to market. We never needed lectures at school to know about the tar in tobacco. After working in it for a few hours, we could roll up marble sized balls of black sticky gum from our hands.

Now the old way of marketing has changed. The farm subsidy program has ended and the money's been used to buy out the farmers who had always raised it. Instead of the old colorful auctions where competitive bids could net a grower top dollar for a particularly attractive sheet of soft golden leaves, tobacco companies now contract directly with the growers for what's pretty much a take-it-or-leave-it offer that can be galling to independent farmers who are more conservative than cats when it comes to change.

My eleven brothers and I had grown up in tobacco without questioning it. Tobacco fed and clothed us, and those who stayed to farm with Daddy—Seth, Haywood, Andrew, Robert, and Zach—pooled their labor and equipment to grow more poundage every year and buy more land until we now collectively own a few thousand acres in fields, woods, and some soggy wetlands.

The morality of tobacco itself was something else we didn't question. Our parents smoked. Daddy and some of the boys still do. But only one or two of their children have picked up the habit. Those grandchildren who hope to stay and wrest a living from the land were hoping to find an economically feasible alternative to tobacco.

Each of my farming brothers has his own specialty on the side. Haywood loves to grow watermelons, cantaloupes, and pumpkins even though he makes so little profit that by the time he pays his fertilizer bills, he's working for way less than minimum wage. Andrew and Robert raise a few extra hogs every year and they get top dollar for their corn-fed, free-range pork. Those two and Daddy also raise rabbit dogs, and Zach's beekeeping hobby now turns a modest profit because he rents his hives to truck farmers and fruit growers. Seth and I have leased some of our piney woods to landscapers who rake the straw for mulch, and Seth's daughter Jessica boards a couple of horses to pay for the upkeep on her own horse.

Today, we were all gathered at Seth and Minnie's to try to reach an agreement as to what the main money crop would be. Outside, the weather was raw and wintry with a forecast of freezing rain. Inside things were starting to heat up. The boys planned to apply for a grant to help make the changeover to a different use of the farm, *if* they could agree on what that use should be.

It was a very big *if* and today was not the first time Haywood and Zach had butted heads on this.

Zach is one of the "little twins," so called because he and Adam are younger than Haywood and Herman, the "big twins," and Haywood does not like being lectured to by a younger brother even if Zach *is* an assistant principal at West Colleton High, where he himself barely scraped through years earlier. Andrew and Robert are even older than Haywood, but they listen when Zach and Seth speak.

Seth is probably the quietest of my eleven older brothers and the most even-tempered. I would never admit to anybody that I love one of them more than the others but I have always felt a special connection to Seth. He didn't finish college like Adam, Zach, and I did, but he reads and listens and, like Daddy, he thinks on things before he acts. Even Haywood listens to Seth.

So far today, we had discussed the pros and cons of pick-your-own strawberries, blueberries, blackberries, or grapes. Someone halfheartedly raised the possibility of timbering some of the stands of pines. That would yield a few thousand an acre but was pretty much a one time sale, given how long it takes to grow a pine to market size. Daddy still mourned the longleaf pines that had to be cut to pay the bills when he was a boy and "Y'all can do what you like about what's your'n," he said firmly, "but I ain't interested in selling any more of mine," which pretty much scotched that possibility since none of us wanted to go against him.

"Too bad we can't grow hemp," Seth said and my brothers nodded in gloomy agreement. Hemp is a wonderful source material of paper and cloth and our soil and climate would make it a perfect alternative to tobacco. If it had first been called the paper weed or something equally innocuous, North Carolina would be a huge producer. With a name like *hemp* though, our legislators are scared to death to promote it even though you'd have to smoke a ton of the stuff to get a decent buzz.

Zach and Barbara's kids had been all over the Internet scouting out alternatives and they had brought printouts to share with us.

"What about shiitakes?" Emma said now, passing out diagrams of stacked logs.

"She-whatys?" asked her Uncle Robert.

"Shiitake mushrooms. You take oak logs, drill holes in them, put the spores in the holes and plug the holes with wax. They grow pretty good here because they like a warm, moist climate and that's our summers, right?"

Her brother Lee added, "We could convert the bulk barns to mini greenhouses and grow them year 'round."

"Right now, a cord of wood can produce about two thousand dollars' worth of mushrooms," said Emma.

"Two *thousand*?" That got Haywood's attention.

Andrew frowned as he looked at the diagrams. "But what's the cost of growing 'em?"

"According to the info put out by State's forestry service, the net return is anywhere from five hundred to a thousand a cord. But they do warn that the profit may go down if a lot of people get into growing them."

"That's going to be the case with anything," said Seth. "What else you find?"

"Ostriches," Lee said.

Across the room, Dwight winked at me and sat back to enjoy the fun.

"Ostriches?" Robert's wife Doris and Haywood were both predictably taken aback by the suggestion.

Andrew's son A.K. laughed and said, "Big as they are, we could let Jessie here put saddles on them and give kiddie rides."

Isabel said, "Ostriches? What kind of outlandish foolery is that?"

"Some of the restaurants and grocery stores are starting to sell the meat over in Cary," said Seth and Minnie's son John, a teenager who hadn't yet committed to farming, but was taking surveying classes at Colleton Community College.

"Oh, well, *Cary*." Doris's voice dripped sarcasm. For most of my family, the name of that upscale, manicured town just west of Raleigh was an acronym: Containment Area for Relocated Yankees, although Clayton, over in Johnston County, was fast becoming a Cary clone with even better acronymic possibilities.

Isabel said, "If y'all're thinking about raising animals, what's wrong with hogs?"

"Ostriches are easier," said Lee. "They don't need routine shots, there's a strong market for their hide and they're a red meat that's lower in fat and cholesterol than pork."

"Plus their waste is not a problem," said Emma, wrinkling her pretty little nose. "They don't stink like hogs."

"Yeah, but hogs is more natural," said Isabel.

"Think of the pretty feather dusters," I said, playing devil's advocate.

"You laugh," said Lee, "but did you know that some manufacturers use ostrich feathers to dust their computer chips? They attract microscopic dust particles yet they don't have any oils like other birds."

"You can even sell the blown egg shells at craft fairs," said Emma.

As they touted the bird's good points, Isabel kept shaking her head. "I'd be plumb embarrassed to tell folks we was raising ostriches."

"But it's something we can think about," Seth said and added them to the list he was making on his notepad.

"What about cotton or peanuts?" asked Andrew. "We'd maybe have to invest in a picker or harvester, but neither one of 'em would be all that different from tobacco."

Robert's youngest son Bobby had been listening quietly. Now he said, "Don't y'all think it'd be good if we could switch over to something that doesn't require tons of pesticides on every acre?"

"Everything's got pests that you gotta poison," said his father.

"Not if we went organic."

The other kids nodded enthusiastically. "The way the area's growing, the market's only going to get stronger for organic foods."

"You young'uns act like we're some sort of criminals 'cause we didn't sit around and let the crops get eat up with worms and bugs and wilts and nematodes," Haywood huffed. "Every time we find something that works, the government comes and takes it away."

"Because it doesn't really work," said Bobby. "All

we're doing is breeding more resistant pests and endangering our own health."

Haywood's broad face turned red. "There you go again. Like our generation poisoned the world."

"Some of your generation has," said Jessie. "Crop dusters filling the air we breathe. PCBs causing cancer. Look at the way some farmers still sneak and use methyl bromide even though it's supposed to be illegal now. And then they make their *guest* workers go in right away."

Her indignant young voice italicized the word "guest." She knows as well as any of my brothers that migrant workers are but the newest batch of laborers to be exploited. I remember my own school days when I first learned that expendable Irish immigrants were used to drain the malaria-ridden swamps down in South Carolina because slaves were too valuable to be risked. To claim that undocumented aliens do the work Americans are unwilling to do ignores the unspoken corollary—"unwilling to do it for that kind of money."

Hey, the balance sheet can look real good when you don't have to pay minimum wage.

But if Haywood was unwilling to be lectured by Zach, no way was he going to be lectured by nieces or nephews.

Or by me either, for that matter.

"We ain't here to argue about what other people are doing on their land," he said hotly. "We're here to talk about what we're gonna do on ours."

Robert sighed. "I just wish we didn't have to quit raising tobacco."

Andrew and Haywood nodded in gloomy agreement.

"We don't," Seth said. "At least not right away. We won't really lose money if we sign contracts for another couple of years."

Andrew brightened. "At least get a little more return outten them bulk barns."

My nieces and nephews looked at each other in dismay at the prospect of sweating out tobacco crops for another two or three years.

"But it wouldn't hurt to start cleansing some of our land," I said. "It takes about five years of chemical-free use to get certified, right?"

Lee shook his head. "Only thirty-six months."

"Well, if you guys want to do the paperwork, you can start with my seven acres on the other side of the creek."

"The Grimes piece?" asked Seth.

I nodded.

"I've got eight acres that touch her piece that you can use," he told the kids, and he and I looked expectantly at Daddy, who held title to the rest of the Grimes land. The field under discussion was isolated by woods on two sides and wetlands on the other, so it would be a good candidate for organic management.

"Yeah, all right," he said. "You can have mine, too. That'll give y'all about twenty-two acres to play with."

Some of the cousins still wanted to grumble, but Lee, Bobby and Emma thanked us with glowing faces. "Wait'll you see what we can do with twenty-two acres!"

Haywood, Robert, and Andrew were still looking skeptical.

"Have some cookies," I said and passed them the cake box.

CHAPTER 6

It is a wonder that everybody don't go to farming. Lawyers and doctors have to sit about town and play checkers and talk politics, and wait for somebody to quarrel or fight or get sick.

—*Profitable Farming in the Southern States,* 1890

On Wednesday morning, the first day of March, I was in the middle of a civil case that involved dogs and garbage cans when my clerk leaned over during a lull and whispered, "Talking about dogs, Faye Myers just IM'd me. The Wards' dog found a hand this morning."

News and gossip usually flies around the courthouse with the speed of sound but these days, with one of the dispatchers in the sheriff's department now armed with instant messaging, it's more like the speed of light.

"A what?"

"A man's hand," the clerk repeated.

"Phyllis Ward's Taffy?" The Wards were good friends of my Aunt Zell and Uncle Ash, and I've known Taffy since she was a pup. They live a couple of miles out from

Dobbs in a section that is still semirural and I drive by their house whenever I hold court here, so I often see one of them out with Taffy when I pass.

"I don't know the dog's name. All Faye said was that a Mr. Frank Ward called in to report that their dog came home just now with a man's hand in its mouth."

Taffy's a white-and-tan mixed breed with enough retriever in her that Mr. Frank had once taken her duck hunting in the hope that she would turn out to be a worker as well as a pet. She loved the thirty-mile drive to his favorite marshland, she loved being in the marsh, she loved splashing in the water, but as soon as he fired the first shot, she took off like a rocket. He called and whistled for hours.

No Taffy.

Eventually, he had to drive the thirty miles back and face Miss Phyllis, who hadn't wanted him to take their house pet hunting in the first place. It was a miserable eternity for him until Taffy finally dragged herself home a week later, footsore and muddy.

Even though he never again took her hunting, the dog did prove to be an excellent retriever. A rutted sandy lane bisects the farm. Locals call it the Ward Turnpike and use it as a shortcut between two paved highways. According to Aunt Zell, Taffy's always coming back from her morning runs with drink cups or greasy hamburger papers that litterbugs throw out. Over the years, she's brought home golf balls, disposable diapers, mittens and ballcaps, a large rubber squeaky frog, a plastic flamingo, the bottom half of a red bikini, and a paperback mystery novel titled *Murder on the Iditarod Trail.*

"Phyllis said it was a right interesting book," Aunt Zell reported.

But a man's hand?

Even though the Wards' place was five or six miles east of Bethel Baptist, surely that hand had to go with those legs that had been found Friday night. Unless we've suddenly thrown up a serial butcher?

Dwight was probably already out there and it would be unprofessional of me to bother him, but I was supposed to be having lunch with Aunt Zell and nobody could fault me for calling her during the morning break to let her know when I'd be there, right? Burning curiosity had nothing to do with it.

(*"Yeah and I've got twenty million in a Nigerian bank I'd like to split with you,"* said the disapproving preacher who lives in the back of my skull. *"Just send me your social security number and the number of your own bank account."*)

"Deborah? Oh, good!" Aunt Zell exclaimed. "Did you hear about Phyllis and Taffy? Is this not the most gruesome thing you've ever heard? First those legs and now this hand? Cold as it is, Phyllis said she had to give Taffy a bath in the garage before she could let her back in the house. I hope you don't mind, but I told her I'd bring them lunch if I could get you to carry me out there? Ash is still up in the mountains and the roads are icy all the way east to Burlington so I made him promise not to drive till it melts."

"Of course I'll take you," I said.

"Thanks, honey. I do appreciate it."

(*"It's always nice to get extra credit for something you*

want to do anyhow," my interior pragmatist said, happily thumbing his nose at the preacher.)

When the clock approached noon, I told the warring attorneys to try to work out a compromise during lunch and recessed fifteen minutes earlier than usual. I called Aunt Zell again from my car and she opened the door as soon as I turned into her drive. The rain had slacked to a light drizzle. Nevertheless, I grabbed my umbrella to shelter her back to the car.

Aunt Zell is my mother without Mother's streak of recklessness or that tart wry humor that kept Daddy off balance from the day he met her till the day she died. Although she never had children, Aunt Zell was the dutiful daughter who did everything else that was expected of her. She finished college. She married a respectable man in her own social rank. She joined the town's usual service organizations and volunteers wherever an extra pair of hands are needed. She not only lives by the rules, she agrees with those rules. Never in a million years would she have shocked the rest of the family and half the county by marrying a bootlegger with a houseful of motherless sons. But she adored my mother and she had immediately embraced those boys as if they were blood nephews. Furthermore, she's always treated Daddy as if he was the same upright pillar of the community as Uncle Ash.

When my wheels fell off after Mother died, she was the one family member I kept in touch with and she was the one who took me in without reproach or questions when I was finally ready to come home.

So, yes, I would drive her to Alaska if she asked me to, whether or not I had ulterior reasons for going to Alaska.

Like me, Aunt Zell wore black wool slacks and boots today, but my car coat was bright red while her parka was a hunter green. She had the hood up against the arctic wind and a halo of soft white curls blew around her pretty face.

"March sure didn't come in like a lamb, did it?" she asked by way of greeting.

I held the rear door for her and she carefully set a gallon jug of tea and an insulated bag on the floor before getting into the front seat. Even though the bag was zipped shut, the entrancing aroma of a bubbling hot chicken casserole filled my car and reminded me that I'd only had a piece of dry toast and coffee for breakfast.

The Ward place was a much-remodeled farmhouse that had been built by Mr. Frank's grandfather when this was a dairy farm. There had once been a smaller house over by the road that took its name from the farm, but when a tree fell on it during a hurricane, the grandfather had sited a larger house on the opposite side of the farm, away from the bustling dairy. The cows and the dairy were long gone, but the hay pastures remained and so did the Wards, who valued heritage over the hard cash the land would probably bring if they ever put it on the market. As I approached, I saw patrol cars down on the turnpike, but I didn't spot Dwight.

("*Not that you're looking for him,*" my inner preacher reminded me sternly.)

As is still the custom out here, I followed the drive around to the back rather than parking out front. A single light tap of my horn brought Mr. Frank to the door and he held it wide for us to run through the icy raindrops. Taffy was right there at his heels ready for a friendly pat or ear scratch and smelling faintly of baby shampoo.

"If she's ever seen a stranger, she's never let us know," said Miss Phyllis, coming out to the sun porch to give me a welcoming hug. "But you've been a stranger lately, Deborah. I do believe this is the first time I've seen you since the wedding."

She's small and bird-boned and always makes me feel like an Amazon even though I'm only five-six. After a quick look of appraisal, she smiled and said, "Married life must suit you."

"It does," I agreed.

"And Zell tells me that you're a full-time stepmother, too? Poor little boy. That's so sad about his mother. How's he doing?"

"Pretty good, everything considered," I said as Mr. Frank took our coats and we went on through the warm and cheerful kitchen to the dining room where the table was set with five places even though there were only four of us. "It helps that his cousins are close by. And Dwight's mother, too, of course. It's not as if he's had to adjust to a bunch of strangers."

"All the same, it has to be hard on him. On you and Dwight, too," Miss Phyllis said wisely. "You've both suddenly become full-time parents without the usual nine months to get used to the idea."

"There are times when I wish I could ask Mother how she did it," I admitted. "At least Dwight and I have known each other long enough to be used to each other's good and bad points, but how on earth did she find time to get to know Daddy with eight young boys in the house?"

"You'll figure it out," said Mr. Frank. "You're a lot like Sue, isn't she, Zell?"

Aunt Zell smiled and squeezed my hand, then we got to work unpacking the lunch. I filled the five glasses with ice cubes and poured tea while she set out a large earthenware casserole, a side dish of baby butter beans that she'd frozen last summer, and a basket of fresh hot yeast rolls. Miss Phyllis brought in butter and a dish of crisp sweet pickles.

By the time we sat down at the table, I had heard all about the severed hand Taffy found.

"I let her out as usual around seven this morning," said Miss Phyllis. "Most days, Frank and I will take a cup of coffee and walk around the edge of the woods with her, but it was so raw and wet this morning that we let her go alone. I have no idea where she went, but as muddy and drenched as she was when she came back, I'm sure she was over splashing in the creek."

"She'll do that if we're not with her," said Mr. Frank, smoothing down silky white hair that still bore the marks of the hat he must have worn earlier. "Doesn't matter how cold it is."

"She was out there a good forty-five minutes," his wife continued, "and I was loading the dishwasher when I saw her, through the kitchen window, coming across the backyard with something in her mouth. At first I thought it was somebody's old brown leather work glove or an oddly shaped piece of wood. As soon as I opened the door for her, I told her to drop it because whatever it was, I didn't want it on my clean floor. She left it on the step and came on in. I keep an old towel out there on the sun porch to wipe her off if she comes back muddy and she knows to stand still for me, but this morning, she kept nosing at the door like she wanted her find.

"I finally opened the door to see what was so interesting to her and as soon as I took a good look, I just screamed for Frank. It was horrible, Deborah! A hand chopped off at the wrist. Yuck!"

"I called 911," said Mr. Frank.

"And I took Taffy right out to the garage for a good soapy bath. I even washed out her mouth. I couldn't bear to think of her licking me with a tongue that had licked at that thing."

She shuddered and almost spilled the glass of tea when she took a sip to steady her nerves.

"Try not to think about that part," said Aunt Zell. "I'm sure her mouth is nice and sweet again."

With a heartiness that fooled no one, Mr. Frank said, "I'm so hungry I could eat a horse. This looks delicious, Zell."

Miss Phyllis allowed herself to be distracted from that grisly image and indicated where we were to sit.

"Is someone else coming?" I asked as I sat down next to the extra chair and unfolded my napkin.

Mr. Frank nodded. "I did tell Dwight that lunch would be here when he was ready to eat, but he said for us not to wait on him."

That was all I needed to hear and as soon as he'd said grace, I excused myself and went out to the sun porch to call. Taffy followed, her fur soft and shining clean. Nevertheless, I did not put my hand out for her to lick.

"Just wanted you to know that lunch is on the table," I said when Dwight answered.

"Sorry, shug. I can't leave now. I'll have to grab a sandwich or something back in town." He let two beats of silence go by, then said, "What? No questions?"

I couldn't help smiling. "No. Mr. Frank and Miss Phyllis have already told me everything."

"Not everything," he said and hung up before I could say another word.

Mindful that I had to get back to court yet solicitous of Dwight who had been out in the cold and wet for hours, Phyllis Ward said she'd carry Aunt Zell back to town if I wanted to swing down and take him some lunch. Because she was already pulling out bread and lettuce and sliced ham from the refrigerator, and because Aunt Zell seemed to be settling in for a nice long visit, I really had no choice except to thank her for her thoughtfulness and do as I was told.

"I hope he's dressed warm enough," she worried aloud as she saw me off. "I'd send him one of Frank's white sweaters if he wasn't twice as big as Frank."

The rain had pretty much stopped as I drove the hundred yards or so down the highway, then turned into the rutted lane. A few yards off the road, a left fork continued on down the slope into the woods and presumably to the creek. The right one ran along the far edge of fields green with winter rye and would eventually lead over to Ward Dairy Road, so named for the original dairy farm. A knot of patrol cars blocked the left lane, which seemed to be the center of activity, so I did a U-turn and backed into the other one.

As I expected, someone alerted Dwight and in a couple of minutes he slung his raincoat in back and eased his tall frame into the front seat beside me with a head-shaking smile. "Couldn't resist it, could you?"

"Not me," I said, handing him the sandwiches and hot coffee. His brown hair was dark from the rain. "I'd've let you stay out here and starve, but Miss Phyllis was worried about you. I think she feels guilty that Taffy brought you out on such a cold wet day."

"Who's Taffy?" he asked around a mouthful of ham and lettuce.

"Their dog. The one that found the hand. Was it a left or right?"

He uncapped the coffee and took a long drink, then grinned at me. "I thought you said the Wards told you everything."

"I forgot to ask them that particular detail. Miss Phyllis was freaking just thinking about it in Taffy's mouth."

"It's a right hand."

"Too bad it wasn't the left. A ring might have given you a lead if he was wearing one."

We both glanced at the gold band gleaming on his own left hand. The words I'd had engraved there wouldn't have helped anyone identify the owner, but the date could narrow it down a bit.

"I just hope the guy's prints are on file." He finished the first sandwich and unwrapped the second.

"The fingertips are still intact?"

"Some of them." He didn't elaborate and I didn't ask. "The cold weather helps. We found the left arm about an hour ago. Makes us think that the other arm and hand might be here but some animal could have dragged them off. Coons or possums or more dogs maybe. Their tracks are all over and something's been at it."

He continued to eat, his appetite unaffected by a situation that would make my skin crawl if I allowed myself to dwell on it.

"This lane connects to Ward Dairy Road," I said.

He nodded, already there before me. "And Ward Dairy runs right by Bethel Baptist, less than five miles from where those legs were found. When we finish up here, I'm going to have our patrol cars eyeball all the ditches between here and there."

I glanced at my watch and realized that I was going to be late if I didn't hurry.

"Yeah, I need to get back to work, too," Dwight said. He put the wrappings in the bag Miss Phyllis had sent the sandwiches in, wiped his mouth with the napkins she'd provided and leaned over to kiss me. "The roads are slick, so don't speed, okay?"

"Okay."

He raised a cynical eyebrow. "You say it, but do you really mean it?"

Fortunately, there were no slow-moving tractors out on the road this first day of March and I made it back to court with a few minutes to spare and without going more than five or six miles over the limit. To my surprise, the litigating parties had indeed decided to settle, and after I signed all the orders, we moved on to the next item on the docket, which was more complicated.

Judson "Buck" Harris, a large commercial grower, had divorced his wife, Suzanne "Suzu" Poynter Harris, a middle-aged woman who might have been attractive in her youth but had now let herself go. A bad hair color was showing at least an inch of gray roots, her skin had faced too many hours of wind and sun without moisturizers, and her boxy navy blue suit and navy overblouse did nothing to disguise the extra thirty pounds she was carrying.

The divorce had been finalized a week or so ago and we were now trying to make an equitable division of their jointly held assets. "Trying to" because, to my annoyance, there was no Mr. Harris at the other attorney's table. Said attorney was my cousin Reid Stephenson, a younger partner at my old law firm and someone who knows me well enough to know when I'm unhappy with a situation.

"Your Honor," he said, giving me a hopeful look of boyish entreaty, "I would ask the court's patience and request one final continuance."

"Objection," snapped Mrs. Harris's lawyer.

Pete Taylor was just as problematic for me as Reid, even though he, too, had agreed to my hearing this case. Pete's the current president of the District Bar Association and he was one of my early supporters when I first decided to run for the bench. And yes, there are times when practicing law in this district can feel almost incestuous. But if every judge recused himself because of personal connections, our dockets would never be cleared.

"Is Mr. Harris ill or physically unable to come to court?" I asked Reid as I looked around the almost empty courtroom.

"Not to my knowledge, Your Honor, but I haven't been able to reach him this week."

Pete Taylor straightened his bright red bow tie, one of dozens that he owns, and got to his feet. "Your Honor, this matter has dragged on three months longer than necessary because Mr. Harris can't seem to remember court dates. Today's hearing is to establish his financial worth and this is the third time that Mr. Lee has been called to testify as to the validity and accuracy of Mr. Harris's bank records. Unless my worthy opponent plans to challenge Mr. Lee's veracity, I submit that there is no substantive reason not to begin without Mr. Harris's presence and hope he will arrive before we get to disputed matters."

"I agree," I said. "Call your witness, Mr. Taylor."

Before he could do so, Mrs. Harris tugged at his sleeve and when he bent to hear what she wanted to ask, it was clear from her body language that she was upset about something and that Pete's answer did not please her. She immediately let go his sleeve and spoke to me directly.

"Your Honor?"

"Yes, Mrs. Harris?"

"Can't this be more private?"

"More private?"

"Mr. Lee's going to be talking about personal stuff, about how much money we have and how much land we own, and I don't see why it has to be said in front of a lot of people."

A lot of people?

At this point, except for the participants in the case, there were only five others in the courtroom, a man and four women. I recognized two of the women, elderly regulars who prefer courtroom drama to afternoon television. The young man sat three rows in front of the third woman, but a current seemed to run between them. No doubt this was the divorcing couple scheduled to follow the Harris hearing. The fourth woman was unfamiliar to me.

In her anger, Mrs. Harris spoke with a good old Colleton County twang like someone raised on a local farm. I didn't know much about the Harrises except by hearsay, but I gathered that she had worked right alongside her husband back when he was out in the fields, plowing and planting and growing the produce that was now sold in grocery chains from Maryland to Maine. There might be diamonds on her big-knuckled fingers and those might be real pearls around her neck, but this was clearly someone who had spent her youth in hard work and plain dealing.

She turned to glare accusingly at the woman seated alone on the last bench in the courtroom. "I don't want *her* here while this is going on."

The woman returned her glare with level eyes that were vaguely—arrogantly?—amused. Wearing jeans and a chocolate brown turtleneck sweater, with a fleece-lined beige leather jacket draped over her slender shoulders, she lounged against the armrest at the end of the bench and seemed completely at ease. From where I sat, she looked to be my age—late thirties. She wasn't classically beautiful, yet there was something that made you take a second look and it wasn't just the flaming red hair that flowed in loose waves to her shoulders.

"I'm sorry, Mrs. Harris. This is a public hearing."

She wasn't the first person to cringe at the realization that what had been private was now going to become public knowledge, but her animosity was so palpable that I had a feeling that the redhead back there must have played a starring role in the disintegration of the Harris partnership.

Mrs. Harris flounced back around in her chair and I nodded to her attorney. "Call your witness, Mr. Taylor."

As expected, that witness was Denton Lee, an executive at Dobbs Fidelity Trust and one good-looking man. Dent's a few years older than me but even though he's a distant cousin by way of my former law partner, John Claude Lee, I hadn't known him when I was growing up, so I was devastated to come back to Dobbs and discover that the most stone-cold gorgeous man in town was happily married and the father of two equally beautiful children. Like all the Colleton County Lees, his hair is prematurely white which goes very nicely with his piercing blue eyes and fair skin.

After firmly reminding myself that I was a married woman now ("*Married but not brain dead*," my interior pragmatist said tartly), I put aside those memories of past regrets and concentrated on his testimony as to the financial holdings of Harris Farms.

In front of me was a thick sheaf of records that detailed the checks deposited and the withdrawals made from the three accounts that the bank handled.

In clear, direct testimony, Dent explained for the record precisely how these statements had been generated, the technology used, the validity and accuracy of the data. This was not the first time he had come to court with such testimony and I was no more inclined to distrust his expertise than was my cousin Reid.

The Harrises may have started with a single thirty-acre farm here in the county, but their tomatoes now grew in huge fields that sprawled from Cotton Grove to the other side of New Bern. Yet, despite the amount of money trundling in and out of their accounts, the Harrises ran what was still basically a mom-and-pop organization. Yes, there was a layer of accountants and clerks to track expenses and taxes; overseers who directed the planting, cultivation, and harvesting out on the land; mechanics who kept the equipment in good repair; managers who kept the migrant camps up to federal standards; and marketing personnel, too, but Harris Farms was a limited liability company, which meant that the Harrises owned all the "shares." Mr. Harris was said to be a hands-on farmer who still got on a tractor occasionally or rode out to the fields himself.

The gross take from fresh produce they'd sold to the grocery chain was astonishing, but my eyes really widened when I saw the size of the check from a major cannery for the bulk of last year's tomato crop. Maybe Haywood was right. Maybe my brothers could do with garden peas what the Harrises had done with tomatoes.

"Thank you, Mr. Lee," Pete Taylor said when the banker finished speaking.

"No questions," said Reid.

Next came testimony from their chief accountant, then Reid asked for a recess to see if he could contact his client.

"Good luck on that!" I heard Mrs. Harris say. "If he's still holed up in the mountains, we don't get good cell service there and he never answers a land line."

As Reid stepped out to place his call, I signaled to the divorcing couple. It was a do-it-yourself filing. Both were only twenty-two. No children, no marital property to divide, no request for alimony by either party. I looked at the two of them.

"According to these papers, you were only married four months before you called it quits. Are you sure you gave it enough time?"

"Oh yes, ma'am," said the woman. "We lived together two years before we got married."

The man gave a silent shrug.

His soon-to-be-ex-wife said, "Marriage always changes things, doesn't it?"

I couldn't argue with that. I signed the documents that would dissolve their legal bond and wished them both better luck next time.

"Won't be a next time," the young man said quietly.

CHAPTER 7

The farmer must be vigilant and sensible to all that happens upon his land.

—*Profitable Farming in the Southern States,* 1890

On Thursday, I had lunch with Portland at a Tex-Mex restaurant that's recently opened up only two blocks from the courthouse. Although the sun was finally shining, the mercury wasn't supposed to climb higher than the mid-thirties, which made chile rellenos and jalapeño cornbread sound appealing to me.

Portland was game even though she couldn't eat anything very hot or spicy.

As we were shown to our table, she tried to remember just how many times this place had changed hands in the last eight or nine years since the original longtime owner died and his heirs put it up for sale.

"First it was Peggy's Pantry, then the Souper Sandwich House, but wasn't there something else right after Peggy's?"

"The Sunshine Café?" I hazarded.

"No, that was two doors down from here, where the new card shop's opened."

Neither of us could remember and our waitress spoke too little English to be of help. She handed us menus, took our drink orders and went off to fetch them.

"I swear I feel just like Clover," Portland complained as she looked through the menu for something bland.

"Clover?"

"You remember Clover. My grandmother's last cow? Every spring she'd get into the wild garlic and the milk would taste awful. That's me these days. Anything fun to eat goes straight through my nipples and gives the baby colic or diarrhea."

With impeccable timing, a plate of something that involved black bean paste arrived at the next table.

"A few less graphics here, please," I said.

"Sorry. I don't suppose you want to talk about body parts either, huh?"

I sighed. "Not particularly. Without the head and torso, Dwight and Bo are beginning to think they may never get an identity. The fingerprints aren't in any official databases and there don't seem to be any men missing who match the body type the medical examiner's postulated, based on two legs, a hand, and an arm."

We ordered, then talked about the baby, about Cal, about Dwight and Avery, about the Mideast situation and the President's latest imbecilic pronouncements until our food came. Our talk was the usual bouncing from subject to subject that friends do when they know each other so well they can almost finish each other's sentences. She laughed when I told her Haywood and Isabel's reaction to the idea of raising ostriches and she shared a bit of catty gossip about a woman attorney that neither of us likes.

We worried briefly about Luther Parker, a judge that we do like, and how it was lucky he'd only twisted his ankle when he fell on the ice yesterday.

"How did he rule on that violation of the restraining order by—what's his name? Braswell? Your client's ex-husband?" I asked.

"James Braswell," she said. "Imposed another fine and gave him ten more days in jail, but since it's to run concurrent with what you gave him, he'll be out again by the middle of next week. If he violates it again, Parker warned him that he could be doing some serious time. I hope this convinces him to stay away because Karen's really scared of him, Deborah."

"Any children?"

"No, but she's got a sick mother that she's caring for, so she doesn't feel she can just cut and run even though that's what her gut's telling her."

This was not the first time we'd had this discussion about why some men can't accept that a relationship is over when the woman says it's over.

"At least Judge Parker's going to take away his guns."

"That's a step in the right direction," I said trying to ignore the dish of butter between us that cried out to be spread on the last of my cornbread.

My back was to the door so I didn't immediately see the woman who spoke to Portland by name as she started to pass our table.

Portland looked up and did a double take. "Well, I'll be darned! Hey, girl! What brings you up to Dobbs?"

"A man, of course," the laughing voice said. "Isn't it always?"

I half-turned in my seat and immediately recognized the redhead who had been in my courtroom yesterday.

"Deborah," said Portland, "do y'all know each other? Robbie-Lane Smith?"

I smiled and shook my head.

"Well, you've heard me talk about her. Deborah Knott, meet Robbie-Lane Smith. She managed that restaurant down at Wrightsville Beach where I worked two summers."

"I thought her name was Flame—? Oh, right. The hair."

The woman laughed. "A lot of people still call me that."

Portland arched an eyebrow at her old roommate. "People of the male persuasion?"

A noncommittal shrug didn't exactly deny it. She wore jeans again today and carried her tan fleece-lined jacket over one arm. Her silk shirt was a dark copper that did nice things for her green eyes and fair complexion even as I realized that she was probably mid-forties instead of the late thirties I'd first thought her.

"Are you by yourself?" Portland gestured to the empty chair at our table. "Deborah and I are almost finished, but why don't you join us?"

"Sorry. I'm meeting someone." She pulled a card from her pocket. "Here's my cell number and e-mail, though, and why don't you give me yours? It looks like I'm going to be around for a couple of days. Maybe we could get together for drinks or something?"

"Sure." Portland rummaged in her purse and came up with one of her own cards.

"Portland *Brewer* now? You're married?"

"And the mother of a two-and-a-half-month-old," she said proudly. "You still at the restaurant?"

"Nope. I own a B&B just two blocks from the River Walk down in Wilmington. We have some serious catching up to do." She turned to follow the waitress who had been waiting to show her to a booth in the back. "Call me, okay? Nice meeting you, Judge."

"Oh, God, look at those hips!" Portland murmured enviously as the other woman walked away. "She's at least five years older than me and I never looked that sexy in jeans. I'm a cow!"

"You are not a cow," I soothed. "Besides, didn't you say you'd lost another two pounds?"

Her face brightened beneath her mop of short black curls. "True. And I didn't eat any bread or butter today."

"There you go, then."

I signaled our waitress that we were ready for our check and we gathered up our coats and scarves.

"How did Flame know you're a judge?" asked Portland as we were leaving.

I explained that she'd been in my court the afternoon before. "The Harris Farms divorce," I said. "And Mrs. Harris was furious that she was there. I get the impression that your friend Flame is Buck Harris's new flame."

"Really? I've heard tales about him for years but I never met him. Is he good-looking?"

"I've only seen him once and he's not our type—musclebound with a thick neck as I recall. I've had to grant four continuances because he just won't come to court. Reid's his attorney and I warned him yesterday that if

Harris doesn't show up next week, I'm going to try the case without him."

"Speak of the devil and up he jumps," said Portland, and we watched as my cousin Reid Stephenson entered the restaurant and went straight on back to join Flame Smith in a rear booth.

"If Buck Harris doesn't get himself down from the mountains and tend to business, he's liable to find Reid warming her bed."

"You're getting cynical in your old age," Portland said. "She's got at least ten years on him."

"You're the one who said how sexy she looked in those jeans," I reminded her. "And we both know Reid's weakness for redheads."

"Not to mention blondes and brunettes," Portland murmured.

"Now who's being cynical?"

At the afternoon break, I called Dwight's number.

He answered on the first ring. "Bryant here." His tone was brusque.

"And hey to you, too," I said. "Does this mean the honeymoon's over?"

"Sorry. I didn't check my screen." Warmth came back into his voice. "I assumed it was Richards calling back. What's up?"

"I just wanted to know if you remembered to pick up Bandit's heartworm pills from the vet? Or should I do it on my way home?"

"Could you?" he asked. "And call Kate to let her know I'm running late?"

"Don't worry. I'll pick Cal up, too."

I heard voices in the background. "What's going on?"

"Another hand's been reported," he said grimly. "At the edge of Apple Creek, just off Jernigan Road."

"Jernigan Road? That's nowhere near Ward Dairy. Was there a wedding ring on the finger?"

"I doubt it," Dwight said. "They say it's another right."

CHAPTER 8

Cold does not injure the vitality of seeds, but moisture is detrimental to all kinds.

—*Profitable Farming in the Southern States,* 1890

DWIGHT BRYANT
THURSDAY AFTERNOON, MARCH 2

Dwight hung up the phone as several officers crowded into his office to get their instructions. Using the large topographical map of the county that covered most of one wall, he located Apple Creek and traced it with his finger till it crossed Jernigan Road. It was well south and east of Dobbs and, as Deborah had just pointed out, nowhere near Ward Dairy Road or Bethel Baptist where the other limbs had been found.

"Here's where the kids found the hand. Most animals won't usually carry something all that far, but it could have washed down, so for starters, I want you walking at least a half-mile up the creek and maybe a quarter-mile down. Both sides. Pay particular attention here and here, where there're lanes that get close enough to the creek that a body could be easily dumped from a vehicle. And keep your eyes open for anything out of the ordinary that might give a clue to whoever did the dumping. Mel, you and your team take it north and the rest of you go south. Richards says it looks like that hand's been out there a while, so take some rods and check anything that looks like a log."

"Not much of a creek, as I remember," said Sheriff Bo Poole when the room was clear. "Just a little offshoot of Black Creek."

"Best I recall, it pretty much dries up every August," Dwight agreed, "but we've had a right wet winter and I've heard it can pool up in places."

Bo nodded. "Beaver dams."

He was a small trim man, but he carried his authority like a six-footer. "I used to run a trapline through there when I was a boy. Muskrats and beavers, even the occasional mink."

He went over to the map and looked at it so intently that Dwight was sure his boss was walking the creek again in his mind.

While Dwight called Detective Mayleen Richards to tell her reinforcements were on the way and how she should deploy them, he watched as Bo put his finger on the creek and traced it a little further west.

"Here's where it flows out of Black Creek. Used to be good trapping along in here, too." He looked up at Dwight. "You fixing to head out there?"

Dwight nodded.

"Let me get my hat. Maybe I'll ride along with you."

After so many gray days, the blue sky was washed clean of all clouds. Even the sunlight seemed extra bright, and they rode out of Dobbs in companionable silence, enjoying the novelty of a clear windshield and no wipers swishing back and forth.

"Everything's going good then?" Bo asked.

"Would be better if somebody'd come forward and tell us who's missing."

"No, I meant at home. You and Deborah and your boy."

"He's handling it better than I would. Bedtimes can be a little rough. That seems to be when he misses Jonna the most."

"How's Deborah handling it?"

"Cal and me, we're real lucky, Bo."

"She got any long-range plans for you?"

"What do you mean?"

"Some women, they think they want a lawman and then when they get him, they don't want the law part."

"That happen with you and Marnie?"

"Naw, but Marnie was special."

"So's Deborah."

"All I'm saying is let me know if I need to start looking me another chief deputy."

"And all *I'm* saying is don't plan on writing a want ad anytime soon."

When they pulled onto the shoulder of Jernigan Road near the little bridge that crossed Apple Creek and stepped out of the truck, a bitter wind whipped through the trees and dead vines that overhung the water. It stung their eyes and cut at their bare faces. Richards walked up from the creekbank to meet them, a wad of tissues in her gloved hand. She had been fighting a drippy cold all week and the tip of her nose was raw from blowing. Tendrils of cinnamon brown hair worked their way loose from her cap and blew across her freckled face until she tucked them back in.

"Nothing yet, sir," she reported. "It's up this way."

Thin crusts of ice edged the creek, which was only about eight feet wide and slow-moving. At this point it was less than eighteen inches deep.

The two men followed as Richards led the way down a narrow rough footpath that paralleled the south bank. Nearly impassable here at the end of winter, one would almost need a bushaxe to get through it in summer. Dried briars tore at their pantlegs and tangled vines caught at their feet. All three of them carried slender metal rods and they used them as staffs to keep their balance and brush back limbs.

Dwight was pleased to see that Mayleen was a savvy enough woodsman to hold back the small tree branches she pushed aside till Bo could grab them in turn and hold them for Dwight, rather like holding open a set of swinging doors to keep them from hitting the person behind in the face. It was a reminder that Mayleen grew up in this area and that Bo knew her people, which is how she talked him into giving her a job.

"Who'd you say found it?" asked Bo, who kept having to duck low-hanging branches to keep from losing his trademark porkpie hat—a dapper black felt in winter, black straw in the summer.

"Three girls from the local high school." Richards paused to blow her nose. "They were looking for early fiddleheads for a science project. One of them's my niece. Shirlee's oldest daughter?"

Bo grunted to acknowledge he knew her sister Shirlee.

"Soon as they realized what it was, she called me on her cell phone and sent me a picture of it. I'm afraid they trampled the ground around it too much for us to see any animal tracks."

Bo shook his head and Dwight knew it was not over the messed up tracks, but that teenagers came equipped these days with cell phones that could transmit pictures instantaneously.

"Getting too high tech for me," he said. "Any day now I expect to hear they've put a chip in somebody's brain so they can tap right into the Internet without having to mess with a keyboard or screen."

A few hundred feet or so in from the road, they reached the scene, a popular local fishing spot, according to Richards. A ring of stones encircled an old campfire and a few drink cans and scraps of paper were scattered around.

"There's actually a way to drive here closer, but it means going around through someone's fields. That's how the girls got here," she said.

Detective Denning was already there taking pictures

and documenting the find. The hand lay at the edge of the water among some ice-glazed leaves.

"My niece said it had ice on it, too, when they first found it," said Richards. "But when they poked it, the ice broke off."

It had been in the open so long that the skin was dark and desiccated around the white finger bones.

"Not gonna be easy getting fingerprints," said Denning as they joined them. "I haven't moved it yet, but just eyeballing it?" He gave a pessimistic shrug inside his thick jacket. "Doesn't look hopeful."

"Were the bones hacked or sawed?" Dwight asked.

"The cartilage is pretty much gone, so it's hard to say. Should I go ahead and bag it?"

Bo Poole deferred to Dwight, who nodded.

Abruptly, the sheriff said, "Tell you what, Dwight. Let's you and me take a little drive. I need to see something."

"Call me if they find anything else," Dwight said, then followed Bo back out to the road and his truck.

"Which way, Bo?" he asked, putting the truck in gear.

"Let's head over to Black Creek."

They drove north along Jernigan Road until they neared a crossroads, at which point, Bo told him to turn left toward the setting sun. As they approached the backside of the unincorporated little town of Black Creek, population around 600 give or take a handful, the empty land gave way to houses.

"Slow down a hair," said Bo and his porkpie hat swung back and forth as he studied both sides.

Dwight knew Bo was enjoying himself so he did not spoil that enjoyment by asking questions.

"There!" Bo said suddenly, pointing to a narrow dirt road that led south. "Let's see how far down you can get your truck."

The houses here were not much more than shacks and the dark-skinned children who played outside stopped to stare as the two white men passed.

The dirt road ended in a cable stretched between uprights that looked like sawed-off light poles. Beyond the cable, the land dropped off sharply in a tangle of blackberry bushes and trash trees strangled in kudzu and honeysuckle vines. A well-worn footpath began beside the left upright and disappeared in the undergrowth.

Bo looked back down the dirt road to the low buildings clustered in the distance, then nodded to himself and struck off down the path.

Dwight followed.

In a few minutes, they reached the creek that gave the little town its name and the path split to run in both directions along the bank. Without hesitation, Bo followed the flow of water that ran deep and swift after so much rain.

They came upon the charred remains of a campfire built in a scooped-out hollow edged with creek stones next to a fallen tree that had probably toppled during the last big hurricane and that now probably served as a bench for the kids who had cleared the site. A dirt bike with a twisted frame lay on the far side of the log. Scattered around were several beer cans, an empty wine bottle, cigarette butts and some fast-food wrappers. There were also a couple of roach clips and an empty plastic prescription bottle that had held a relatively mild painkiller, which Dwight picked up. The owner's name was no longer legible, but the name of the pharmacy was there and so was most of the prescription number. If this was all the kids were into though, things weren't too bad in this neighborhood.

He pocketed the bottle for later attention and hurried after Bo, who had not paused at the campfire, but kept walking as if he were late for his own wedding, ducking beneath the tree branches, his small trim body barely disturbing the bushes on either side of the path that pulled at Dwight's bulk as he tried to pass.

The creek deepened and narrowed and the path made by casual fishermen and adventurous kids petered out in even rougher underbrush, yet Bo pushed on.

When Dwight finally caught up, his boss was standing by the water's edge. At his feet was what at first appeared to be a half-submerged log.

"Over yonder's where Apple Creek wanders off," he told Dwight, pointing downstream to the other side of the creek just as one of their people broke through the underbrush and stopped in surprise in seeing them on that side of the fork. Then he looked down at the remains that lay in the shallows. "And here's where poor ol' Fred Mitchiner wandered off to."

CHAPTER 9

The world seeks no stronger evidence of a man's goodness of heart than kindness.

—Profitable Farming in the Southern States, 1890

Deborah Knott
Thursday Evening, March 2

I did not repeat what Dwight had told me, but at adjournment, I asked my clerk if she'd heard anything more about that first set of body parts, figuring that if fresh rumors were circulating through the courthouse about another hand, she would mention it. Instead, she shook her head.

"And Faye's off today, so I wouldn't anyhow. Lavon's on duty and he never talks."

As I left the parking lot behind the courthouse, I didn't spot Dwight's truck, but there seemed to be no more activity than the usual coming and going of patrol cars. A second hand though? Where were the bodies? I thought of that crematorium down in Georgia that stashed bodies all over its grounds rather than committing them to the fire, and a gruesome image filled my head of a pickup truck bumping around the county, strewing body parts as it went. Careless drivers are forever hauling unsecured loads of trash that blow off and litter our roadsides. Was this another example?

I switched my car radio to a local news station, but heard nothing on this latest development.

After picking up Bandit's heartworm pills at the vet's, I swung by Kate and Rob's to collect Cal. The new baby was fussing and Kate had dark circles under her eyes.

"He got me up four times last night," she said, jiggling little R.W. on her shoulder with soothing pats as Cal went upstairs with Mary Pat to retrieve his backpack. Through the archway to the den, I saw young Jake watch them go, then he settled back on the couch and turned his eyes to the video playing on the TV.

"I thought he was sleeping six hours at a stretch now."

"So did I," she said wearily. "I was wrong."

A middle-aged Hispanic woman came down the hall. Kate's cleaning woman, María, whose last name I can never remember. She wore a heavy winter coat and drew on a pair of thick knitted gloves. She gave me a shy smile of greeting and said to Kate, "I go now, *señora*."

"Thanks, María. See you on Monday?"

"Monday, *sí*."

She let herself out the kitchen door and Kate said, "I don't know how I'd manage without her."

She transferred the fretful baby to her other shoulder. "Before this one, I only needed her every other week and still put in a twenty-five-hour week in my studio." Kate was a freelance fabric designer and had remodeled the farm's old packhouse into a modern studio. "Now she's here twice a week and I still haven't done a lick of drawing since R.W. was born."

"Slacker," I said.

She gave me a wan smile.

"Kate, he's not even two months old. Give yourself a break. Are you sure it's not too much to have Cal here every afternoon?"

"He's no real extra trouble."

"But?" I asked, hearing something in her voice.

"It's only the usual bickering," she sighed. "The four-year age difference. And it's probably Mary Pat's fault more than Cal's. She's just not as patient with Jake now that she has Cal to play with. He's so happy when they get home from school and it really hurts his feelings when they exclude him. I had to give her a time-out this afternoon and we're going to have a serious sit-down tonight after Jake goes to bed, so maybe you could speak to Cal?"

"I'll tell Dwight," I said.

Kate shook her head in disapproval. "Come on, Deborah. I'm not asking you to beat him with a stick or send him to bed without supper. I'm just asking you to reinforce the scolding I gave him and Mary Pat."

"But Dwight's the one to speak to him. He's his father," I protested weakly.

"And you're his stepmother. *In loco maternis* or whatever the Latin phrase would be. Sooner or later, you're going to have to help with discipline and you might as well get started now. Besides, if you think Cal's going to resent your talking to him about something this minor, imagine how he's going to feel if you tattle to Dwight and it gets blown out of proportion."

I knew she was right. Nevertheless, I was so apprehensive about this aspect of parenting, that we were almost to the turn-in at the long drive that leads from the road to the house before I got up enough nerve to say, "Aunt Kate tells me that you and Mary Pat are having a problem with Jake."

Cal gave me a wary glance. "Not really."

"That's not what she says."

"I'll get the mail," he said, reaching for the door handle as I slowed to a stop by the mailbox. I waited till he was back in the car with our magazines and first of the month bills, then drove on down the lane, easing over the low dikes that keep the lane from washing away.

"She says that you and Mary Pat aren't treating him very nicely. That you don't want him to play with you."

"He can play, but he doesn't know how. He's a baby."

"He's four years old," I said gently. "If he doesn't know how, then you should take the time to teach him."

"But he can't even read yet."

"I know it's hard to be patient when he can't keep up, Cal, but think how you'd feel if you went over there and he and Mary Pat wouldn't play with you. Think how it makes Aunt Kate feel. This is a stressful time for her with a fussy new baby. If you won't do it for Jake, do it for Aunt Kate."

He was quiet as he flicked the remote to open the garage door for us.

"Are you going to tell Dad?"

"Not if you and Mary Pat start cutting Jake some slack, okay?"

"Okay," he said, visibly relieved.

Inside the house, he hurried down to the utility room to let Bandit out for a short run in the early evening twilight and I let out the breath I'd been metaphorically holding.

"*See? That wasn't bad,*" said my internal preacher.

"*Piece of cake,*" crowed the pragmatist.

By the time Dwight got home, smothered pork chops and sweet potatoes were baking in the oven, string beans awaited a quick steaming in a saucepan, the rolls were ready to brown and I was checking over Cal's math homework while he finished studying for tomorrow's spelling test.

I was dying to hear about the latest developments, but I kept my curiosity in hand until after supper when Cal went to take his shower and get into his pajamas before the Hurricanes game came on. Tonight was an away game and Cal didn't want to miss a single minute before his nine o'clock bedtime.

"The thing is," Dwight said as he got up to pour us a second cup of coffee, "are you likely to be the judge for a half-million civil lawsuit?"

"Probably not," I said, my curiosity really piqued now. "Something that big usually goes to superior court. Unless both parties agree to it, most of our judgments are capped at ten thousand."

"Okay then," he said and settled back to tell me how Bo Poole started thinking about his teenage years when he used to run a trapline along the creeks in the southern part of the county, especially Black Creek.

"He wasn't the only one and it dawned on him that Fred Mitchiner used to trap animals and sell the pelts, too."

"Who's Fred Mitchiner?"

"That eighty-year-old with Alzheimer's who wandered away from the nursing home right before Christmas, remember?"

I shook my head. "That whole week was a haze. Except for our wedding and Christmas itself, about all I remember is that you took two weeks off and Bo wouldn't let you come into work."

Dwight cut his eyes at me. "That's all you remember?"

I couldn't repress my own smile as his big hand covered mine and his thumb gently stroked the inside of my wrist.

"Don't change the subject," I said, with a glance into the living room where Cal seemed absorbed by the game. "Fred Mitchiner."

"Once Mitchiner slipped away from the nursing home, it would have been a long walk for him, but they do say Alzheimer's patients often try to find their way back to where they were happy. Bo figures the old guy probably thought he'd go check his traps, fell in the water, and either drowned or died of exposure. High water and animals did the rest. It wasn't murder."

"But it does sound like negligence," I said. "Is that what his family feel?"

He shrugged. "We haven't told them yet. Bo wants to wait till we get an official ID; but yeah, that's the talk."

CHAPTER 10

There is something always preying on something, and nothing is free from disaster in this sublunary world.

—*Profitable Farming in the Southern States,* 1890

Friday's criminal court is usually a catchall day for me—the minor felonies and misdemeanors that don't fit in elsewhere. Sometimes I think Doug Woodall, our current DA, goes out of his way to see that the weird ones wind up on my Friday docket. On the other hand, sometimes his sense of humor matches mine and when I entered the courtroom that morning and saw Dr. Linda Allred seated in the center aisle, it was hard not to smile.

"All rise," said Cleve Overby, the most punctilious of the bailiffs, and before she'd finished giving him a rueful hands-up motion from her motorized wheelchair, he grinned and added, "all except Dr. Allred. Oyez, oyez, oyez. This honorable court for the County of Colleton is now open and sitting for the dispatch of its business. God save the State and this honorable court, the Honorable Judge Deborah Knott presiding. Be seated."

I ran my finger down the calendar and found the case

she was probably there for, then sat back and listened as ADA Kevin Foster pulled the first shuck on Anthony Barkley, a nineteen-year-old black kid who had ridden through a parking lot on his bicycle and tried to snatch a woman's purse. Before the shoulder strap fully left her arm, she gave it a sharp yank, which sent him sprawling into the path of a slow-moving car. The car immediately flattened his bike and the man who jumped out to see what was going on had proceeded to flatten the youthful thief.

"Fifteen days suspended, forty hours of community service," I said.

Next came a Latino migrant, one Ernesto Palmeiro, age thirty, who had gotten drunk, "borrowed" a tractor, and headed east, plowing a half-mile-long furrow across several semi-rural lawns before the highway patrol could head him off.

"He deeply regrets his actions," said the interpreter, "but he went a little loco when his wife left him and went home to Mexico. He's already repaired most of the damage and throws himself on the mercy of the court."

I rather doubted if that was what he'd said, but what the hell? "Fifteen days suspended on condition that he finishes putting all the yards back the way they were, including any plantings that he might have destroyed."

I looked at his boss, a Latino landscaper, who'd spoken on his behalf. "And I'd suggest, sir, that you teach him how to lift the plows before you let him near another tractor."

I sent the exhibitionist for a mental health evaluation and gave the guy who'd tried to steal an antique lamppost from the town commons ten days of jail time.

The woman who bopped her boyfriend over the head with the Christmas turkey while it was still on the serving platter? Ten days suspended if she completed an anger management course.

Finally, Kevin called, "Raymond Alito, illegally parked in a handicap space in violation of G.S. 20–37.6(e)."

A heavyset white man of early middle age rose and came forward. He was neatly dressed in black slacks and a gray nylon windbreaker worn over a red plaid shirt. His black hair was thinning over the crown and there were flecks of gray in his short black beard. He did not look familiar to me, but if Linda Allred was here, then he'd probably been cited for at least one earlier infraction of the code.

"I see you have chosen not to use an attorney, Mr. Alito. How do you plead?"

"Your Honor, could I just tell you what happened?"

"Certainly, sir, as soon as you tell me whether you're pleading guilty or not guilty."

"Not guilty then, ma'am."

"Mr Foster?"

"Your Honor, we will show that on December twenty-third of last year, Mr. Alito illegally parked in a space reserved for the handicapped at the outlet mall here in Dobbs. Mr. Alito is not physically disabled and he does not possess a handicap permit. The ticketing officer called for a tow truck, which impounded his car. This is Mr. Alito's second ticket for this infraction."

With appropriate gravity, I asked, "And is the ticketing officer in court?"

"She is, Your Honor. I call Dr. Linda Allred to the stand."

"Huh?" said Alito as Allred steered her motorized chair over to a position in front of the witness seat, which was one step above floor level. "She's the one who gave me a ticket? She's no police officer."

"You'll have your chance to speak, Mr. Alito," I told him. "The witness may swear from her own seat."

The bailiff handed her the Bible and my clerk swore her in.

Dr. Allred is a dumpling of a woman with short straight gray hair parted high on the left and piercing eyes that usually cast jaundiced looks over the top of her glasses. Although her doctorate is in psychology and she teaches statistical analysis on the college level, she lives in Dobbs and in her heart of hearts, she's Dirty Harry. Or maybe I should say Betty Friedan because a lot of her work is rooted in women's issues.

Her particular pet peeve, however, is able-bodied drivers who park in spaces reserved for those with impaired mobility. Any time she spots one, she writes up a ticket, something that she's officially allowed to do, as Kevin's next question made clear.

"Dr. Allred, are you a sworn law officer?"

"No, Mr. Foster, but I was made a special deputy and given ticket-writing authority by Sheriff Bowman Poole and I try not to abuse it."

"Would you describe what happened on the twenty-third of December?"

"Certainly." She took a small laptop computer from a pocket on the side of her chair and opened it to a screen full of photographs. "On the afternoon of December twenty-third, a friend and I were finishing up our Christmas shopping at the outlet mall. I was just getting out of my van when Mr. Alito pulled into the only empty slot. It was directly in front of ours. I immediately noticed that his car did not display a handicap tag on the rearview mirror, so I took out my camera and snapped the first picture."

The bailiff handed me her laptop. There, in glorious color was a view of Alito in his late-model black Honda with the edge of the blue warning sign just visible. His rearview mirror was dead center. Nothing dangled from it except a set of rosary beads.

"Mr. Alito then got out of his car and had no trouble walking into the Gifts and Glass Warehouse. That's the second picture on the screen, Your Honor. Now if you'll click to the third picture?"

I clicked as directed.

"My friend helped me with my wheelchair and I went around to the rear of his car and took a third picture of his license plate. As you see, it is a standard North Carolina plate, not one issued to the disabled. At that point, I called for a tow truck and wrote out the citation."

I signaled for the bailiff to show the laptop to Mr. Alito, who looked at the pictures with a distinctly sour expression.

"What did you do next, Dr. Allred?" Kevin asked.

"The parking lot was quite crowded. There were regular spaces way off to the side, but all the other nearby handicap spaces were legally taken. An elderly couple with a tag asked us if we were coming or going so they could have my spot, but I told them just to wait a few minutes and that the one in front of me would be opening up as soon as the tow truck got there. Then my friend and I went inside and finished our Christmas shopping. When we came out, Mr. Alito's car was gone and the other car was parked there."

"No further questions," Kevin said.

"Your turn, Mr. Alito," I said. "Do you wish to question the witness?"

He blustered a moment, then said, "I'd just like to ask her if she followed me in the store and saw what I bought?"

"No, sir," Dr. Allred responded promptly.

"Well, if you had, you'd've seen me buy a Christmas present for my eighty-nine-year-old mother and she *does* have a handicap tag. Her heart's so bad she couldn't walk across this room without her oxygen tank."

Dr. Allred looked at him over the top of her glasses. "I'm sorry to hear that, sir, but she wasn't in the car with you, was she?"

Alito turned to me. "Ma'am, can I just explain what happened in my own words?"

"Certainly," I said. "But first, I have a question for Dr. Allred."

She looked at me expectantly.

"Dr. Allred, you say you try not to abuse the authority Sheriff Poole gave you. It's my understanding that you usually just write a ticket. Could you tell me why you called a tow truck for Mr. Alito's car?"

"Because this is the second time I've caught him in a handicap space." Her fingers played over the keyboard.

"According to my records, I ticketed him on the fourth of September in front of a grocery store."

Alito's mouth dropped open when he heard that.

"Thank you, Dr. Allred. No further questions. You may come up and take the witness stand, Mr. Alito."

They passed in the space before my bench and I heard Alito mutter, "Bitch!"

"Did you say something, sir?" I asked.

"No, ma'am. Just clearing my throat." He took the Bible and promised to tell the truth, the whole truth and nothing but the truth.

"Yeah, I know I shouldn't have parked there, but I really was just going in to buy a present for my poor old mother. I bet I wasn't in there ten minutes. Well, twenty if you count the time I had to wait in line to check out."

"One present?" I said. "That was all?"

"Well, maybe I did pick up a couple of little things on my way back to the front, but my mother's present was really all I went in for. I got back outside, I almost had a heart attack myself. I thought my car'd been stolen, but when I called the police and they saw where I'd been parked, they told me to call the county's towing service. Cost me a hundred-fifty to get it back, and what I don't understand is how come this ticket's for two-fifty, when the first one was only fifty."

He paused briefly to glare at Dr. Allred but there was a whine in his voice when he turned back to me and said, "So what I'm saying here is yes, I did wrong, but I don't see why it's got to cost me four hundred dollars. It was Christmas and the parking lot was jammed. She says there were spaces further out, but by the time I parked out there and walked to the store, I could have already been in and out. Can't we just let the towing charges take care of everything?"

I shook my head. "Sorry, Mr. Alito. If this were your first citation, I might have been inclined to let you off more lightly. But this is your second offense here in this district. If I were to have my clerk run your license plate, would I find that you'd collected more tickets elsewhere? Say in Raleigh?"

By the way his jaws clamped tight, I was pretty sure I'd hit home.

"Those spaces aren't there for the convenience of the able-bodied. The State of North Carolina reserves them for its citizens who are not as fortunate as you are, sir. I find you guilty of this infraction and fine you the full two-fifty plus court costs."

"Court costs!" he yelped. "That's outrageous! That's highway robbery! That's—"

"That's going to be a night in jail if you make me hold you in contempt," I warned him. "The bailiff will show you where to pay."

As he stomped out in one direction and Dr. Allred serenely rolled out the other way, two middle-aged sisters came forward to argue over a pair of diamond earrings valued at about three hundred dollars. According to the younger sister, their mother had given her the earrings before she died. The older sister did not dispute that their mother might have let her borrow them, but that her mother's will left them to her. When the younger sister refused to give them up, the older one had taken them from the other's house, whereupon the younger sister called the police and charged her with theft. The earrings were nothing more than two small round diamonds set in simple gold prongs. Identical earrings could be found in any discount jewelry store in any mall in America, so I did the Solomon thing. I threw out the larceny charge and awarded each sister one earring. "Why don't you two ladies go have lunch together, buy a pair to match these and then think of your mother whenever you wear them. I bet she'd be horrified to think you'd let these two little rocks destroy your relationship."

I had hoped for sheepish looks and murmurs of reconciliation. What I got were glares and snarls as they both huffed off, still mad at each other and now mad at me as well.

I sighed and adjourned for lunch.

As I went down the hallway to the office I was using that week, I heard hearty laughter coming from within. I pushed the door open and there sat Portland and Dr. Allred munching on bowls of pasta salad. Portland immediately pulled out a third disposable bowl and waved a plastic fork. "She got one for you, too."

"Thanks," I said, unzipping my robe. "I meant to bring my lunch today, but Cal couldn't find his spelling book this morning and I didn't have time. Good to see you again, Dr. Allred."

She rolled her eyes at Portland. "When is she going to start calling me Linda?"

"Probably when you stop hauling assholes up before her in court," Portland said, and speared a cherry tomato on the end of her fork. "Wonder if the baby's allergic to tomatoes?"

"Yes," I said, and plucked it from her fork. Like most tomatoes this time of year, it had been picked way too early and was almost tasteless, but the morning's session had left me hungry and soon I was digging into my own salad.

"So what were y'all laughing about?" I asked.

"Tell her," Portland urged.

The professor smiled and an impish gleam lit her face. "It was outside the café where I picked up our salads just now. First this dilapidated wreck of a pickup with a crushed front fender and a closed-in topper slides into the curb and parks."

"In a handicap spot?"

"Yep. And no, they didn't have a tag."

"Are we to assume a tow truck's on the way even as we eat?"

Dr. Allred shook her head. "I didn't have the heart. See, the driver's door opens and a grizzled old man gets out. He's got one foot in a cast and his arm's in one of those rigid slings where his elbow is on the same level as his shoulder."

She demonstrated the awkward angle.

"Then the passenger door opens and out comes a pair of crutches, followed by a woman with both legs in casts."

I laughed. "You're making that up."

"Word of honor. They then help each other hobble around to the back, open up the door and a dog jumps out."

"Don't tell me the dog's wearing a cast?"

"No, but it's only got three legs."

"No way," I protested.

Eyes twinkling, she crossed her heart. "True story. Now how could I write those poor folks a ticket?"

"You're all heart," I told her.

She laughed and finished off the last of her salad. "Gotta go. If you need any more data, Portland, just give me a call. Good seeing both of you."

I held the door for her, but more than that she would not allow. Fortunately the courthouse is completely accessible and I knew that her van was equipped with full hydraulics so that she could manage easily.

"What was all that about?" I asked when she was gone.

Portland wiped a small dollop of mayo from her upper lip and handed me a manila folder. "She brought me a rough draft of the statistical analysis she's doing on domestic violence. Especially as it relates to threats made and threats carried out."

I leafed through the graphs and charts and row of numbers that were meaningless to me.

"Bottom line?" Portland said grimly. "Once physical violence accelerates, if the violent partner threatens to kill the significant other, there's damn little the authorities can do to stop it. I plan to show these figures to Bo and Dwight and see if they can't prove her wrong in the case of Karen Braswell."

CHAPTER 11

If all farmers were true to principle with respect to the disposal of their products, there would be less perversion of the good and useful.

—*Profitable Farming in the Southern States*, 1890

Friday night found Dwight and me heading in opposite directions. Uncle Ash had brought home a mess of rainbow trout from the mountains and Aunt Zell had invited us to supper, but the Canes were back in Raleigh for a home game, so Dwight said he'd pick Cal up and head on into town for a supper that was something other than pizza.

"Did Portland talk to you about her client?" I asked.

It was my afternoon break and I had caught him still at his desk, reading through reports.

"And that ex-husband who keeps harassing her? Yeah. Like I told her though, there's not much we can do if he decides to punch her out, but at least Portland doesn't have to worry about him shooting her client. Judge Parker sent over an order for us to search Braswell's place and confiscate any guns we found. We got a shotgun, a .22

rifle and a .9-millimeter automatic. It's too bad though, that she and her mother can't move to another state before he gets out next week."

"Why should she be the one to run?" I asked indignantly. "He's the problem, not her."

"Hey, I'm not saying she's at fault," he said, holding up his hands to fend off my irritation. "I'm just saying we can't provide round-the-clock protection and if the woman's that worried . . . Be fair, Deb'rah. You live on the beach and you know a hurricane's coming, you know you need to move to high ground till the storm's over, right?"

"I guess," I said glumly.

"Well, she needs to get out of his way till he gets over her. Give him time to get interested in another woman or something. And that's what Bo and I told Portland."

I could just imagine what her response to that had been.

When I got to Aunt Zell's that night, I found that she had taken pity on my cousin Reid and invited him to join us. He claims not to know how to boil water and he's always glad to accept the offer of a home-cooked meal. The grilled trout were hot and crispy and Aunt Zell had made cornbread the way Mother and Maidie often did it: a mush of cornmeal, chopped onions, and milk poured into a black iron skillet after a little oil's heated to the smoking point, then baked at 400° till the bottom is crusty brown. Turned onto a plate and cut into pie wedges, it doesn't need butter to melt in your mouth.

Uncle Ash is tall and slim. Like his brother, who is Portland's dad, he had the Smith family's tight curly hair, only his was now completely white. He had brought home a copy of the *High Country Courier* because it carried a story about a murder that had taken place when I was up there last October. One killer had been sentenced to twelve years after pleading guilty. The other was going to walk away free.

No surprises there.

We caught up on family news. Uncle Ash's whole career had been with the marketing side of tobacco and he was interested to hear that my brothers were going to tread water by growing it on contract for another year.

"But if they're really interested in doing something different, the first cars ran on alcohol, you know," he said with a sly grin. "Kezzie say anything about y'all maybe distilling a little motor fuel?"

"Oh, Ash," said Aunt Zell, who is always embarrassed for me whenever anyone alludes to Daddy's former profession.

"Now, Uncle Ash, you know well and good that my daddy wouldn't do anything illegal like that," I said, unable to control my own grin. "Besides, to run a car, it'd have to be a hundred-and-ninety proof, almost pure alcohol. I don't think he ever got anything that pure."

"Would they really legalize the home brewing of something that potent?" asked Reid, helping himself to another wedge of cornbread.

"If gas keeps going up, who knows?" said Uncle Ash. "Soon as you mention alcohol, though, lawmakers get nervous. It's like when they made farmers quit growing hemp about seventy years ago."

Industrial hemp was one of Uncle Ash's favorite hobby horses and he was off and riding.

"We spend millions importing something that we could grow right in our own country, right here in Colleton County. You can make dozens of useful things from it—paper, food, paint, medicine, even fuel. And they say that hemp seed oil is one of the most balanced in the world for the ratio of omega-sixes to omega-threes. It's friendly to the environment, doesn't take a lot of water or fertilizer to grow, and it's easy to harvest. But those spineless jellyfish who call themselves statesmen? Soon as they see the word 'hemp,' they're afraid their voters will see 'cannabis.'"

"Ash, dear, you're raising your voice again," said Aunt Zell.

"Sorry," he said sheepishly and got up to help her make coffee and bring in the pecan pie I had seen cooling in the kitchen earlier.

"So what's with you and Flame Smith?" I asked Reid as I set out coffee cups.

"You know her?"

"Not me. Portland. She ran into us at lunch yesterday. Just before you got there. Please tell me you're not putting the moves on your client's girlfriend."

His blue eyes widened innocently. "It was strictly business and excuse me, Your Honor, but should we be having this *ex parte* discussion?"

I hate it when he scores a legal point off my curiosity.

I was home by nine and immediately switched on the hockey game. Amazing how much easier it was to follow now that I'd attended an actual game. During the commercials, I managed to wash and dry two loads of laundry and had piles of folded underwear on the couch beside me by the time Dwight and Cal returned. The game had been a blowout. Unfortunately, it was the Canes that got stomped.

Aunt Zell had sent the rest of the pie home for them and Cal had taken his into the living room to watch WRAL' s recap of the game when Dwight's phone rang. He listened intently, then said, "I'm on my way."

I quit pouring his milk. "What's happened?"

Dwight reached for his jacket with a grim face. "They just found another damn hand."

CHAPTER 12

While money making is one of the great desiderata with most men, it is not the chief good in life, neither does it constitute the sum total to earthly happiness as men, by their lives, seem to regard it.

—*Profitable Farming in the Southern States,* 1890

Dwight Bryant
Friday Night, March 3

At Ward Dairy Road again, but this time it was not a dog or a human who found a body part

It was a buzzard.

"Damnedest thing," said the man who had called them. "My wife and I were running late this morning and as we headed out to the car, there were some buzzards over there in those weeds at the edge of the field. One of them flew up with something when I started the engine and then I heard a clunk on the top of the car. Sounded almost like a rock, only not as heavy, you know? My wife saw it bounce way under the holly bushes over there but we didn't have time to stop and see what it was. After work, we went out to supper and a movie, but as soon as we got home, my wife wanted me to take the shovel and find whatever it was before we let the dogs out and they got into something nasty. They're bad for rolling in roadkill."

He had left his find on the shovel by the holly bushes and their flashlights showed a large and presumably male left hand, much the worse for wear. It seemed to be frozen solid, yet flesh had been pecked from the bones and several finger joints were missing. If the third finger had ever worn a wedding band, there was no sign of one now. Dwight was surprised the buzzard hadn't come back for it. Unless there was something else out there beyond their flashlights?

They would have to wait for the ME's determination, but it looked to him like the mate to the first hand they had found exactly one week ago.

A full week and they were no nearer an identity.

The man indicated the general area where he had first seen the buzzards and they approached gingerly, sweeping the ground before them with their lights. They saw nothing of interest in the weeds and nothing on the shoulder of the road, but when they walked in the opposite direction, shining their flashlights in the ditches, Detective Jack Jamison noticed that water had ponded up and frozen solid behind a clogged culvert. He started to walk on, but something seemed to be embedded in the dirty ice.

"I think it's the other arm!" he called.

The others quickly joined him on the edge of the road. Three flashlights focused on the ice, and the shape was so similar to what they hoped to find that it took a poke with the shovel to confirm that the object was only part of a tree branch that had broken off and lodged there.

Disappointed, they walked on.

"At least it's on a line with the other parts," Deputy Richards said. Despite a red nose and cheeks, her cold seemed to be drying up and she had turned out when Dwight paged her, even though technically not on duty.

There was something different about her tonight, Dwight thought. She wore jeans instead of her usual utilitarian slacks and the turtleneck sweater peeping out of her black suede jacket was a soft pink. And was that perfume drifting on the chill night air?

He gave himself a mental kick in the pants. Of course! Friday night? Young single woman?

"Sorry for messing up your evening," he said.

She shrugged. "That's okay. Goes with the job, doesn't it?"

And that was something else new. Heretofore, whenever he addressed a personal remark to Richards, she usually turned a fiery red. He realized now that it had not happened in the last few weeks. She was a good officer, but he had begun to think she was never going to be able to join in the department's easy give-and-take, yet she had finally adapted and he had not even noticed.

Just as Dwight was ready to call it a night, Jamison's light caught something amid a curtain of dead kudzu vines that entangled a clump of young pines growing on the ditchbank. He thought at first that it was an old weatherstained cardboard box. Nevertheless, he walked over to check it out.

"Oh dear Lord in the morning!" said Richards, who had crossed the road to shine her own light on his find.

There, hidden from casual view was a naked torso that was armless, legless, and headless as well. Because it was lying on its back, it took them a moment to orient themselves, to realize that the three black stumps nearest them were probably the neck and what was left of the upper arms, which meant that the opposite end should have been the sex organs. It was probably male like the earlier parts they had found. There was a mat of hair between the flat breasts, but nothing was left in the genital area except a dark ugly gouge.

Denning drove the crime scene van down to the site and set up his floodlights. As he surveyed what was left of the body before taking pictures, he shook his head and said to Dwight, "You know something, Major? We got ourselves one pissed-off killer."

Every man in the group felt a painful twinge of sympathetic horror as they gazed down at the mutilated victim. Dwight, too. Once again, he thought of the church sign where they had found the first hand.

With what measure you mete, it shall be measured to you again.

What the hell had the guy done to wind up like this, with his personal parts strewn across the county?

At the other end of the state, Flame Smith turned off the main highway and shifted to low gear. The engine protested against the steep climb ahead and her tires spun against the loose gravel, before they gained traction and began to inch upward.

Tree branches brushed either side of the car. Normally she enjoyed the roller-coaster effect of this drive, but that was in daylight. Tonight, the sky was overcast. No moon. No stars. Only her headlights to illuminate the opening between the trees. Driving up here to Buck Harris's mountain retreat had been an impulse fueled by bourbon and anger.

That he could be so cavalier as to go off to sulk about the money he was going to have to give up in this divorce settlement! Did he really think that staying away from court would somehow make that fat greedy wife of his settle for less? And even if she did wind up with a full half of their assets, how much money did a person need? As someone who had been forced to scrabble for every dime, Flame was ready to settle down and be taken care of by a man with an ample bank account. It did not have to be billions. A modest five or six million invested at six percent would do just fine. She could live very happily on that.

But land and money were how men like Buck kept score. The sale of Harris Farms, if it came to that, would leave him cash rich. He could keep his yacht, buy two more houses to replace the two he would have to give up, and still have enough spare change to fly first class to Europe or Hawaii whenever he wanted. Nevertheless, it galled him to know that Suzu Harris could, if she chose, force the sale of the land they had so painstakingly acquired in their early years. Could even hold his feet to the fire over their first tomato field, the thirty acres that had been in his family since before the Civil War.

By the time she reached Wilkesboro, Flame was stone cold sober and beginning to think that running Buck into the shallows was probably a mistake. She had played him like a fish these last two years, giving him enough line to let him think it was his idea to come to her. Start reeling in too hard and she was liable to have him break the line or spit out the hook. As long as she had come this far, though, it was easier to go on than turn back.

"Thank God it's not icy," she muttered as she steered to avoid a hole where the gravel had washed out and almost scraped the car on an outcropping of solid rock. Another quarter-mile and the drive ended in a circle in front of a large rustic lodge built of undressed logs. She did not see his car, but the garage was on the far side of the house. Nor were there any lights. Not that she expected any. Not at—she pressed a button on the side of her watch and the little dial lit up. Not at one-thirty in the morning.

The front door was locked and she rang the bell long and hard until she could hear it echo from within.

To her surprise, the interior remained dark.

She rang again, leaning on the bell so long that no one inside could possibly sleep through it.

Nothing.

A long low porch ran the full length of the house and she retrieved a door key that was kept beneath the second ceramic pot. Within minutes, she was inside the lodge, fumbling for the light switches.

"Buck, honey? You here?" she called.

No answer.

With growing apprehension, she mounted the massive staircase that led to the bedrooms above.

In the small hours of Saturday morning, Detective Mayleen Richards drove through the deserted streets of Dobbs. The only other person out at that time was a town police officer, who gave her a friendly wave from his cruiser that indicated he'd be glad to share a cup of coffee from his Thermos and kill some boring time. Another night and she might have. Tonight though, she merely waved back and continued on to her apartment, a one-bedroom over a garage on the outskirts of Dobbs where town and suburbs merged.

The elderly couple who lived in the main house spent their winters in Florida and were glad to have a sheriff's deputy there to keep an eye on things. Richards was glad for the privacy their absence gave her. Even when the owners were in residence, they went to bed early and seemed singularly uninterested in their tenant's irregular comings and goings.

Not that there had been anything very irregular about her personal life before this. She pulled her shifts. She attended a Spanish language course two nights a week out at Colleton Community College. She visited her family down in Black Creek almost every weekend. She harbored no regrets for ditching either that dull computer programming job out at the Research Triangle nor the equally dull marriage to her highschool sweetheart who had achieved his life's goal when he traded farm life for a desk job. Except for fancying herself in love with Major Bryant, law enforcement had absorbed and satisfied her.

Richards could smile to herself now and see that recent

adolescent crush for what it was—attraction to an alpha male, generated by proximity and nothing more than the needs of a healthy body that had slept alone for way too long.

She coasted to a stop beside a shiny gray pickup with an extended crew cab and cut the ignition, then hurried up the wooden steps that led to a deck and to the man who waited inside.

"I thought you'd be gone," she said, absurdly happy that her prickly reaction to his first overtures had not sent him away.

"No." He carefully unzipped her jacket and eased the soft pink sweater over her head, then buried his face in the waves of her dark red hair as his hands unhooked her bra.

"*Muy hermosa*," he murmured.

Later, lying beside him in her bed, brown legs next to white, she was almost on the brink of sleep when she remembered. "McLamb said he saw you at the courthouse today?"

Miguel Diaz nodded, one hand lazily moving across her body. "One of the men from the village next to my village back home. He took a tractor and I was there to speak for him."

"Tractor? Was he the guy who plowed up a stretch of yards out toward Cotton Grove?"

"Ummm," he murmured, kissing her shoulder.

"He works for you?"

"For now. The other place, they fired him when he took the tractor."

Mayleen Richards laughed, remembering the jokes the uniformed deputies had made. "What was he thinking? Where was he trying to go?"

She felt him shrug. "Who knows? It was the tequila driving. Maybe he thought he could get to his woman."

"She's in Dobbs?"

"No. Their baby died and she went back to Mexico."

"Oh, Mike, that's so sad."

"Yes. But our babies will be strong and healthy."

"*Our* babies?" This was only their third time together and he was already talking babies?

"Our red-haired, brown-skinned babies," he said as he gently stroked her stomach.

The image delighted her, but then she thought of her parents, of her family's attitude toward Latinos, and she sighed.

Intuitively, he seemed to understand. "Don't worry, *querida*. Once the babies come, your family will grow to like me."

CHAPTER 13

A man can't throw off his habits as he does his coat; if contracted in youth they will stick in manhood and old age, whether they be good or bad.

—*Profitable Farming in the Southern States,* 1890

DEBORAH KNOTT
SATURDAY MORNING, MARCH 4

Dwight got home so late Friday night that I slipped out of bed next morning without waking him, and Cal and I tiptoed around until it was nine o'clock and time for me to go pick up Mary Pat and Jake.

"Are the children ready to go?" I asked when Kate answered the phone.

"No, I'm keeping them home today," she said and her voice was cool.

I was immediately apprehensive. "Is something wrong?"

"Did you speak to Cal like I asked you?"

"Absolutely. Don't tell me—?"

"I'm sorry, Deborah, but I am not going to have Jake treated the way Dwight used to treat Rob."

"*What*?"

"You must know that when they were kids and Dwight went over to play with your brothers, half the time he wouldn't let Rob come."

I heard Rob's voice protesting in the background and heard Kate say, "Well, that's what you told me he did. Isn't that why he's not taking this seriously?"

Rob's reply came faintly, "Kate, honey, that's what kids *do*."

"Not in this house," Kate said firmly, and I knew she was laying down the law to both of us, and probably to Mary Pat, too, if the child was within hearing distance.

"Kate, I'm so sorry," I said, "but unless you spoke to Dwight yesterday when he came by for Cal, he doesn't know anything about this."

Cal had only been half listening, but when he heard me say that, he froze and guilt spread across his face.

At her end of the phone, I heard the baby begin to cry.

"Look, I promise that Mary Pat and Cal will include him today," I said, fixing Cal with a stern look. "Let me come and get them. You need the break, okay?"

There was a long silence, then a weary, "Okay, but if I hear—"

"You're not going to hear," I promised.

As soon as I hung up, I called Dwight's mother and when Miss Emily finished exclaiming over those body parts she kept hearing about on the local newscast—"And now a whole body?"—I asked if she could possibly drop by Kate and Rob's and offer to sit with little R.W. during his morning nap so that Rob could take Kate out for an early lunch. "I'll keep the children overnight, but she sounds as if she could stand to get out of the house."

"What a good idea," said Miss Emily. "I'll walk over there right now. Isn't it nice that we're finally getting a taste of spring after all that cold?"

"Are we? I haven't been outside yet." I glanced out the window. Sunshine. And the wind was blowing so gently that the leaves on the azalea bushes Dwight and I had set out in the fall barely stirred. "Maybe we'll see you in a few minutes."

Cal headed for the garage door.

"Sit," I said quietly.

He sat down at the kitchen table and I took the chair across from him. "You want to tell me what happened yesterday?"

He shrugged, twined his feet around the legs of the chair, and tried to look innocent. "I don't know."

"I think you do."

His brown eyes darted away from mine. "Nothing really."

I waited silently.

"We were just playing."

"And?"

"He kept bugging us. Aunt Kate wouldn't let us use the PlayStation because she said we weren't letting Jake have enough of a turn and when we let him play Monopoly with us, he couldn't count his money, so—" He hesitated.

"So?"

"So we said we'd play hide-and-seek and then . . ." His voice dropped even lower than his head. "I guess we sorta hid where he couldn't find us and we didn't come out even when he said he gave up and then he started crying and Aunt Kate got mad and made Mary Pat go to her room." He looked up with a calculated glint in his eyes that more than one defendant had tried on me. "But then I did read Jake a story."

I wasn't any more impressed with that than I generally was in the courtroom when the defendant says, "But I only hit him twice with that tire iron and then I did take him to the hospital."

"You think that makes up for getting Aunt Kate upset again?"

He shrugged, but his jaw set in a mulish fix that was so reminiscent of Dwight that I might have laughed under different circumstances.

"You promised me on Thursday that you were going to be nicer to Jake and cut him some slack."

"Sorry." It was a one-size-fits-all, pro forma apology. "But Mary Pat—"

"No, Cal, this isn't about Mary Pat. This is about you. You gave me your word and you broke it."

"I don't care!" His head came up angrily. "You're not my mother and you're not the boss of me!"

It was the first time he'd snapped at me and we were both taken aback. Defiance was all over his face, but I think he had shocked himself as well.

I took a deep breath. "You're absolutely right, Cal. I'm not your mother, but now that you're living here—"

"I didn't ask to come here and I don't have to stay." His eyes filled with involuntary tears and he wiped them away with an impatient fist. "I can go back to Virginia and live with Nana."

"No, you can't," I said with more firmness than I felt. "That's not an option and you know it. I may not be your mother, but I *am* married to your father and that gives me the right to haul you up short when you step over the line."

He glared at me.

"Unless you want me to let him handle it?"

That got his attention.

"No! Don't tell him. Please?"

Uncomfortable as this was for both of us, I knew that something had to be done, but this was going to take more than a simple time out or an early bedtime. Besides, there was no way I could send him to bed early without Dwight's knowing and for now I was willing to respect Cal's plea that he not be involved.

"You know that what you did was wrong?"

He gave a sulky half nod.

"When your mother punished you for something serious, what did she do?"

His eyes widened and he turned so white that the freckles popped out across his nose. "You're going to spank me?"

Even though my parents had occasionally smacked our bottoms or switched our legs when it was well deserved, I was almost as horrified as he. "No, I'm not going to spank you. But you know we can't let this go."

He thought a moment. "I could not watch television for a whole month."

"And what'll you tell your dad when the Hurricanes play an away game and you don't watch it with him?"

As soon as I'd said that, I knew what would be appropriate.

"Here's the deal," I told him. "You hurt Aunt Kate's feelings when you left Jake out and made him cry, so now it's your turn to miss the fun. You'll stay home from the next Canes game and I'll go with your dad. You can say it was your idea and you have to make him believe it or else he'll ask you for the whole story. If that happens, you'll have to tell him yourself and you'll still stay home. Is it a deal?"

He nodded and by his chastened look, I knew I'd gotten through to him.

"If I hear from Aunt Kate that you're not trying to turn this situation around with Jake, you're going to miss the next game after that as well. Three strikes and you're out of all the others the rest of the season. Is that clear?"

"Yeah."

"*Yeah?*" I said sternly, unwilling to let him get away with that deliberate show of disrespect.

"Yes, ma'am," he muttered.

"Just because Mary Pat is six months older than you doesn't mean you have to let her lead you around by the nose."

"But then she may not want to play with me," he protested.

"I seriously doubt that, Cal. You're smart and funny and you can think up lots of games that take three people. You don't have to play what she wants every time. Isn't there anything besides television that you like that Jake can do, too?"

Again that shrug, but then he grudgingly admitted that Jake was getting pretty good at Chinese checkers. "He almost beat me last week. And when we played with the blocks, his tower was higher than Mary Pat's."

"There you go then. See? You guys are going to know

each other the rest of your lives and the older you get, the less it's going to matter that he's four years younger. By the time you get grown, four years won't make a smidgin of difference. Your dad's six years older than me and that doesn't matter to either of us, does it?"

"What doesn't matter?" asked Dwight, who came into the kitchen yawning widely.

"That you're an old man and I'm your child bride," I said as I got up to pour him a cup of coffee. "Rough night?"

"Tell you about it later," he answered. "You two look awfully serious. What's up?"

"Guess what?" I said brightly. "Your son's giving me his ticket for the next Canes game."

"Really?" He looked at Cal and I could tell that he was half pleased, yet half puzzled. "You sure, son?"

Cal nodded. "She likes them, too, and I heard Grandma talking with Aunt Kate 'bout how y'all haven't been out together since . . . since" —his eyes suddenly misted— "since I came to live here."

I was stricken, knowing that he was thinking of Jonna again and that he probably felt a stab of heartsick longing for his mother, for the way things had been all his life. Another moment and I might have weakened. Fortunately for the cause, Dwight beamed and tousled Cal's hair. "Thanks, buddy. We really appreciate that, don't we, Deb'rah?"

"We do," I agreed. "Right now, though, Cal and I are on our way to pick up the others. We can swing past a grocery store if you want something special for supper?"

"Don't bother. By the time you get back, I'll be dressed

and they can ride with me to see if the nursery's got in those trees I ordered. I'll pick up some barbecue or something."

Cal was quiet on the drive over to Kate's, but shortly before we got there, he said in a small voice, "I really am sorry we were mean to Jake and got Aunt Kate mad."

"You might want to tell that to Aunt Kate next time you catch her alone," I said, not being real big on public apologies. As a child, I much preferred a few quick swats on my bottom to the galling humiliation of having to apologize to someone in front of everybody. There were no cars behind us, so when we came to the stop sign, I paused and turned to face him. "And just for the record, Cal, as long as you try to do right by Jake, this is over and done with so far as I'm concerned."

"You're not still mad at me?"

I smiled at him. "Nope, and I don't hold grudges either."

His look of relief almost broke my heart.

"Look, honey. Stuff happens. I know you wish things could be the way they used to be, but they aren't and there's no way anybody can change it back. Your dad and I know this isn't easy for you. There're going to be times when you think you hate everybody and that everybody hates you. When you make bad choices and do things you know you shouldn't, then yeah, I may get mad for the moment. But you need to know right now that I do love you and I love your dad and I don't care how mad we all get at each other, I'm not going to stop loving either one of you. Okay?"

It could have been a Hallmark moment.

In a perfect world, he would have leaned over and given me a warm spontaneous hug while someone cued the violins, and bluebirds and butterflies fluttered around the car.

Instead, he stared straight ahead through the windshield for a long moment, then sighed and said, "Okay."

Hey, you take what you can get.

CHAPTER 14

In the country, we can wear out our old clothes and go dirty sometimes, without fear of company. A little clean dirt is healthy; city folks wash their children too much and too often.

—*Profitable Farming in the Southern States,* 1890

When he first suggested marriage, back when we agreed it would be a marriage of convenience and for pragmatic reasons only, Dwight said he was tired of living in a bachelor apartment, that he wanted to put down roots, plant trees.

I thought that was just a figure of speech.

Wrong.

No sooner was his diamond on my finger than he borrowed the farm's backhoe and started moving half-grown trees into the yard from the surrounding woods. I had built my house out in an open field. The only trees on the site were a couple of willows at the edge of the long pond that sits on the dividing line between my land and two of my brothers'. Now head-high dogwoods line the path down to the water. Taller oaks and maples would be casting shade over both porches this summer. Pear trees, apples, two fig bushes and a row of blueberry bushes marked the beginning of a serious orchard. He had built a long curved stone wall to act as extra seating for family cookouts and we had planted azaleas and hydrangeas behind the wall. The azalea buds were already swelling despite Tuesday night's freezing rain.

Saturday's warm sunshine and soft western breezes had brought everything along, and in a protected corner on the south side of the house, buttercups were up and blooming. Flowering quince and forsythia were showing their first flush of pink and yellow and if the weather held, they would explode into full bloom by the middle of the week.

It was a jeans and muddy workshoes weekend. Dwight and the children and I spent most of it out in the yard, and some of my brothers and a couple of sisters-in-law stopped by to help set out a row of crepe myrtles on either side of the long drive out to the hardtop. Their twigs were bare now but Dwight promised that by late July we would be driving in and out through clouds of watermelon red.

It wasn't all work. The year before, my nephews and nieces had installed a regulation height basketball hoop at the peak of the garage roof so that they could use the concrete apron in front for a half-court. Dwight lowered the hoop from ten feet to eight, inflated four of the collapsed balls stashed in a bushel basket beneath the work bench, and showed the kids the hook shot that could have let him play for Carolina had he not joined the army instead.

Cal and a chastened Mary Pat were on their best behavior with Jake. Being outdoors in the milder weather helped, of course. Running, jumping, digging in the dirt, riding their bikes, or using the hose to water in the new plants doesn't take fine motor skills and there's no squabbling over balls when every kid has one. It also helped that Robert had brought his grandson Bert along and that Bert was the same age as Jake. It took a lot of pressure off the two older children.

Some of the farm dogs showed up and there was a flurry of snarls and growls and bared teeth before they backed down and acknowledged that Bandit did indeed own the territory around the house, territory he'd spent the last few weeks assiduously marking.

Will and his wife Amy came out from town and Will got sucked into work while I stomped the dirt off my shoes and went inside with Amy. Will's three brothers up from me; Amy is his third wife. She's also the head of Human Resources at Dobbs Memorial Hospital and she was in the process of writing a grant proposal to fund a pilot program for servicing their Hispanic patients. I had told her that I would vet the proposal and that we could use my Lexis Nexis account to look up pertinent case law as it pertains to undocumented aliens.

"Documented or not, we're getting so many people in our emergency room and at the well-baby clinic that we need more interpreters to work every shift," she said. "It scares the bejeebers out of some of the doctors and nurses when they're trying to explain a complicated drug regimen and the only interpreter may be the patient's first-grade child. How can they be sure that a six-year-old understands enough to tell her mother that she needs to take the pills in increasing and decreasing dosages? And don't get me started on ID cards. We almost killed a man the other day. The record attached to that particular ID card said that he wasn't allergic to penicillin, but guess what? The man who presented the card that day was deathly allergic. We almost lost him."

I showed her how to get into the site and suggested key words that might pull up the info she was after.

I like Amy. She's small and dark and claims to have Latin blood somewhere in her background despite not speaking a word of anything except English. She has a firecracker fuse and gets passionate about causes, but she also has a raucous sense of humor, all necessary traits to stay married to Will.

He's the oldest of my mother's four children and a bit of a rounder. Will's good-looking and has a silver tongue that could charm birds out of the trees or dollars out of your pocket, which is why he's such a good auctioneer and just the person you want if you're selling off the furnishings of your grandmother's house. He doesn't exactly lie, but damned if he can't make your granny's circa 1980 pressed glass pitcher sound almost as desirable as a piece of Waterford crystal.

While Amy roamed the Internet looking for factoids to bolster her proposal, I read over what she had so far, put some of her layman's language into more precise legalese, and marked a few places where specific examples would help illuminate the point she was making.

As she printed out the pieces she wanted to save, we talked about the migrant problem. Floods of undocumented aliens have poured into North Carolina in such a very short time and not all are "Messicans" as Haywood calls any Latino.

"I heard Seth telling Will about y'all's meeting last Sunday." She grinned. "Ostriches?"

We giggled about Isabel's thinking hogs would be more natural and about Robert's reaction to the idea of shiitake mushrooms.

"Seth said something about giving the kids some land to grow some chemical-free crops?"

"They won't be able to market their crops as organic for a few years," I said, "but it's a start."

"And bless them for it." Amy gathered up the printouts, blocked their edges, and pushed back from the computer. "It absolutely infuriates me to see how cavalier some of the growers are with pesticides."

"Well, Haywood and Robert can remember when they had to worm and sucker tobacco by hand," I said as we moved into the living room. I added another log to the fire and we sat down on the couch in front of the crackling flames. "No wonder they love being able to run a tractor through the fields pulling a sprayer that'll take care of everything chemically."

"Better living through chemistry?" Amy slipped off her boots and tucked her short legs under her. "Except that it isn't. I wish they had to see some of the migrants who come into the emergency room, covered with pesticides, their clothes green with it. The rashes on their skin. The coughs. The headaches and memory loss and God alone knows how many strokes, cancers, and heart attacks have been triggered by careless handling. They're not supposed to go back in the fields for forty-eight hours after some of those chemicals are used, yet we've had women tell us that they've actually been sprayed while they were out there working. Most times they don't even know what they've been doused with. Birth defects are up. It's criminal. We've called EPA and the US Department of Agriculture on some of the employers, but there's not enough teeth in the laws to make the growers back off."

Her tirade broke off as the children came in, hungry and needing to use the bathroom. I had set out a tray of raw vegetables and sliced apples with a yogurt-based dip, but Mary Pat spotted the bowl of oranges and immediately asked if I'd cut a hole in the top so she could suck out the juice. The three boys thought that was a great idea and they all headed back outside, oranges in hand, noisily sucking.

"She's a pistol, that one." Amy laughed. "Kate's going to have her hands full."

"She already does," I said ruefully.

We took the children back to Kate and Rob's on Sunday evening, tired and dirty and ready for bath and bed. Kate, on the other hand, looked the most relaxed I'd seen her since R.W. was born. There was color in her pretty face and her honey brown hair had been cut and styled since yesterday morning. The haircut echoed her old glamour and reminded me that she had been a New York fashion model before she married Jake's dad and switched from modeling clothes to designing the fabric for those clothes.

"You could still be a model," I said when we were

alone together in the kitchen, putting together coffee and dessert while Dwight and Rob discussed the virtues of planting more than two varieties of blueberries.

She made a face. "For what? Plus sizes? Thanks, but no thanks."

"You're not fat," I protested. "And you were way too skinny before. In fact, the first time Bessie Stewart saw you she told Maidie they could just stick two grains of corn on a hoe handle and use that as your dress form."

Bessie Stewart is our mother-in-law's housekeeper and a plainspoken country woman.

Kate laughed. "I know. She's still trying to fatten me up. You certainly don't think I made this custard pie, do you? Skinny or fat, I'm comfortable where I am, though, and I appreciate you and Miss Emily giving me this weekend to put it all in perspective. I'm not superwoman and I've been hovering over the kids too much instead of letting them work it out. I'm sorry I snapped at you yesterday."

"No, you were right to. It doesn't hurt to teach older children to be patient with younger ones. All the same, Kate, you need to understand—"

"You don't have to say it. Rob admits that he was a pain in the butt to Dwight and Beth, and that Nancy Faye used to irritate the hell out of all of them in turn. I never had brothers or sisters, so I never saw that give and take. Anyhow, things are going to get better. Rob's finally convinced me that the children won't grow up to be axe-murderers if I get back in my studio and work on some designs I've been mulling around in my head."

She filled the cream pitcher with half-and-half and added it to the tray.

"We haven't touched Lacy's room since he died last year." A shadow flitted across her face for that cantankerous old man, her first husband's uncle.

Lacy Honeycutt had initially resented Kate as an interloper who bewitched Jake and kept him in New York almost against his will. It had been hard for Lacy to realize that it was Jake's competitive zest for the New York Stock Exchange and not Kate alone that kept him away from the farm. When Kate inherited the place after his death and came down to await little Jake's birth, she had needed all her persuasive charm to bring Lacy around. He had approved of Rob, though, and so adored his infant great-nephew that he continued to live in the room he'd been born in, even after Kate and Rob were married.

"We're going to fix up Lacy's room and hire a live-in nanny," Kate said. "Mary Pat's trustees have already agreed to kick in with part of the cost."

"Great!" I said. "But does this mean that we have to find another place for Cal after school?"

She shook her head and gave me a mischievous smile. "Nope. It does mean that I'm going to bill you and Dwight for a prorated share of her salary, though."

"Deal," I said.

We solemnly shook hands on it, then carried the pie and coffee out to the living room.

Cal went to bed soon after we got home, but before Dwight and I called it a night, we let Bandit out for a run and walked outside ourselves to admire what we'd accomplished that weekend.

The night breeze lacked the bone chilling edge it had carried only two days ago, yet the cool air still required jackets and gloves. A quarter moon gave enough light to see where we were putting our feet and I could almost smell spring in the air.

In one of our few quiet moments the day before, Dwight had explained why he was so late getting back Friday night.

"I can't believe we've had this whole weekend without somebody finding another body part," I said. "I was sure you were going to get called out for the missing head."

"I just hope the ME's preliminary report's on my desk tomorrow morning and that it says they've found a tattoo or a prominent scar or anything that'll help us make a positive ID. The only thing halfway unique to this guy is that an X-ray of his right arm shows that he broke the ulna about ten years ago. I bet at least twenty percent of the guys in this country have broken a right arm sometime in their lives."

He told me that the Alzheimer patient's family had been notified and yeah, he'd heard that they'd retained Zack Young to file a civil suit against the nursing home.

I told him that Kate and Rob were going to hire a live-in nanny and that we'd need to share the cost. "It'll still be cheaper than putting Cal in formal after-school care. Better for him, too."

"You ever gonna say what yesterday morning was all about?"

"What do you mean?"

"C'mon, Deb'rah. I may not have been a full-time dad after Jonna and I divorced, but I got up there at least twice a month and I know my son well enough to know he wouldn't pass up a Canes game on his own."

I was silent.

"He's not giving you a hard time, is he? Talking back when I'm not around? Disobeying?"

"Nothing like that. Honest. It was just a little bump in the road and we agreed that this is the way to smooth it out. If it was something serious, I'd certainly tell you, but I gave him my word and I don't want to go back on it, okay?"

"You're sure?"

"I'm sure."

He looked down at me with a rueful smile. "Got more than you bargained for, didn't you, shug?"

"I'm sorry Jonna's dead," I said honestly. "And I'm sorry for the way this happened, but Portland and I had already planned on getting the custody arrangement amended so that you could have Cal here for holidays and summers."

He shook his head. "Poor Jonna. She wouldn't have stood a chance with you two." Then his smile faded. "I'm just glad we didn't have to put Cal through a court battle, glad he didn't have to choose between us."

I squeezed his hand and we walked down the drive to where the young crepe myrtles began. In this silvery light, they were a double row of pale slender sticks and leafless twigs.

"I'll probably be sore tomorrow from all the work we did today, but they're going to be beautiful," I said.

Dwight turned and looked back toward the house. "I was thinking we could put more pecans on the south side. They'll shade both bedrooms in the summer, but they won't interfere with the solar panels or the power lines."

I smiled.

"What?" he said with an answering smile.

"I was just thinking how old we'd be before any trees get tall enough to interfere with the wires."

"Less than fifteen years if we keep them watered and fertilized." He gave a contented sigh. "We really are married, aren't we?"

I laughed out loud. "It takes trees to convince you?"

He stopped and I turned to look up into his face. What I saw there made my heart turn over.

"Dwight? Sweetheart?"

He put his arms around me and his voice had a sudden rough huskiness. "I used to try and imagine what it would be like if hell froze solid and I actually got you to marry me."

"And?"

"And this is better than I ever imagined."

Our lips met in the moonlight.

"Much better," he said and kissed me again.

Despite the cool night air, I began to feel warm all over.

Dwight never needed to have a diagram drawn for him. "Why don't we take this inside?" he murmured and whistled for the dog.

CHAPTER 15

We must take things as we find them, making a choice of such as seem to us, by the use of our best judgment, to contain the most good and the fewest evils.

—*Profitable Farming in the Southern States,* 1890

Flame Smith
Monday Morning, March 6

Flame Smith was tired, angry, and fighting a dull headache, the direct result of driving east with the morning sun in her eyes for three hours. All weekend she had waited at Buck Harris's mountain lodge, willing him to pull up in the drive and honk the horn exuberantly upon seeing her car there.

It never happened and she was now so furious with Buck that had she met him as she drove down the winding private road, she would have rammed her Jeep into his BMW hard enough that the hood would be smashed all the way back to the steering wheel in such neat little even pleats that he would be playing it like an accordion.

The image gave her a sour pleasure. So did the image

of chasing him back down the mountain with the .357 Magnum she kept in the console beside her.

In her forty-odd years, she had been chased by many men. Had even let a few catch her. Usually on her terms. Wasn't that why God had given her a mane of fiery red curls, flawless skin with a light dusting of freckles across an upturned nose in the middle of a lovely face, a nicely proportioned body with a twenty-inch waist, and a low sexy laugh that men wanted to hear again and again?

She had passed forty with every asset still intact, so why was she chasing around the state of North Carolina looking for this particular man? Yes, he had money and yes, she was tired of worrying about how she was going to pay the mortgage on Jackson House, her B&B down in Wilmington; but he was not the first man with money to want to put a ring on her finger and another one through her nose. He was not classically handsome, he needed to lose at least twenty pounds, he could be crude and rough, and like many self-made men she had known, he seemed to have the ethics of a polecat. But he was hung like a prize bull, he was surprisingly unselfish in bed, and he made her laugh.

The older she got, the more important that was becoming.

All the same, if he thought she was going to sit around cooling her heels while he took his sweet time to let her know why he'd broken both their date and his word, he had another thought coming, she told herself. It could have been fun for both of them, but *c'est la* damn *vie*. Enough was enough.

She stopped for gas on the east side of Raleigh and

bought a Coke for caffeine and a BC powder for her headache. To hell with Buck Harris. She would go back to Wilmington, make sure things continued to run smoothly at Jackson House, and then maybe she would give ol' what's-his-name a call. The guy who had developed one of the first planned communities along the river. The one who kept sending her orchids and roses. What the devil *was* his name? He wasn't as rowdy as Buck, but what the hell? Maybe solid and dependable would wear better in the long run.

As I-40 veered southeast through Colleton County, her headache eased off and she flipped on the radio, turning the dial to an amusing local country station. Solemn organ music played softly beneath a somber voice that enunciated proper names, followed by the name of a funeral home.

Flame had to laugh. Just what she needed—the local obituaries. "Add Mr. Effin' Buck Harris to your list," she told the announcer. "From now on that SOB is dead to me."

Obituaries were followed by the latest county news: the weekend had produced four car wrecks and a motorcycle accident for a total of three deaths. Several computers had been stolen from a Dobbs middle school. An employee with the county's planning board had been charged with embezzling almost four thousand dollars.

Stupid cow, thought Flame. Wreck your life for a paltry four thousand?

Still no identification for the dismembered body of a muscular Caucasian male. The Colleton County Sheriff's Department again urged the public to report any missing man between the age of thirty and sixty.

Eighteen dogs had been confiscated in Black Creek and their owner charged with felony dog fighting and animal cruelty, while—

"Wait a damn minute here!" Flame exclaimed. She was almost past the Dobbs exit, but she flashed her turn signal, yanked on her steering wheel and slid in front of a van that was trying to make its own sedate exit. The van honked angrily and veered to avoid rear-ending the Jeep, but Flame barely heard.

It was crazy, but what if that bitch was even less willing than Buck to share what they had built?

"Major Bryant?"

Dwight looked up to see one of the department clerks standing in his doorway.

"Mr. Stephenson's here with a client and they'd like to speak to you if you have a minute?"

"Sure," he said, laying aside the ME's report on the torso, a report which confirmed that it really was part and parcel of the other appendages they'd collected. If there had been scars, tattoos, or anything else unique to this body, they were obliterated by animal depredations or by the heavy blade that had dismembered it. Said blade, incidentally, appeared to be approximately six inches wide with a slight curvature of the cutting edge, all consistent with an ordinary axe.

Nevertheless, in addition to the broken right ulna earlier X-rays had discovered, the torso did carry two markers that might help distinguish this body from another.

First, there was a small mole just below the navel.

Second was what the ME described as "a protrusive umbilicus."

"Thanks for seeing us, Major Bryant," Reid Stephenson said formally as he held the door open for a very attractive redhead. A handsome six-footer himself, Reid was well-known for his penchant for knockout redheads, but this one was even more gorgeous than usual.

Where the hell did he keep finding them? Dwight wondered as he stood and shook hands with Deborah's cousin and former law partner.

"This is Ms. Smith," Reid said. "Flame Smith, from Wilmington."

"Major Bryant," she said, offering a firm handshake.

Up close, she was still gorgeous, if not quite as young as her flowing hair, slender figure and tight jeans implied at first glance. There were laugh lines around her wide mouth and small crinkles radiated from eyes as green as the snug sweater she wore beneath a beige leather jacket.

"What can I do for y'all?" he asked when they were seated.

Reid leaned forward. "That man, the one with his legs in one place and his body in another—has he been identified yet?"

"Why do you ask?"

"Because my client has been missing for over a week now and he fits the general description that's been released to the media."

Dwight frowned. "I thought you said Ms. Smith here is your client."

"Actually, I'm his client's girlfriend," said the redhead in a smoky voice that seemed to have Reid enthralled. "We were supposed to meet here in Dobbs this week for his divorce settlement, but he never showed up and I can't find anyone who's seen him lately. It's weird to think it might be Buck you've found, but if it is—"

"I see," said Dwight. "Does he have any identifying marks that you know of?"

"Identifying marks?"

"Like a tattoo or scars or something?" Reid said helpfully.

Flame Smith shook her head.

"Wait a minute!" said Reid. "Isn't he missing the tip of one of his fingers?"

"That's right!" She held up a beautifully manicured finger. Her long nails were painted a soft coral. "His right index finger. It got caught in a piece of farm equipment when he was a teenager."

They looked at Dwight expectantly. The big deputy frowned as he leafed through the file on the body. "The right hand we found is missing the tip of the index finger, but it's also missing some other joints."

Flame Smith winced, but she did not go dramatic on them. Dwight had the impression that this was a woman who could, when necessary keep her emotions in check, but he was willing to bet she could also take advantage of a redhead's reputation for a blazing tongue and temper if it suited her.

"You say no one's seen him," he said. "Who have you actually asked?"

"Well, first I tried everybody around here I could think

of. I even drove over to the main office in New Bern thinking something might have come up, but no one's seen him there since week before last. His wife's been living at their New Bern place since they split and he's been staying here."

"Here?"

"At the old farmhouse he got from his granddaddy. It was their first tomato farm."

"Oh yes," said Dwight. "I remember now. It belonged to his mother's people, didn't it? The old Buckley place?"

"I guess. That's his middle name. Judson Buckley Harris, but everybody calls him Buck." She pushed a tress of hair away from her eyes. "I tried there first thing on Wednesday and again on Friday. No sign of him and the housekeeper says she hasn't heard anything in over a week either. But in court Wednesday, I heard his wife say he might be holed up in the mountains."

"Deborah's doing the Harris ED," Reid murmured in an aside.

"Deborah?" asked Flame. "Judge Knott? You know her?"

With a repressive glance at Reid, Dwight nodded. "So then you—?"

"—drove up to his lodge in the mountains?" she asked, finishing his question. "Yes. But he wasn't there and when I finally caught up with the caretaker Sunday afternoon, he said he hadn't heard from Buck in at least three weeks."

"You try calling him?"

"Of course I did," she said impatiently. "That's why

I drove up to Wilkesboro. The lodge is in an area where reception is spotty and he never answers a land line. I thought sure that's where he'd be."

"When did you last speak to him, Ms. Smith?"

"Sunday before last. He was all riled up about the settlement and said he was going to be too busy to come down to Wilmington, but we set it up for me to come here. He said the divorce would be final by then and we could name our wedding date."

"You didn't worry when he didn't call?"

"I give my men a long leash," she said with a rueful smile. "Buck hates to talk on the phone and I don't push it."

"What about you?" Dwight asked Reid.

Reid shrugged. "As she said, Mr. Harris doesn't like to talk on the phone. I left messages on all his answering machines and at his office. When Ms. Smith came in today, I checked with my secretary. According to our records, the last time he actually spoke to me was Friday the seventeenth. I told him that the judge was running out of patience and he promised to be in court this past Wednesday."

Dwight turned back to Flame Smith. "Do you know if Mr. Harris ever broke his arm?"

"No, but I just remembered. He has a tiny little mole, right about here." One coral-tipped finger touched an area of her jeans halfway below her waist. "Oh, and he's an 'outie,' too," she added with an electric smile.

Dwight reached for a notepad. "Tell me the name of his housekeeper out at the Buckley place." He glanced at

Reid. "And maybe you'd better give me his wife's contact numbers, as well."

"Oh God!" Flame Smith moaned. Her peaches-and-cream complexion had turned to ivory. "It *is* Buck, isn't it?"

CHAPTER 16

City folks eat their meals more from habit than hunger, but country folks love to hear the horn blow.

—*Profitable Farming in the Southern States*, 1890

Deborah Knott
Monday Morning, March 6

Monday morning and my turn to handle felony first appearances. The State of North Carolina is obligated to bring an accused person before a judge within ninety-six hours of arrest and incarceration in the county jail or at the next session of district court, whichever occurs first. First appearance is where the judge informs the accused of the charges, sets the bond if bail is deemed appropriate, appoints an attorney if so requested, and calendars a trial date. Innocence or guilt is irrelevant. Neither plea can be accepted. This is just to get the case into the system and onto a calendar so that it can be moved along in a judicious manner.

When I first came on the bench, Monday mornings might bring me twenty or thirty people—forty after a real hot August weekend if it followed a week of unremitting heat. (Heat and humidity cause tempers to flare and differences are too often settled with baseball bats, knives, handguns, and the occasional frying pan.)

Between the building boom, and Colleton County's exploding population growth, fifty's no longer an unusual number, even on a Monday morning after some beautiful early spring weather. Here were the hungover drunks, the druggies coming down from their various highs, the incompetent burglars, the belligerent citizens and aliens alike, with attitudes that hadn't softened after a night or two on a jail cot.

Coping with all this is one judge and one clerk. If we're lucky, we may have a fairly skillful interpreter on hand for the whole session, but that's about it.

North Carolina is forty-eighth in the country in its funding of the whole court system, so take a guess where that leaves its district court? Last year 239 district court judges like me disposed of 2,770,951 cases. While upper court judges are plowing through their lighter load in air-conditioned tractors equipped with cell phones, iPods, and hydraulic lifts, district court judges are out in the hot sun, barefooted, following the back end of a mule.

I worked straight through the morning without even a bathroom break. Around 10:30, a clerk handed me a note from Dwight. "*Lunch here in my office*?"

I sent word back that I'd be down at noon and managed to gear it so that I actually recessed at 12:07.

Lunch in Dwight's office when he's buying tends not to be soup or a healthy salad, so it was no surprise to smell chopped onions and Texas Pete chili sauce as I turned into his hallway.

Detectives Mayleen Richards and Jack Jamison were on their way out and we paused to speak to each other. Like Kate, Richards had a new haircut, too. Her cinnamon-colored hair still brushed her shoulders, but there was a softer, more feminine look to the cut.

"Looks great," I told her. "You didn't get something that uptown here in Dobbs, did you?"

"As a matter of fact I did," she said. "There's a new stylist at the Cut 'n' Curl."

I made a face. "Too bad. That's where I go when I need a quick fix. Ethelene would kill me if I went to someone else in the same shop."

"How long since you were last there?" Richards said. "I think the new girl might be her replacement."

"Really? Thanks."

New hairdo? New air of confidence? Heretofore she could barely look me in the eye without turning brick red.

"You give Richards a promotion or has she got a new boyfriend?" I asked Dwight as soon as the door was closed behind me.

He popped the tops on a couple of drink cans. "No promotion."

"Boyfriend, then," I said. "Somebody here in the courthouse?"

"Don't ask me, shug. That's Faye Myers's department. Dispatchers seem to keep up with that stuff."

He handed over the sack from our local sandwich shop. "I got extra napkins."

"Thanks." I took the chair beside his desk and unwrapped a hot dog, being careful not to let it drip on my white wool skirt.

I know it's full of nitrates and artificial coloring and probably a dozen other coronary-inducing additives, but a frankfurter tucked into a soft roll with onions, chili, and coleslaw is difficult to resist and I didn't try.

"Cheers," Dwight said, touching his can to mine. "So how come you didn't tell me that Buck Harris is missing?"

"Huh?"

"Or did the sight of Dent Lee in your courtroom run it right out of your head?" he asked sardonically.

I groaned. "Do you remember every comment I ever made about every guy I ever lusted after?"

The corner of his lips twitched.

"If I'd realized I was going to wind up married to you, I'd've kept my mouth shut when we used to hang out together. You've never heard me say a single word about Belle Byrd, have you? Or Claudia Ward or Mary Nell Lee? Or Loretta Sawyer or—"

His grin was so wide at that point that I had to laugh, too. He'd suckered me again. "You must have been talking to Reid."

"Yep."

"Guess he's in no hurry to have his client show up. Have you seen the client's girlfriend? Anyhow, why should I have told you how some self-important millionaire keeps ditching his court dates? I *will* tell you this, though. If he doesn't come to court next week, I'm going to hear the case without him and he can whistle down the wind if he thinks I've acted unfairly. Until then—"

I looked at him in sudden dismay as the last dime finally dropped.

"Those body parts. Buck Harris?"

He gave a grim nod. "It's not a hundred percent positive, but it's on up there in the nineties." He finished his first hot dog and started on the second. "Nobody seems to have seen your missing Buck Harris since those legs were found last week. He had a mole just below his navel; so does the torso we found Friday night. His navel was an outie and so is this."

"His girlfriend—Flame Smith—does she know?"

"She's the one told me about the mole and the 'protrusive umbilicus,' as the ME put it. She contacted Reid and they were both in this morning. We're getting a search warrant for the old Buckley place. That seems to be the last place he was seen."

"The old Buckley place," I said slowly. "It's on Ward Dairy Road."

"Yeah," said Dwight.

That big bull of a man reduced to chunks of hacked-off arms and legs? My hot dog suddenly turned to ashes. I set it back on the paper plate and took a long swallow from the drink can.

"You know this Smith woman?" he asked.

"Not really. Portland's the one who introduced us the other day. They used to work together down at the beach. She was surprised to see Por here and I think they were going to get in touch with each other, have dinner or something."

"How far along was Harris's divorce?"

"It was final last month, but we're still working on the ED. There's a lot of money, property, and real estate to divide. That's why Dent was there to testify."

"Was it going amicably?"

"Not particularly. Mediation didn't work for them. That's why their case came to me. I can't quote you chapter and verse but the one time they were in court together, you'd've needed a chainsaw to cut the hostility. They split hairs and argued every point. But what do Pete and Reid care? If their clients want to waste time sniping at each other and not cooperating, that's just more billable hours. Wednesday, though, Mrs. Harris was furious that Flame was even there at all. Whether or not she's the primary reason they split, I get the impression that Mrs. Harris blames her for the divorce. You've seen her."

"Oh yes indeed," said Dwight with just a little more enthusiasm than I might have preferred.

"Mrs. Harris is fifty-two and wears every year on her face. Flame Smith doesn't look much over forty, does she? Buck Harris wouldn't be the first man to trade in an old wife for a new model and try to give the back of his hand to the old one."

"Was she mad enough to do something about it?"

"You mean kill him and then butcher him like a hog?"

"More people are killed by their loved ones than by total strangers," he reminded me.

"I only saw him the one time he came to court, but yeah, her anger was pretty obvious. He was big, but she is too. They say that in the early years, she was out on the tractors, plowing and spraying and hoisting boxes of vegetables right alongside him till they were making enough to hire migrant labor for all the physical stuff, so I imagine there's a lot of muscle underneath those extra pounds of fat."

"Kill him and she would get the whole company," Dwight said.

"Kill him before the divorce is final and then take a dismissal of her ED claim, she would," I corrected. "Assuming rights of survival. At this point, though, the ED will proceed as if he were still alive."

"Really?"

"I'll have to look it up. There's a similar case on appeal to the state supreme court but I'm pretty sure that's how it would work. But since they're divorced—"

"When was it final?" he interrupted.

"Sometime within the last two weeks or so. I'd have to check the files. I'm pretty sure it was a summary judgment, so neither of them came to court. Reid just handed me the judgment and I signed it, so it's a done deal."

"Today's March sixth. What with the cold weather and no insect damage, the best guesstimate we have for time of death is sometime between the morning of Sunday, February nineteenth, when Ms. Smith said she last spoke to him, and Wednesday the twenty-second, two days before we found the legs. You gonna eat the rest of that?"

I shook my head and the last third of my hot dog followed his first two.

"Tonight we stop somewhere for something healthy," I warned.

He gave me a blank look.

"You haven't forgotten have you? The Hurricanes? You and me?"

"Is that tonight?"

"It is. Jessie and Emma are going to pick Cal up after school and keep him till we get home, so no getting sidetracked, okay? You've got good people, darling. Trust them. What's the point of being a boss if you're going to roll out for every call?"

I finished my drink and stood to go. He stood, too.

"Wait, there's a spot of chili on your tie."

I tipped the carafe on his desk to wet a napkin and sponged it off before it had a chance to stain.

"I'll be finished by five or five-thirty," I said. "That gives you an extra ninety minutes. My car or your truck?"

"You'll come in early with me tomorrow?"

"Sure." I laced my hands behind his neck and pulled him down to my level. He smelled of mustard and chili and Old Spice. "I'd come to Madagascar with you."

"What's in Madagascar?"

"Who cares? You want to go, I'll go with you. As long as you come with me to tonight's game."

He laughed and kissed me. "My truck. Five-thirty. And don't forget to find me that divorce date."

CHAPTER 17

Horace argued both sides, and wound up by saying "the city is the best place for a rich man to live in; the country is the best place for a poor man to die in."

—*Profitable Farming in the Southern States,* 1890

Mayleen Richards
Monday Afternoon, March 6

On the drive out to the farmhouse that Buck Harris had inherited from his maternal grandfather, Jack Jamison was unusually silent. Normally, the chubby-faced detective would be throwing out a dozen theories, cheerfully speculating as to what they would find at the house, formulating possible motives. For the last few days though, he had seemed a million miles away and worry lines had begun to settle between his eyebrows.

"Everything okay at home?" Mayleen Richards asked him.

"Yeah, sure."

"Baby okay?"

As a rule, the mere mention of Jack Junior, now called

Jay, was enough to get her colleague talking non-stop. Today, all it got was an "Um."

"Guess Cindy's got her hands full now that he's starting to crawl."

"Yeah."

It was a sour response and Mayleen backed off. If Jack and Cindy were having marital problems, best she stay out of it. She turned the heater down a notch and concentrated on keeping up with Percy Denning, who was in the car ahead of them.

"Her sister's husband got a big raise back around Christmas," Jamison burst out suddenly. "They bought a new house. New car. And now she's told Cindy that they're going to have an in-ground swimming pool put in this summer."

He did not have to say more. Cindy and Jack lived in a doublewide next door to his widowed mother. Although Jack had never specifically said so, Mayleen was fairly sure that he gave Mrs. Jamison some financial help with her utility bills and car repairs in return for using her well and septic tank.

"She knew what the county pays when she married me."

Knowing it's one thing, Mayleen thought. Living on it's something else.

"She ever think about going back to work?"

"While Jay's still nursing?" He sounded shocked at the idea.

"I was just thinking that if she wants a bigger place or—?"

"Not if it means leaving our son."

Mayleen glanced over at him. "Well, then?"

"I could maybe get on with the Wake County sheriff's department, but it wouldn't pay that much more."

"Plus you'd lose any seniority," she said. "Anyhow, you're happy here, aren't you? Money's not everything."

"Right," he said with more sarcasm than she had ever heard from him. "It's just new houses, new cars, and fancy swimming pools." He sighed. "Police work's all I ever wanted to do. But if it won't pay enough here, then maybe I should—"

He broke off as they saw Denning flip on his turn signal upon approaching two dignified stone columns that marked a long driveway up to a much-remodeled farmhouse.

The housekeeper was expecting them and opened the door before they rang. Short and sturdy with dark brown skin, wiry salt-and-pepper hair pulled back in a bun, and intelligent brown eyes, Jincy Samuelson wore a spotless white bib apron over a long-sleeved blue denim dress. She brushed aside the search warrant they tried to give her and led them immediately to her employer's home office. Paneled in dark wood, the room looked more like a decorator's idea of a gentleman farmer's office than a place where real work was done by a roughneck, up-from-the-soil, self-made millionaire. The only authentic signs that he actually used the room were a rump-sprung leather executive chair behind the polished walnut desk, a couple of mounted deer heads, a desktop littered with papers, and a framed snapshot of a child who sat on a man's lap as he drove a huge tractor.

"That him?" Richards asked.

The housekeeper nodded. "And his daughter when she was a little girl."

It was their first look at the victim's face and the two deputies stared long and hard at it. He was dressed in sweaty work clothes, and only one hand was on the steering wheel. The other arm was curved protectively around the child who smiled up at him.

"He doesn't want anybody to do anything in here except run a dust cloth over the surfaces, vacuum the rug, and wash the windows twice a year," said Mrs. Samuelson. "Once in a while his secretary from over in New Bern might come by, but for the most part, he's the only one who uses this room. If you want to be sure it's just his fingerprints . . ."

"Not his bedroom or his bathroom?" Mayleen wondered aloud.

"Those rooms the maid or I clean regularly. Besides," she added with a small tight frown, "he occasionally takes—*took*—company up there."

Percy Denning had brought a small field kit and was soon lifting prints from the desk items.

Dwight Bryant arrived while they were questioning Mrs. Samuelson about Buck Harris's usual routine. He found them in the kitchen, a kitchen so immaculate that it might never have cooked a meal or had grease pop from a pan even though he could smell vanilla and the rich aroma of freshly brewed coffee. Heavy-duty stainless steel appliances and cherry cabinets lined the walls and the floor was paved with terra cotta tiles. Only the long walnut table that sat in the middle of the room looked old, so old that its edges had been rounded smooth over the years and there were deep scratches in the polished top. He would later learn that it was, as he suspected, the same kitchen table that had belonged to Buck Harris's great-grandparents and that it had stood in this same spot for over a hundred years.

While Denning labored in Harris's office, Richards and Jamison were enjoying coffee and homemade cinnamon rolls at that table.

Dwight joined them in time to hear Mrs. Samuelson tell how Mrs. Harris had originally hired her some six or eight years earlier to live in an apartment over the garage out back and act as both housekeeper and general caretaker.

"Sid Lomax manages this farm and the migrant camp. Whenever I need someone to do the grounds or help with the heavy work here in the house, he'll lend me a couple of Mexicans."

She told them that the Harrises lived together in New Bern before the separation and divorce. "But this house is the one he loves best—it was his grandfather's—and he wanted it kept so that he could walk right in out of the fields if he felt like staying over. She always called if they were both coming, but a lot of times he'd just show up by himself and expect fresh sheets on the bed, the rooms aired, and for me to have a meal ready to eat pretty quick, just like his grandmother did for him. I always keep something in the freezer that I can stick in the microwave. I don't look anything like his old granny, but he loved my stuffed peppers and they freeze up good. Meatloaf, too."

"So he was a demanding employer?" Mayleen asked.

Mrs. Samuelson smoothed the bib of her crisp white apron. "That's what he was paying me for. I've worked for worse."

"And you went on working for him after he and Mrs. Harris separated?"

"She asked me to come with her to New Bern, but we both knew that was because she wanted to mess it up here for him." A bit of gold gleamed in her smile. "Both my sons are just down the road and so are my grandbabies. Nothing in New Bern worth moving there for. Besides, when I told him she wanted me to go, he raised me a hundred a month if I'd stay."

Dwight's phone buzzed and as soon as he'd checked the small screen, he excused himself to take Deborah's call. "I checked the records, Dwight. The Harris divorce became final on the twentieth of February."

Twentieth of February. The day after Flame Smith said she last spoke to him.

He turned back to Mrs. Samuelson and said, "When did you see him last?"

"Saturday morning, three weeks ago," she answered promptly as she set a mug of coffee in front of him. It was so robust that he had to reach for the milk pitcher. "Saturday the eighteenth. Reason I remember is that's my sister's birthday. On weekends, I only work a half day on Saturday. I gave him his breakfast as usual and I left vegetable soup and a turkey sandwich for his lunch. When I came in on Monday morning, I saw by the mess he'd left in the kitchen that he'd fixed himself breakfast on Sunday morning, but that was the last meal he ate here."

"Did he sleep here Sunday night?"

She thought a moment, then frowned. "I don't know. I made the bed while he was eating breakfast and it had been slept in when I got here that Monday morning, but whether he slept here one night or two, I just can't say."

"But you're positive you didn't see him again after you left at noon on Saturday?"

"No sir, I didn't."

"What about children? The Harrises have any?"

"Just one girl. Susan. She was grown and gone before I started working here, but she's been here with them for Christmas a time or two. You could tell that she was his eyeballs, he was that foolish about her, but she was breaking his heart. Her husband was killed in Nine-Eleven and it changed her. Mrs. Harris says she used to love pretty dresses and parties and flying off to Europe. First time I saw her, though, she was skinny as a broomstick and she was wearing stuff that looked like it came from the Goodwill. Turned her away from God. She sat right here at this table and told them both that if God made the world, he wasn't taking very good care of it and it was up to people like them—people who had money—to do the work God should've been doing. I believe she still lives in New York. No children though. I think he used to take off and go see her two or three times a year."

"And you didn't see the need to notify her or Mrs. Harris that he was missing?"

"I didn't know that he was. He could have been at his place in the mountains or he might've been working over in the New Bern office. Like I say, he never lets me know where he was going or when he was coming back. He'd take a notion and he'd be gone and the only way I'd know was if I happened to be out there in the hall when he was leaving. 'Back in a few days.' That's all he ever told me. But you can ask Sid—Mr. Lomax."

She passed the plate of cinnamon rolls down the table and Jamison took another. Dwight and Richards passed.

"Do you know Ms. Smith?" Dwight asked. "Flame Smith?"

Mrs. Samuelson was too disciplined to sniff, but the expression that crossed her face was one that reminded him of Bessie Stewart, his mother's housekeeper who had helped raise him. He would not have been surprised to hear a muttered, "Common as dirt."

"I've met her," she admitted.

"And?"

"And nothing. If she was here in the mornings, I fixed her some breakfast, too. Wasn't any of my business what went on upstairs, although I have to say that she was always polite to me. Not like some of them he brought home."

Dwight paused at that. "He had other women?"

"He used to. When he and Mrs. Harris were still living together. This last year though, it's only been her. That Smith woman."

"Do you know their names?"

Mrs. Samuelson cupped her mug in her workworn hands as if to hold in the warmth and her brown eyes met Dwight's in a steady look. "If you don't mind, sir, I'd just as soon not say."

"I'm sorry, ma'am, but if Mr. Harris has been murdered, we need to know who might have hated him enough to do it."

The housekeeper nodded to the two detectives. "They say those hands and legs y'all've been finding might be him?"

"I'm afraid so."

She shook her graying head. "I don't see how any woman could do that. That takes a hateful and hating man."

"Like a husband who finds out his wife's been cheating on him?"

She thought about it, then nodded slowly. "Only one of them was married, but yes, her husband might could do it. A gal from El Salvador. Said her name was Strella. I think her husband's name is Ramon. Mr. Lomax can tell you. They live in the migrant camp on the other side of the field. She was here twice last summer. First time was to help me turn all the mattresses and he came in and saw her. Second time, I guess she was stretched out on one of the mattresses."

"Who else, Mrs. Samuelson?"

Reluctantly, she gave up two more names. "Both of 'em white, but I haven't seen either of them in this house in over a year. Mrs. Smith pretty much had a lock on him."

They all looked up as Denning came to the kitchen door. There was a smudge of fingerprint powder on his chin, more on his fingers. He crossed to the sink to wash his hands and Mrs. Samuelson immediately rose and tore off some paper towels.

"Thanks," he said, drying his hands.

"Any luck?" Dwight asked.

"It's a match. No question about it. The state lab can take a look if you want, Major, but it's Harris."

While Mrs. Samuelson showed Richards and Denning over the house and the nearer outbuildings, Dwight called Reid Stephenson as he had promised and asked him to notify the Harris daughter before it hit the news media. "And you might as well tell Pete Taylor so he can pass the word on to Mrs. Harris."

Then he and Jamison drove along a lane that was a shortcut over to the farm manager's home. Trim and tidy, the white clapboard house appeared to date from the late thirties and sat in a grove of pecan trees whose buds were beginning to swell in the mild spring air. No one appeared when Dwight tapped the horn, but through the open window of the truck, they could hear the sound of tractors in the distance and they followed another lane past a line of scrubby trees and out into a forty- or fifty-acre field. Two tractors were preparing the ground for planting. A third tractor seemed to be in trouble. It was surrounded by a mechanic's truck, two pickups with a Harris Farms logo on the doors, and several Latino and Anglo men.

As the two deputies drew near, a tall Anglo detached himself from the group.

"Mr. Lomax?" Dwight asked. "Sid Lomax?"

The man nodded in wary acknowledgment. He wore a billed cap that did not hide the flecks of gray at his temples and his face was weathered like the leather of a baseball glove, but if the muscles of his body had begun to soften, it was not evident in the way he moved with such easy grace.

"Lomax," Dwight said again. "Didn't you use to play shortstop for Fuquay High School?"

Lomax looked at Dwight more carefully and a rueful grin spread across his face. "I oughta bust you one in the jaw, bo. You played third for West Colleton, didn't you? Can't call your name right now, but damned if you weren't the one got an unassisted triple play off my line drive in the semifinals with the bases loaded, right?"

"Dwight Bryant," Dwight said, putting out his hand. "Colleton County Sheriff's Department."

"Yeah?" Lomax took his hand in a strong clasp. "Reckon I'd better not punch you out then."

"Might make it a little hard for my deputy here," Dwight agreed as Jamison smiled.

"Man, we were supposed to go all the way that year," he said, shaking his head. "Oh well. What can I do for you?"

"You've heard about the body parts been scattered along this road?"

"Yeah?"

"I'm afraid it's your boss."

"The hell you say!" His surprise seemed genuine. "Buck Harris? You sure?"

"We've just compared the fingerprints with those in Harris's study here. They match."

"Well, damn!"

"When's the last time you saw him?"

Lomax pulled out a Palm Pilot and consulted his calendar. "Sunday the nineteenth at the Cracker Barrel out on the Interstate. I was having dinner with my son and his wife after church and he stopped by our table on his way out. I walked out to the car with him because he wanted to firm it up about moving most of the crew on this place to one of our camps down east. We've had tomatoes here the last two years, so this year we're planting these fields in soybeans. Beans don't take a lot of labor."

"So did you move them yet?" Dwight asked.

"All but these guys you see here. Why?"

"Any women or children left in the camp?"

"A couple to cook for the men. Three or four kids and they all go to school. We encourage that. We don't let 'em quit or work during the school year. Mrs. Harris is pretty strict about that."

"Not Mr. Harris?"

"Well, you know Buck." He paused and looked at them dubiously. "Or do you?"

"Never met him that I know of," said Dwight.

"Me neither," said Jamison.

"Buck didn't mind cutting corners if it would save a few dollars."

"In what way?"

Lomax shrugged. "Hard to think of any one thing. He's one of those up-by-his-bootstraps guys. Always saying he started with nothing and built it into something. Wasn't completely nothing though, was it? He had what was left of his granddaddy's farm. Gave him a place to stand while he leveraged the rest. Not the most patient man you'd ever want to meet. Couldn't bear to see any workers standing around idle if the clock was running. Thought they ought to keep picking tomatoes or cutting okra even if it was pouring down rain because that's what he did when he first started. Always pushing the limits."

"You got along with him though?"

"Enough that I never quit him. Came close a couple of times. But he paid good wages for hard work and he knew he didn't have to be breathing down my neck every minute to make sure I was keeping to the schedule. And most of the time he could laugh about things. He liked to keep tabs on whatever was going on. He'd come out here in the fields and get his hands dirty once in awhile or plow for a few hours. That man did love to sit a tractor."

"Yet you weren't surprised when he didn't show up for two weeks?"

Again the shrug. "I knew he and Mrs. Harris were fighting it out in court. I figured that's where he was."

"You have a couple here named Ramon and Strella?"

"Ramon? Sure. Only they're not on the place now." Once more he consulted his Palm Pilot. "They moved over to Harris Farm Three back around Thanksgiving. That's down near New Bern."

"Any objection if we question the people still here?" Dwight asked.

"No problem. Either of you speak Spanish?"

As both deputies shook their heads, Lomax unclipped the walkie-talkie on his belt. "Let me get Juan for you. He's pretty fluent in English." When the walkie-talkie crackled, the farm manager said, "Hey, Juan? Come on in, bo."

Immediately, one of the tractors broke off and headed in their direction.

Before it reached them, though, Dwight's own phone buzzed again.

"Hey, Major?" Denning said. "You might want to get back over here. We've found Harris's car. I think we've also found the slaughterhouse."

CHAPTER 18

A good barn is essential, and no farmer can afford to be without one, which should be of sufficient size for all the purposes to which it is to be appropriated.

—*Profitable Farming in the Southern States,* 1890

Dwight Bryant
Monday Afternoon, March 6

Sid Lomax followed Dwight and Jack Jamison back to a cluster of outbuildings, which were screened from sight of the farmhouse and garage by a thick row of tall evergreen trees and bushes. In addition to the usual shelters, several of the sheds held specialized equipment for the different crops. The two trucks pulled up in front of a shed where Richards was already cordoning the place off with a roll of Denning's yellow crime scene tape. This shed was built for utility, not beauty: a concrete slab flush with the ground, steel studs, steel framing, a tinned roof that sloped from front to back, no windows. One of the tall double doors stood open and gave enough light to see that a silver BMW was parked inside.

"What's this shed used for?" Dwight asked Lomax as they walked closer.

"It's where we store the tomato sprayers, but we sent them on to the other farms before Christmas because we're going to grow beans here this year. It's supposed to be empty right now."

"Watch where you put your feet and don't touch anything," Richards cautioned him as he started to follow them inside.

Not that there was that much to touch. The car was the only object of any size in a space designed to hold at least two large pieces of machinery.

As they entered, Dwight paused and examined the door fastenings. The hasp was a hinged steel strap that slotted over a sturdy steel staple meant to hold a padlock and secure the strap. A wooden peg hung from a string but there was no padlock in sight and no sign that the doors had been forced.

Lomax followed his eyes. "We keep the sheds locked if there's something worth stealing in them," he said, "but we don't bother when they're empty, just peg the doors shut. I doubt I've stuck my head in here since Christmas."

Carefully, Denning used a screwdriver to pull a chain that released the catch for the other door and let it swing wide, then used equal care to switch on a couple of bare lightbulbs overhead that immediately lit up the gory scene at the rear of the shed.

Blood, lots of blood, had pooled at a slight low spot and blow flies and maggots were busily churning it on this mild spring day. Small dried chunks were scattered around.

"Bone," Denning said succinctly.

The bloody axe had been flung to one side but there were deep gouges in the concrete floor where the blade had come down heavily.

But that wasn't the worst.

The real horror was a length of bloody rusty iron chain that lay in heavy loops, the links caked in blood and gore, the two ends secured with a lock.

"Dear God," Lomax murmured. "He was alive and conscious when the hacking started?"

Denning nodded grimly. "Looks like it."

"And after it was finished," said Dwight, "the killer didn't need to open the lock. He just pulled away the pieces."

Lomax turned away and bolted for the door. They heard him retching, but there were no grins from any of them for a civilian's involuntary reaction.

Except for Denning, all of them had grown up on working farms where food animals had been routinely slaughtered to fill the family freezer for the winter, but that sort of killing was done cleanly and as humanely as possible.

This though—!

I'm getting too hardened, Richards thought sadly. *What would Mike think of me that I'm not out there throwing up, too?*

"Looks like his clothes over here," said Denning.

Jockey shorts lay tangled with a jacket, shirt, and pair of pants. Shoes and socks had been tossed into a corner.

"No blood," said Richards. "So he was stripped naked before the chain went on."

Jamison was appalled by the level of cruelty. "Somebody really hated his guts, didn't they?"

"But where the hell's the head and penis?" asked Dwight. "Either of y'all check the car?"

"Not there," Richards said. "The keys are in the ignition though."

Dwight peered through the windshield. The steering wheel sported a black lambswool cover, so no chance of fingerprints from it.

"Y'all open the trunk?"

"Not yet," Richards admitted.

They waited for Percy Denning to dust the door handle. "Too smeared," he reported.

After gingerly extracting the key from the ignition, he fitted one of them into the trunk lock.

Richards held her breath as the lid lifted and immediately realized she was not the only one when the others collectively exhaled.

The trunk was upholstered in dark gray and, except for the spare tire, appeared at first to be empty. And then they took a second look.

"Shit!" said Denning. He got his camera and took pictures of the stains on the floor and lid of the trunk and of the once-white undershirt with which the killer had probably wiped the worst of the blood from his hands. "This was the delivery truck."

CHAPTER 19

With a zest, seasoned and heightened by congenial companionship, let him have at times . . . such festivities as sweep from the brain the cobwebs of care.

—*Profitable Farming in the Southern States,* 1890

Deborah Knott
Monday Afternoon, March 6

After lunch, I finished up the first appearances. Normally, unless an address is familiar for other reasons, I don't pay much attention to the ones given by the miscreants who come before me, but so soon after talking with Dwight and with the Harris divorce on my mind, I looked closer at the Latino who had been picked up Saturday night and was charged with possession of two rocks of cocaine.

"Ward Dairy Road?" I asked through the interpreter. "Harris Farms?"

"Sí," he said and followed that with a burst of Spanish. The only word I caught was *Harris* and the interpreter, a young woman going for an associate degree in education out at Colleton Community, confirmed that he lived in the Harris Farms migrant camp out there on the old Buckley place.

I appointed him an attorney, set his bond at five thousand, and before remanding him to the custody of the jailer, asked if he knew Mr. Harris.

"*¿Conoce el Señor Harris?*"

From the negative gestures and the tone of his reply, I was not surprised to hear that this guest worker knew the "big boss" by sight but had never had direct dealings with him.

The rest of his reply was almost lost to me as a distraught white woman burst through the doors at the rear of the courtroom with a wailing infant. There was a huge red abrasion on the side of her face and blood dripped from her cut lip onto the dirty pink blanket wrapped around the baby.

A uniformed policewoman hurried in after her, calling, "Ma'am? Ma'am?"

"Please!" she cried as the bailiff moved out to intercept her. "He's going to kill me and the baby, too! You got to stop him! You *got* to! Please?"

Between us, we got her calmed down enough to speak coherently and give me the details I needed to issue an immediate domestic violence protection order. Someone from the local safe house was in the courtroom next door and she volunteered to take the woman and her baby to the shelter.

As things returned to normal, I finished the last of the first appearances and sent them snuffling back to jail to await trial or try to make bail. While the ADA got ready to pull the first shuck on today's criminal trials, I asked my clerk to check on when I'd signed the summary judgment for the Harris divorce.

At the break, I phoned Dwight, who was out at the old Buckley place by then and gave him the date—Monday, February 20. "Four full days before those legs were found," I said.

"So if he died before then, maybe the wife decided she'd rather inherit everything instead of having to divide it with his heirs?"

"Only if she withdraws her request for the ED," I reminded him.

"Who are they, by the way?"

"I haven't a clue," I said, resisting the urge to go into all the possible legalities that could complicate his simplistic summation. "Reid might know. Am I still going to see you in a couple of hours?"

"I'll be there," he promised.

I adjourned at 5:30, then got held up to sign some orders, so that I went downstairs prepared to apologize for being a little late. I needn't have worried.

Melanie Ashworth, the department's recently hired spokesperson, was holding forth about something to reporters in the main lobby, so I crossed out of camera range and asked the dispatcher on duty what was up.

"They just identified all those body parts," he whispered. "It's Buck Harris."

I walked on down the hall. Dwight was in Bo's office with a couple of deputies, and they seemed to be discussing something serious. He held up a with-you-in-a-minute finger and I signaled that I'd wait for him in his office. It did not look good for the home team. Even though Cal and I both needed for me to follow through on this, I should have known better than to try to set up an evening with Dwight when he was in the middle of a sensational murder investigation.

Fortunately, I had brought along some reading material, although it didn't make me happy to read that a colleague had been reversed on an earlier ruling. She had ordered the divorced father of minor children to turn in all his guns until the children were grown. This was after he himself testified that yes, he did keep a loaded handgun on the dash of his truck and loaded long guns in the house and no, he didn't plan to lock them up in a gun cabinet or have them fitted with trigger locks because *his* kids knew better than to mess with them.

The father had appealed and the higher court had sided with the dad. I just hoped my friend would never have to send those judges the obituary of one of those kids with an "I told you so" scribbled across it.

I had rendered a similar judgment almost a month ago, but so far that father hadn't appealed. With a little luck, he might never hear that there were higher courts that would let him put his preschoolers in harm's way. I certainly wasn't going to tell him.

Dwight was still tied up when I finished reading the official stuff, so I pulled out *Blood Done Sign My Name*, my book club's selection for March.

I know, I know. My club is always behind the curve, but hey, sometimes it's helpful to let the first waves of enthusiasm wash out what's trendy and leave what's solid. We've spared ourselves a lot of best sellers that weren't worth the trees it took to print them. With this book, the first sentence grabbed me by the throat and was so compelling that I was deep into it by the time Dwight finally got free

"Sorry about supper, shug," he said when he joined me. To my surprise, it was five past seven "I guess we'll have to get something at the game."

I slid my book into the tote bag that held my purse and papers. "You're not going to blow me off?"

"Nope. You're right. We've got good people. Let 'em run with the ball."

He picked up his jacket, held my coat for me, and switched off the light behind us.

"Enjoy the game," Bo called as we passed his office.

Happily, the lobby was now bare of reporters.

"They were all over the Harris story when I got here. Y'all hired Melanie Ashworth just in time, didn't you?" I said, holding out my hand for his keys. Late as it was, we didn't have time to meander in to Raleigh with him behind the wheel.

He handed them over without dissenting argument and said tiredly, "You don't know the half of it. It's been one hellacious day. Remember that second right hand we found?"

"The Alzheimer's patient who drowned in Apple Creek?"

Dwight nodded. "The autopsy report just came in. The body's definitely Fred Mitchiner, but it turns out that an animal didn't just pull the hand loose. Somebody cut it off."

"What?"

"Yeah. That hand had been in the water so long that the connective tissues were pretty much gone, but there was a ligament that must have still been intact because it was only recently cut off. Not when he first died."

"Someone killed him?"

"Hard to say. The ME doesn't think so. There's no evidence of trauma to the body, but he'd been in the water so long that there's no way to know if he drowned by accident or if someone held him under."

I gave Dwight my tote bag to stash behind the seat and unlocked the truck. Although we were in danger of missing the opening face-off, we would also miss the rush hour traffic.

"Another cute thing," Dwight said as we pulled out of the parking lot behind the courthouse. "A lot of Alzheimer's patients will try to get away, but the nursing home has said all along that Mitchiner wasn't one to wander off. For some reason the place reminded him of spending the summers at his grandparents' house with a bunch of cousins, so he was pretty content there."

"So content that they didn't put an electronic bracelet on him?"

"Exactly. Another reason that the family's claiming negligence. You do know that the town's speed limit is thirty-five, don't you?"

I braked for a red light and adjusted his mirrors while I waited for the green. "When's the last time a Dobbs police officer stopped a sheriff's deputy for speeding?"

"That's because we don't speed unless we've got a blue light flashing."

"Hmmm," I said, and reached as if to turn his on.

He snorted and batted my hand away. "You try that and I'll write you up myself."

"Any theories as to how and why he wound up in the creek? Who profits?"

"Nobody. That's the hell of it. He was there on Medicaid. No property. No bank account. His nearest relatives are the daughter who's suing and a sixteen-year-old grandson and everybody says they were both devoted to the old man. One or the other was there almost every day for the last two years, ever since she had to put him there because they couldn't handle him at home anymore what with her working and the kid in school. Wasn't like the Parsons woman."

"That the one down in Makely?"

"Yeah. She had children and grandchildren, too, but when she went missing, none of them noticed till the nursing home told them. They say nobody from the family had come to visit her in nearly a year."

"Didn't stop them from trying to get damages for mental anguish, though, did it?" I said, recalling some of the details.

He laughed and relaxed a little as I merged onto the interstate where it's legal to go seventy and troopers usually turn a blind eye to seventy-five.

"What about Buck Harris's place?" I asked. "Anything turn up there?"

"Oh yes," he said, his jaw tightening. "He was butchered in one of the sheds back of the house."

Without going into too many of the grisly details, he hit the high spots of what they had found—a locked chain, the fact that Harris had been naked and probably conscious when the first axe blow fell, how the killer must have used the trunk of Harris's car to strew the body parts along Ward Dairy Road.

I mulled over the chronology and tried not to visualize what he had described. "Nobody saw him after that Sunday, the divorce was final on Monday, his legs weren't found till Friday and the ME's setting the time of death as when?"

"Originally between Saturday and Thursday, but that's been narrowed down to Sunday as the earliest possible day."

"Because Flame talked to him then?"

"And because his farm manager saw him on Sunday around noon. If the body was in that unheated shed from the time of death till the night they were found, then Sunday's more likely. If somebody held him prisoner for a few days first though, it could be as late as Thursday. Denning's taking extra pains with the insect evidence in the blood."

Insect evidence?

Read maggots.

"Is that going to be much use? Cold as it was all that week, would there have been blowflies?"

"Remember the foxes?"

I smiled and lifted his hand to my lips. Of course I remembered.

It had been a chilly Sunday morning back in early January. The temperature could not have been much over freezing, but the sun was shining and when he asked if I'd like to take a walk, I had immediately reached for a scarf and jacket. Hand in hand, we had rambled down along the far side of the pond, going nowhere and in no hurry to get there, enjoying the morning and sharing a contentment that had needed few words. On the right side of the rutted lane lay the lake-size expanse of dark water; on the left, a tangle of bushes, trash trees, and vines edged a field that had lain fallow since early summer. Some farmers hate to see messy underbrush and are out with weed killers at the first hint of unwanted woody plants, but we've always left wide swaths for the birds and small mammals that share the farm with us.

That morning, sparrows and thrashers fluttered in and out of the hedgerow ahead of us as we approached and our footsteps flushed huge grasshoppers that had emerged from their winter hiding to bask in the warm sun. At a break in the bushes, we paused to look out over the field and saw movement in the dried weeds less than fifty feet away. A warning squeeze of his hand made me keep still. At first I couldn't make out if they were dogs or rabbits or—

"Foxes!" Dwight said in a half-whisper.

A pair of little gray foxes were jumping and pouncing. With the wind blowing in our direction, they had not caught our scent and seemed not to have heard our low voices.

"What are they after?" I asked, standing on tiptoes to see. "Field mice?"

At that instant, a big grasshopper flew off from a tuft

of broomstraw and one of the foxes leaped to catch it in mid-flight.

Entranced, we stood motionless and watched them hunt and catch more of the hapless insects until they spooked a cottontail that sprang straight up in the air and lit off toward the woods with both foxes close behind.

So no, not all insects died in winter.

"There are always blowflies in barns and sheds," Dwight reminded me. "They may hunker down when the mercury drops, but anything above thirty-five and they're right back out, especially if there's blood around."

We rode in silence for a few minutes. I was carefully keeping under the speed limit. With all he'd had to cope with today, I didn't need to add any more stress. So what if we missed the opening face-off?

"If it turns out Harris died on Sunday, what's this going to do to your ED case?" he asked.

"Not my problem. If it can be proved that he died before I signed the divorce judgment, then that judgment's vacated. If he died afterwards, then it proceeds unless Mrs. Harris dismisses her claim."

"And if nobody can agree on a time of death?"

"Then Reid and Pete get to argue it out. They or the beneficiaries under Harris's will. With a little bit of luck, some other judge will get to decide on time of death." I thought about Flame Smith, who had clearly planned on becoming the second Mrs. Harris. "I wonder if he made a will after the separation? Want me to ask Reid?"

"Better let me," Dwight said. "Could be the motive for his death."

"I rather doubt if Flame Smith swung that axe," I said.

"You think? I long ago quit saying what a woman will or won't do."

After such a harrowing day, I was glad to see Dwight get caught up in the hockey game. We ordered hamburgers and beers that were delivered to our seats and found we had only missed the first few scoreless minutes. Soon we were roaring and shouting with the rest of the fans as the lead seesawed back and forth. Each time one of our players was sent to the penalty box, the clock ticked off the seconds with a maddening slowness that was just the opposite of the way time whizzed by if it was our chance for a power play. Near the end, the Canes pulled ahead 3 to 2 and when Brind'Amour iced the cake with a slap shot that zoomed past their goalie, Dwight swept me up and spun me around in an exuberant bear hug.

Canes 4 to 2.

Yes!

CHAPTER 20

Those farmers who are generally dissatisfied with their condition and imagine that they may be greatly benefitted by a change of place, will find, in the majority of cases, that the fault is more in themselves than in their surroundings.

—*Profitable Farming in the Southern States,* 1890

Dwight Bryant
Tuesday Morning, March 7

The clouds that had intermittently obscured the moon on the drive home last night had thickened in the early morning hours and now a heavy rain beat against the cab of the truck as Dwight and Deborah waited with Cal at the end of their long driveway for his schoolbus to arrive.

Normally, thought Dwight, the three of them would be laughing and chattering about last night's game, but his attempt to get Cal to speak of it earlier went nowhere. "The Canes won, you know."

"I didn't watch it," Cal had said, concentrating on his cereal.

Yes, they had watched the beginning of the game, he said, but then it was his bedtime. Yes, it was good the Canes had won. Yes, he'd had a good time with Jessie and Emma. When pushed for details, he allowed as how they had taken him over to Jessie's house for a couple of hours to ride horses across the farm. These boots that he was wearing today? "Jess said I could have them since they don't fit anybody else right now."

"That was nice of her," Dwight said heartily.

Cal shrugged. "I have to give them back when they get too tight, so that maybe Bert can wear them."

He wasn't openly sulking, and he wasn't rude. He did and said nothing that Dwight could use as a launching pad for a lecture on attitude.

Sitting between them while the rain streamed down and fogged the truck windows, Deborah was pleasant and matter-of-fact. Had he not known her so intimately, he could almost swear that it was a perfectly ordinary morning. He did know her though, and he sensed her conscious determination to keep the situation from becoming confrontational.

He also sensed the relief that radiated from both of his passengers when they spotted the big yellow bus lumbering down the road. Cal immediately pulled on the door handle.

Although his hooded jacket was water-repellent, Dwight said, "Wait till she stops or you'll get soaked," but his son was out the truck so quickly that he had to wait in the downpour for a moment before the driver could get the door open.

Dwight sighed as the bus pulled off and he gave a

rueful smile to Deborah, who had not moved away even though the other third of the truck's bench seat was now empty. "Sorry about that."

She laid a hand on his thigh and smiled back. A genuine smile this time. "Don't be. If he wasn't mad because I made him miss the game, I'd be worried. I like it that he's feeling secure enough to show a little temper."

"You're still not going to tell me what it was all about?"

"One of these years, maybe. Not now though."

"All the same," he said as he pulled onto the road and headed the truck toward Dobbs, "I think he and I are due to have a little talk this afternoon."

She considered the ramifications for a moment, then said, "That might not be a bad idea. It won't hurt for him to hear again from you that he's supposed to listen to me when you're not around so that he'll know we're both on the same page, but please make it clear that you don't know any details and that you're not asking for any, okay?"

"Gotcha."

She sighed and leaned her head against his shoulder. "Poor kid. I think it's really starting to sink in that Jonna's gone forever and he's stuck here with us."

"That still doesn't mean—"

"No," she agreed before he could finish the thought. "But it does mean I'm not going to take it too personally and you shouldn't either. Mother used to tease me about the time I stomped my foot and yelled that I was purply mad with her."

"*Purply* mad?"

"I knew purple, I didn't know perfect. The point is, she

was my mother. Not my stepmother, yet I absolutely hated her at that moment. Nothing we can say or do changes the fact that Jonna's dead. That's the cold hard reality Cal has to deal with, but it's something he's going to have to work through on his own. All we can do is give him love and security and let him know what the rules are."

Her face was turned up to his and he bent his head to kiss her. "Anybody ever tell you you ought to run for judge?"

When they got to the courthouse, it was still pouring, so he dropped her at the covered doorway to the Sheriff's Department and she waited while he parked and made his way back with a large umbrella. Despite the rawness of the day, this felt to him like a spring rain, not a winter one.

"I know Cletus and Mr. Kezzie have a garden big enough to feed everybody," he said happily, "but don't we want a few tomato plants of our own? And maybe some peppers? Oh, and three or four hills of okra, too?"

She shook her head in mock dismay. "Are tomatoes the camel's nose under the tent? Am I going to come home and find the south forty planted in kitchen vegetables? I'm warning you right now, Major Bryant. You can plant anything you want, but I don't freeze and I certainly don't can."

Because it was early for her, they walked down to the break room and as they emerged with paper cups of steaming coffee, they met a damp Reid Stephenson.

"Got an extra one of those?" he asked.

"You're out early," Deborah said.

"I've had Flame Smith on my tail since last night. What about it, Dwight? When did he die? Before the divorce or after?"

"Now that I can't tell you for sure. We may not ever know."

"Guess I'd better go talk to Pete Taylor," he said.

"Was there a will?" Deborah asked.

Dwight frowned at her and she grinned unrepentantly. "It's going to be a matter of public record sooner or later. So *cui bono*, Reid? Or weren't you the one who drew it up?"

"Oh, I did one. It was about a week after he initiated divorce proceedings over here. Both the Harrises decided to hire personal attorneys instead of using the New Bern firm that handles their combined business interests."

"Does Flame inherit anything?"

"Goodbye, Deborah," Dwight said, sounding out every syllable of her name.

She laughed and turned to go. "See you for lunch?"

"Probably not." He motioned for Reid to follow him into his office.

"I really ought not to tell you anything till I put the will in for probate," the younger man said.

Dwight took his seat behind the desk and asked, "Who's his executor?"

"His daughter up in New York." Reid pulled up a chair and set his coffee on the edge of the desk. "She was pretty upset when I called her yesterday, but she called back this morning and she's flying in this afternoon."

"Whether or not the divorce was final won't affect the terms of the will, will it?"

"Actually, it probably will. From the documents he

gave me—and you might want to check with their company attorneys—their LLC was set for shared ownership with rights of survival."

"If one of them dies, the other gets full ownership?"

"That's my understanding. I'm sure Mrs. Harris's attorney will argue that the divorce doesn't really matter because there had been no formal division of property yet so the terms of the LLC will still be in effect. On the other hand, if the divorce was finalized before he died, then the ED could go forward, with his estate taking whatever he was awarded. It could be a pretty little legal problem. Of course, he did own property and money in his own name and his will should stand as to the disposition of that part of his estate."

"How much are we talking?"

"His personal estate? Maybe three million, give or take a few thousand."

"So answer me Deb'rah's question. Who inherits?"

"I can't tell you that, Dwight."

"Sure you can. Like she said, it's all going to be public record soon enough. Is Flame Smith in the will?"

Reid thought about it a minute, then threw up his hands in surrender. "Oh yes. To the tune of half a million. Except for a few small bequests, the daughter gets everything else, which he thought was going to be half of Harris Farms."

Dwight leaned back in his chair. "What was Buck Harris really like, Reid?"

"He was okay. Blunt. To the point. Knew what he wanted and was willing to pay for it. Expected full value for his money though."

"So why would someone take an axe to him like that?"

"Damned if I know." Reid took a first swallow of his coffee and grimaced. "Y'all need to let Julia Lee start buying your coffee beans. This stuff's like battery acid."

"I doubt if Bo's budget runs to a coffee grinder and gourmet beans," he said, remembering how he used to look for excuses to drop by the firm of Lee, Stephenson and Knott, before Deborah ran for the bench. Coffee was always good for one visit a week and they did have the best coffee of any office in town.

Not that he was ever there for the coffee.

After Reid left, Dwight phoned Pete Taylor. "I'd appreciate it if you could get Mrs. Harris to come in and see me this afternoon?"

Taylor promised that he would try.

Down in the detectives' squad room, he gave out the day's assignments as to the lines he wanted pursued and the people they should interview.

"One thing, boss," said Denning. "I found a hammer at the back of the shed. There was blood on the peen and one strand of hair that I compared with hairs from the comb in Harris's bathroom. I've sent them both to the state lab, but the hairs look like a match to me."

"Which means?"

"He was probably coldcocked over the head with the hammer first. We'll have to wait till we find the head to know for sure."

As Dwight returned to his office and the rat's nest of

paperwork awaiting his attention, he heard Jamison say, "Talk to you a minute, Major?"

"Sure. Come on in."

The deputy followed and closed the door. There was a troubled look on his round face.

"What's up?" Dwight asked. He gestured to the chair Reid Stephenson had vacated, but Jamison continued to stand.

"I need to tell you that I'm resigning, sir."

"*What?*"

"Yes, sir. Effective the end of next week, if that's okay with you."

"What the hell's this about? And for God's sake, sit down."

The detective sat, but he looked even more uncomfortable and was having trouble meeting Dwight's eyes.

Dwight studied him a long moment. "What's going on, Jack? If it's a better offer from another department, you're about due a raise. I don't know that we can match Raleigh, but—"

"It's not Raleigh, Major. It's Iraq."

Dwight frowned. "I didn't realize you're in the Guard."

"I'm not. It's DynCorp. They're a private security company that—"

"I know what DynCorp is." He realized that he should have seen this coming. Police departments all over the area had lost good men to private security companies. First war America's ever had to contract out, he thought sourly.

"They've accepted me into their training program. If I qualify, I'll be helping to train Iraqi police officers."

"And that's what you want to do?"

"Not really but the pay's too good to pass up, Major. We're just not making it on thirty-seven thousand a year. Cindy wants things for our son and I want them, too. Over there, I can start at around a hundred-thirty."

Dwight leaned back in his chair, feeling older and more tired than he had in a long time. "No, we certainly can't match that. But you say you want things for your son. What about a father? Civilian personnel are getting killed over there."

Jamison nodded. "I know. But like Cindy says, police officers are getting shot at over here, too."

"You ever been shot at?"

"Well, no sir, but it does happen, doesn't it? A couple or three inches more and Mayleen could have died back in January. Anyhow, I figure two years and we'll be out of debt with enough saved up to put a good down payment on a real house. It's worth the risk." He took a deep breath. "And if I do get killed, she'll get a quarter million in insurance. That should be enough to get Jay through college."

Dwight shook his head. "Do the math, Jack. Divide a quarter million by eighteen years. Cindy won't have enough left to pay your son's application fees."

By the determined look on Jamison's face, his mind was clearly made up.

"So. The end of next week?"

"Yes, sir."

"Okay. I'm really sorry you feel you need to do this, but notify human resources and make sure your paperwork's caught up."

Jamison came to his feet. "Thank you, Major. And I really do appreciate all you've done for me, making me a detective and all. Maybe when I get back . . ."

"We'll see. You're not gone yet though, and I expect another full week of work from you, so get out there and see what you can dig up on thc Harris murder."

CHAPTER 21

It is a matter of paramount importance to the prosperity of any community or State to have its surplus lands occupied by an industrious, enterprising, and moral population.

—*Profitable Farming in the Southern States,* 1890

Deborah Knott
Tuesday Morning, March 7

Because I had nearly forty-five minutes to kill after leaving Dwight and Reid, I stopped by the dispatcher's desk out in the main lobby where Faye Myers was on duty.

Faye's in her early thirties, a heavyset blonde who strains every seam of her uniform. She has a pretty face, a flawless complexion that seems to glow from within, and the good-hearted friendliness of a two-month-old puppy. She's married to Flip Myers, an equally plump EMS tech, and between them, they have a finger on almost every emergency call in the county, which means she also has the best gossip—not from maliciousness but because she genuinely likes people and finds them endlessly fascinating.

"New hairdo?" I asked with what I hoped was a guileless tone. "Looks nice."

She immediately touched her shining curls. "Well, thank you, Judge. No, it's the same style I've had since Thanksgiving. I did get a trim yesterday but I might should've waited 'cause this wet weather's making it curl up more than usual."

"Detective Richards tells me she goes to the Cut 'n' Curl. You go there, too?"

"No, I just get my sister to clip it for me. She cuts everybody in the family's hair."

"Lucky you," I said. "You must save a ton of money."

She beamed.

"But the new stylist at the Cut 'n' Curl did a great job on Mayleen Richards, didn't she? She looks like a different person these days."

"Yeah, well . . ." Myers gave me a conspiratorial look. "She's real happy right now."

"Oh?" I encouraged.

Within moments, I was hearing how Richards had recently become involved with a "real cute Mexican guy," who ran a landscaping business "out towards Cotton Grove," someone she'd met last month when investigating a shooting over that way. A Miguel Diaz. "Mayleen calls him Mike."

A naturalized citizen, he had been in North Carolina for eight or nine years and had bootstrapped himself up from day laborer to employer who ran several crews around the area, contracting with some of the smaller builders to landscape the new developments that were springing up all over the county.

Faye was under the impression that he wanted to marry Richards but that she was hanging back because of her family.

"They're sort of prejudiced, you know," the dispatcher confided. "But I told Mayleen that's probably just because they don't really know any Mexicans. Think they're all up here to take away our jobs and get drunk on Saturday night. Not that some of 'em don't. Get drunk, I mean. But Mike— Oh, wait a minute! You know something, Judge? You actually talked to him."

"I did?"

"That guy that stole the tractor and messed up a bunch of yards 'cause he didn't know how to lift the plows? Wasn't he in your court Friday?"

"That's her new boyfriend?"

"No, no. Mike was there to speak up for him, least that's what one of the bailiffs told me anyhow."

"Oh yes. I remember now. The Latino who said he'd see that the rest of the damage was repaired?"

"That's the one. It's real nice when people take care of their own, isn't it?"

I couldn't exactly recall Miguel Diaz's face, but I did retain an impression of responsibility and I remember being surprised by how fluent his English was.

"Mayleen says Mike felt so sorry for the man, what with all his troubles, that he's hired him on after he got kicked out of the camp he was staying at."

"That's right," I said, as more of the details came back to me. "His wife left him, didn't she?"

"Went right back to Mexico after their baby died." Faye looked around to make sure no one was near and leaned even closer. "I might not ought to be telling this, but Flip was on call that night and he helped deliver the baby and *he* said—"

Her phone rang then and, judging by the sudden professional seriousness of her voice, it sounded like an emergency for someone, so I gave her a catch-you-later wave because Reid walked past at that moment.

He held the door for me and we walked around to the stairs. When we reached the atrium on the ground floor that connects the old courthouse to the new additions, the marble tiles were slick where people had tracked in muddy water. A custodian brought out long runners and laid them down to cover the most direct paths from one doorway to another before tackling the floor with a mop.

We paused to speak to a couple of attorneys, then sat on the edge of one of the brick planters filled with lush green plants to finish our coffee and enjoy the rain that was sluicing down the sides of the soaring glass above us. At least, Reid was enjoying it. My agenda was to get him to tell me everything he'd told Dwight.

"I suppose his daughter scoops the lot? His housekeeper told Dwight that he was close to her. Poor Flame Smith."

"Not too poor," said Reid, half-distracted by the weather he was going to have to brave to keep an appointment back at his office. "The daughter's the residual beneficiary, but Flame'll get half a million. I don't suppose you've got an umbrella you could lend me? Flame took mine and John Claude keeps his locked up for some reason."

I had to laugh. I know exactly why John Claude keeps his umbrella in a locked closet and I immediately began to chant the exasperated verse our older cousin always quoted whenever he discovered that Reid had once again "borrowed" his umbrella:

"The rain it raineth every day
Upon the just and unjust fellow,
But more upon the just, because
The unjust hath the just's umbrella."

"Very funny," Reid said grumpily as he stood to dump our cups in the nearest trash bin. He spotted Portland Brewer coming up the marble steps outside and, ever the gentleman, he rushed over to hold the heavy outer door for her. Her small red umbrella hadn't warded off all the wet, but she was so angry, it's a wonder the raindrops didn't sizzle as soon as they touched any exposed skin. "Dammit, Deborah! I thought Bo and Dwight were going to take away all of James Braswell's guns!"

"Huh?" I said.

"He got out of jail yesterday morning and last night he shot up Karen's condo."

"*What?* Is she okay?"

"No, she's freaking *not* okay! She's scared out of her mind."

I made sympathetic noises, but Por was too wound up to be easily calmed. The rain had curled her black hair into tight little wire springs. Reid took her dripping umbrella and made a show of holding it over the green leaves.

"You in court this morning?" he asked her.

"After I get through blasting Dwight and Bo. Why?" Too riled to give him her full attention, she continued venting at me. "The only reason Karen's still alive is that she's been staying at her mother's. She could have been killed for all they care."

"Now wait a minute," I said. "That's not fair. They can't put a twenty-four-hour watch on her. And besides, how do you know it was Braswell?"

"Who else would it be? You think a sweet kid who works at a Bojangles and takes care of an invalid mother has that kind of enemies? Hey! Where're you going with my umbrella?" she called as Reid pushed open the door for one of our clerks and kept walking.

"I'll drop it off at your office," he called back and hurried down the marble steps and out into the unrelenting rain, Portland's umbrella a small circle of red over his head.

As Por stormed off in one direction, I was joined on my walk upstairs by Ally Mycroft, a prisspot clerk who had pointedly worn my opponent's button during the last election whenever she had to work my courtroom.

Making polite chatter, I asked, "You working for Judge Parker today?"

"No," she said, with equally phony politeness. "I'll be with you today."

I made a mental note to drop by Ellis Glover's office sometime today, see if it was me our Clerk of Court was annoyed with or Ally Mycroft.

"In fact," Ally said, "Mr. Glover has assigned me to your courtroom for the rest of the week."

In my head, Brook Benton began singing his world-weary "Rainy Night in Georgia."

"Lord, I feel like it's rainin' all over the world."

CHAPTER 22

I've got an old mare who will quit a good pasture to go into a poor one, and it's just because she got into a habit of letting the bars down.

—*Profitable Farming in the Southern States,* 1890

DEPUTIES MCLAMB AND DALTON
TUESDAY MORNING, MARCH 7

"Better not block the driveway," Deputy Raeford McLamb said and Sam Dalton, the department's newest detective trainee, parked at the curb in front of a shabby little house in sad need of paint. A white Honda stood in the driveway. On the small porch, a young man in a UNC hoodie with a black-and-silver backpack dangling from his shoulder shifted his weight from one foot to the other as an older woman carrying a big red-and-green striped umbrella came out and locked the door behind her. He held out his hand and she gave him the keys. Both of them looked at the detectives suspiciously as McLamb got out of the prowl car and approached in the pouring rain.

"Mrs. Stone?"

"Yes?" A heavyset, middle-aged black woman, she wore a clear plastic rain bonnet over her graying hair.

"Colleton County Sheriff's Department, ma'am. Could we step inside and talk a minute?"

Mrs. Stone shook her head. "Is this about my daddy again?"

"Yes, ma'am."

"What is it?"

"Ma'am—"

"I'm really sorry, Officer, but if I don't go on now, I'm gonna be late for work and they told me if I'm late again, they're gonna lay me off. Whatever you got to say's just gonna have to wait till this evening. I'll be back at five."

"Where do you work? Maybe we could drive you?"

She paused indecisively and the teenager jingled the keys impatiently. "Let 'em drive you, Mom. I'm gonna be late for school myself if you don't."

"All right," she said, but as the boy dashed through the rain to the Honda, she called after him. "You better be on time picking me up today, you hear? You not there when I come out, you're not getting the car for a week. You hear me, Ennis?"

But he was already backing out of the drive and into the street.

"Boys!" she said, shaking her head. "Soon as they turn sixteen, they start climbing Fool's Hill. Let 'em get to talking to their friends, flirting around with the girls, and they forget all about what they're supposed to be doing and where they're supposed to be. I believe to goodness he had more sense when he was six than he's got now that he's sixteen."

McLamb smiled, having heard the same words from his own mother when he first started driving. He motioned to Dalton, who drove up to the porch so that they wouldn't get too wet. McLamb helped Mrs. Stone into the front seat and he climbed in back.

"So what's this about?" Mrs. Stone asked after she had told them where she worked and they were under way.

As gently as possible, McLamb told her that the medical examiner over in Chapel Hill was pretty sure that her father's hand had been detached from his wrist not by an animal, but by human intervention.

Mrs. Stone turned in the seat and faced him, her face outraged. "Somebody cut off my daddy's hand?"

"Well, not the way you're probably thinking. Mostly they say the flesh was so—" He searched for an inoffensive word that would not sicken the woman. "—so degraded, that the hand probably pretty much pulled loose by itself when it was lifted, but there was a ligament that was holding it on and when the pathologist looked at the edges under a microscope, he could tell that it was definitely a recent cut. You're his only relative, right?"

"Me and Ennis, yes."

"Can you think of anyone who might have wanted your dad dead?"

Mrs. Stone shook her head. "The only person who couldn't get along with him was my mother and she passed six years ago, come June. You can let me out right here," she said and opened the door as soon as Dalton slowed the car to a stop in front of the motel where she worked.

McLamb hopped out to hold the door for her. She handed him her umbrella and waited for him to open it.

"Mrs. Stone—"

"I told you. I can't be late today!" she snapped and hurried inside.

"You didn't ask for her alibi," Dalton said, handing him some paper towels to mop the worst of the rain from his jacket.

"Yeah, I know. Looks like we have to catch her this evening after all."

From Mrs. Stone's place of work to Sunset Meadows Rest Home at the southern edge of Black Creek was just over ten minutes and Dalton parked the car as close as he could get it to the wide porch that ran the full width of the building.

"Here's good," said McLamb. A slender man of medium height, he prided himself on staying in shape and usually looked for opportunities to take a few extra steps, but not when it was raining this hard. His navy blue nylon jacket had COLLETON CO. SHERIFF'S DEPT. stenciled in white on the back and he pulled the hood low over his face before making a dash for it.

Dalton followed close behind in an identical jacket. Younger and chunkier than McLamb, at twenty-four, he was still kid enough to be excited by his recent promotion to the detective squad. "Provisional promotion," he reminded himself as he took a good look at the facility accused of letting one of its patients wander off to drown back before Christmas.

"Don't just look at what's there," McLamb had told him on the drive out. "Look at what's not there, too."

Although certified and licensed by the state, the nursing home had begun as a mom-and-pop operation and was a drab place at best. Built of cinder blocks, the utilitarian beige exterior was at least three years overdue for a new coat of paint. The shades and curtains looked sun-faded, and the uninspired shrubs that lined the porch needed work, too. Cutting them back to waist height would make them bush up at the base and would also allow anyone standing at the doorway an unobstructed view of the parking lot. As it was, the privet hedge was so tall and straggly that a casual observer might overlook someone leaving without authorization, especially if it was getting on for dark on one of the shortest days of the year.

The porch was a ten-foot-wide concrete slab set flush with both the paved entrance walk and the sills of the double front doors beyond. Easy wheelchair access, thought Dalton, but also easy for unsteady old feet to walk off without stumbling.

The fifteen or so rocking chairs that were grouped along the porch were worn and weather stained, but they were a thoughtful amenity for men and women who had grown up when porches were a place for socializing, for shelling beans, for watching children play, for resting after lunch in the middle of a busy day. Indeed, despite the cool spring morning and the pouring rain, three of the rockers were occupied by residents swaddled in blankets from head to toe who watched their approach with bright-eyed interest.

Not a lot of money to spread around on paint and gardeners, thought Dalton, but enough money to pay for staff who would help their patients out to the porch and make sure they were warm enough to enjoy the fresh air, even to tucking the blankets around their feet. The nursing home where his grandmother had recovered from her hip replacement was beautifully landscaped and maintained, but there had been a persistent stench of urine on her hall and she complained that her feet were always cold. Somehow he was not surprised to follow McLamb into the building and smell nothing more than a slight medicinal odor overlaid with the pungency of a pine-scented floor cleaner.

Immediately in front of them was a reception area that doubled as a nursing station. Long halls on either side led away from the entrance lobby with a shorter hall behind. Sam Dalton soon learned that Sunset Meadows Rest Home was basically one long rectangle topped by a square in back of the middle section to accommodate a dining room, lounge, kitchen, and laundry. Each of the forty "guest" rooms held two or three beds and there was a waiting list.

"Does that sound like we're careless and neglectful?" demanded Mrs. Belinda Franks, the owner-manager. A large black woman of late middle age, her hair had been left natural and was clipped short. She wore red earrings, black slacks, and a bright red zippered sweater over a white turtleneck. The sweater made a cheerful splash of color in this otherwise drab setting. She possessed a warm smile but that had been replaced by a look of indignation as she glared up at the two deputies from her chair behind the tall counter.

"Would people be lining up to put their loved ones here if they thought we were going to let them come to harm?"

"No, ma'am," Raeford McLamb assured her. "And we're not here to find fault or put the blame on you or your people, Mrs. Franks. We came to ask for your help."

"Like how?"

"We're now treating Mr. Mitchiner's demise as a suspicious death."

"Suspicious?" Her brow furrowed. "Somebody took that sweet old man off and *killed* him?"

"Too soon to say for sure, but someone did disturb his body after he was dead, and we need to find out who and why. I know you and your staff gave statements at the time, but if we could just go over them again?"

Mrs. Franks sighed and rolled her chair back to a bank of filing cabinets, from which she extracted a manila folder.

Standing with his elbows on the counter between them, McLamb looked in both directions. The front edge of the counter was on a line with the inner walls of the hall. Although he could clearly see the exit doors at the end of each hallway, there was no way someone behind the desk could.

"I know, I know," Mrs. Franks said wearily when McLamb voiced that observation. "We're going to curve this desk further out into the lobby this spring when we get a little ahead so that anybody on duty can see these three doors. Right now, though, we had to borrow money to set up the monitor cameras."

She motioned to the men to come around back of the counter where a split screen showed the three doors now under electronic watch.

"What about a back door?"

"That's kept locked all the time now except when somebody's actually using it."

"But it used to be unlocked before Mr. Mitchiner walked off?"

She nodded. "You have to understand that we're not a skilled nursing facility. Most of our people are just old and a little forgetful and not able to keep living by themselves, and we have a few with special problems. My first daughter was a Downs baby and we couldn't find a place that would treat her right. That's how my husband and I started this home. We wanted to take care of Benitha right here and have a little help once she got too big for us to handle. We still have a couple of Downs folks, the ones who can't live on their own, but mostly it's old people who come to us. We see that everybody takes the medications their doctors have prescribed and we keep them clean and dry, but we're not equipped for serious problems and we only have one LPN on staff. The rest are aides who have had first aid training, CPR, that sort of thing. We wouldn't have kept Mr. Mitchiner here except that his family was always in and out to help with him and he had a sweet nature. Eventually, he would have had to transfer into a place with a higher level of care. They knew that. But this was convenient for now. His grandson could ride his bicycle over after school and his daughter could stop in before or after work."

"Who last saw him that day?" asked McLamb.

"We just don't know," the woman said, with exasperation both for the question and her lack of a definitive answer. "We don't make visitors sign in and out. We want people to feel free to come in and sit with their loved ones, bring them a piece of watermelon in the summertime or some hot homemade soup in the winter. Put pretty sheets on their bed. Bring them a new pair of bedroom slippers. I think it makes them feel good to know that they can pop in any time to check up on us because we have nothing to hide. It's just like they were running in and out of their grandmother's house, you know?"

The men nodded encouragingly and Dalton said, "Sounds like a friendly place."

"It *is* a friendly place. You ask anybody. The only person with any complaints is Miss Letty Harper. She says our cook scrambles the eggs too dry, but that's because she always wants a fried egg with a runny yolk. All the same, Ramsey'll cook one like that for her if he's not too jammed up."

She opened the folder and took out copies of the statements she and her staff had given back in December. "Mary Rowe. She's due back any minute. She gave him his heart pills that morning. Then Ennis Stone. That's his grandson. He just got his driver's license around Thanksgiving and he took Mr. Mitchiner out for a ride and got him a cheeseburger for lunch. That man did love cheeseburgers. Then Ennis brought him back here and put him in his room for a nap. His room was down there on the end and Ennis usually came in that end 'cause it's closer. He could park right next to the door. His roommate, Mr. Thomas Bell, says Mr. Mitchiner was asleep on the bed when he came back to take a nap himself; but he wasn't there when he woke up."

"No one else saw Mitchiner that afternoon?" Dalton

asked, thumbing through the statements McLamb had read back in December.

"Not to remember. But it's not like anyone would unless it was his family. He was in his own world most of the time, so he didn't have any special friends here. A real nice, easygoing man, but you couldn't carry on much of a conversation with him. He kept thinking Mr. Bell was his cousin and he's white as you are."

"Could we speak to Mr. Bell?" McLamb asked.

"Well, you *can*," she said doubtfully, "but he's had another little stroke since then and his mind's even fuzzier than it was at Christmas."

She led them into the lounge where several men and women—mostly black, but some white—sat in rockers or wheelchairs to watch television, something on the Discovery Channel, judging by the brightly colored fish that swam across the screen. In earlier years, Mr. Bell had probably been strongly built with a full head of hair and shrewd blue eyes. Now he was like a half-collapsed balloon with most of the air gone. His muscles sagged, his shoulders slumped, his head was round and shiny with a few scattered wisps of white hair, his blue eyes were pale and rheumy. Large brown liver spots splotched his face and scalp.

This is what ninety-four looks like, Sam Dalton told himself. Pity and dread mingled in his assessment as Mr. Bell struggled to his feet at Mrs. Franks's urging. *We all want to live to be old, but, please, God! Not like this! Not me!*

The old man steadied himself on his walker and obediently went with them to the dining room where the deputies could question him without the distraction of the television.

While Dalton steadied one of the straight chairs, McLamb and Mrs. Franks helped him lower himself down. He kept one hand on the walker though and looked at them with incurious eyes as Mrs. Franks tried to explain that these two men were sheriff's deputies.

"They need you to tell them about Fred Mitchiner," she said, enunciating each word clearly.

"Who?"

"Fred Mitchiner. Your roommate."

"Fred? He's gone."

"I know, sweetie, but did you see him go?"

"Who?"

"Remember Fred? He had the bed next to you."

Mr. Bell frowned. "Jack?"

"No, sweetie. Before Jack. Fred. Fred Mitchiner."

Silence, then unexpected laughter shook the frail body. "My cousin."

"That's right." Mrs. Franks beamed. "That was Fred."

"Where'd he go, anyhow? I ain't seen him lately."

Raeford McLamb leaned in close. "When did you last see him, Mr. Bell? Your cousin Fred?"

"He ain't really my cousin, you know. Crazy ol' man. He's blacker'n you are." He paused and looked up at Mrs. Franks. "Idn't anybody else gonna eat today?"

Mrs. Franks sighed. "It's only nine-thirty, sweetie. Dinner won't be ready till twelve."

McLamb sat back in frustration and Dalton pulled his chair around so that his face was level with Mr. Bell's.

"Mr. Bell? Tom?"

"Thomas," Mrs. Franks murmured.

"Thomas? Tell us about the last time you saw Fred."

The old man stared at him, then reached out with a shaky hand to cup Dalton's smooth cheek. Sudden tears filled his eyes. "Jimmy?" His voice cracked with remembered grief. "Jimmy, boy! They told me you was dead."

In the end, Sam Dalton had to help Mr. Bell to his room. The confused nonagenarian would not let go of his arm until they persuaded him to lie down on the bed and rest. Eventually, he calmed down enough to close his eyes and release his unexpectedly strong grip on Dalton's arm.

"Who's Jimmy?" Dalton asked as he walked back down the hall with Mrs. Franks to rejoin McLamb.

"His son. He got killed in a car wreck when he was thirty-one. I don't think Mr. Bell ever got over it."

Back in the lobby, at the central desk, McLamb was interviewing Mary Rowe, the LPN who oversaw the medication schedules. A brisk, middle-aged blonde who was going gray naturally, Rowe wore a white lab coat over black slacks and sweater. She shook her head when told that Mitchiner's death might not have been as accidental as they first thought, but she was no more help than Mr. Bell.

"I'm sorry, Officers, but like I said back when he walked away, I gave him his meds right after breakfast and I think I saw him in the lounge a little later, but there was nothing new on his chart so I didn't take any special notice of him."

It was the same story with the housekeeping staff

who cleaned, did laundry, and helped serve the plates at mealtimes.

"I made his bed same as always while he be having breakfast," said one young woman, "and somebody did lay on it and pull up the blanket between then and when they did the bed check, but I can't swear it was him. Some of our residents, they're right bad for just laying down on any bed that's empty, whether it's their own or somebody else's."

CHAPTER 23

It takes time to revolutionize the habits of thought and action into which a people have crystallized by the practice of generations.

—*Profitable Farming in the Southern States,* 1890

Tuesday Morning (continued)

"What took you so long?" Mayleen Richards asked when Jack Jamison finally slid in beside her in the unmarked car they were using this morning.

"Handing in my resignation," he said tersely.

She laughed as she turned on the windshield wipers and shifted from park to drive, but the laughter died after taking a second look at his face.

"Jeeze! You're not joking, are you?"

"Serious as a gunshot to the chest," he said, in a grimmer tone than she had ever heard him use.

"So where're you going? Raleigh? Charlotte?"

"Texas first, then Iraq if I pass the physical."

Richards was appalled. "Are you out of your gourd?"

She had seen the flyers, had even visited the Web sites. "You're going to become a hired mercenary?"

He flushed and said defensively, "I'm not signing up for security. I'm signing up to help train Iraqis to become good police officers. And in case you haven't noticed, you and I are already hired mercenaries if that means keeping the peace and putting bad guys out of business."

"We don't have a license to kill over here," she snapped. "And the bad guys aren't lying in wait to ambush us for no reason. I can't believe you're going to do this."

"Believe it," he said. "I'm just lucky I can go as a hired hand. I can quit and come home. Soldiers can't and they get paid squat."

Richards did not respond. Just kept the car moving westward through the rain.

Eventually her silence got to Jamison. "Look, in two years, I'll have a quarter-million dollars. Enough for Cindy and me to pay off all our bills and build a house. And it's not like Jay'll even know I'm gone. I'll be back before he's walking and talking good."

"Be sure you get one of those life-size pictures of yourself before you go," she said angrily. "Cindy can glue it to foam board and cut it out and Jay can have his own Flat Daddy for when you get blown up by a car bomb."

"That's not very damn funny, Mayleen."

"I didn't mean for it to be."

"Easy for you to talk," he said resentfully. "No kids, your dad and mom both well and working. You've even got brothers and a sister to help out if one of them gets sick or dies."

His words cut her more than he could ever realize,

Mayleen thought. No kids. No red-haired, brown-skinned babies. Because if she did have kids, then she would have no brothers and sister. No mother or father either. They had made that very clear.

She had gone down to Black Creek last night expecting to celebrate a brother's birthday and they had been waiting, primed and ready to pounce. No nieces or nephews, no in-laws around the birthday table, just her parents, her two brothers, and her sister, Shirlee. Her mother had been crying.

"What's wrong?" she had asked, immediately alarmed, wondering who was hurt, who might be dying.

"There's been talk," her father said, his face even more somber than when she had told them nine years ago that she was divorcing a man they had known and liked since childhood, a hard-working, steady man who didn't use drugs, didn't get drunk, didn't hit her or run around on her. That had been rough on them. There had never been a divorce in their family, they reminded her. Leave her husband? Leave a good town job that had air-conditioning and medical benefits after growing up in the tobacco fields where her father and brothers still labored? Ask Sheriff Poole to give her a job where she'd carry a gun and wear an ugly uniform instead of ladylike dresses and pretty shoes?

"You ain't gay, are you?" her brother Steve had asked bluntly.

She had slapped his freckled face for that. Hard.

"What kind of talk, Dad?"

"Somebody saw you at a movie house in Raleigh," he said. "They say you was with a Mexican and he had his arm around you. Is it true?"

"Is he Mexican?" Steve demanded.

"Would that make a difference?" she said coldly.

"Damn straight it would!" said her brother Tom.

"I'm thirty-three years old. I'm divorced. I'm a sheriff's deputy. Who I choose to see is my own business."

"Oh dear Jesus!" her mother wailed, bursting into tears again. "It *is* true!"

Her father's shoulders had slumped and for the first time, she realized that he was getting old. Suddenly there was more white than red in his hair and the lines in his face seemed to have deepened overnight without her noticing.

While her brothers fumed and her sister and mother twittered, he held up his hand for silence.

"Mayleen, honey, you know we're not prejudiced. If you're seeing this man, then he's probably a good person."

"All men are created equal, Dad. That's what you always told us."

He nodded. "And they've got an equal right to everything anybody else does. But there's a reason God created people different, honey. If He intended us to be just one color, with one kind of skin and one kind of hair, then that's how He would have made us. He meant for each of us to keep our differences and stay with our own."

"So how come you didn't marry another redhead, Dad?"

It was an old family joke, but no one laughed tonight.

"That ain't the same, and you know it, honey."

"It *is* the same," she said hotly. "Mike's skin's a little darker than ours and his hair is black, but it's no different from Steve and Tom and Shirlee being freckled all over and marrying people with no freckles."

"We're *white*!" Steve snarled. "And we married white people. White Americans. I bet he's not even here legally, is he? He probably wants to marry you so he can get his citizenship."

"He's been a citizen for years," she snarled back. "And believe it or not, butthead, he wants to marry me because he loves me. He even thinks I'm beautiful. So maybe you're right. Maybe there *is* something wrong with him. Maybe he's loco."

But all they heard was *marry*.

"Oh Mayleen, baby, you can't *marry* him!" her mother sobbed.

"You do and you'n forget about ever setting foot in *my* house again!" Steve had shouted.

"Shirlee?"

Her sister's eyes dropped, but then her chin came up. "Steve's right, Mayleen. I'd be ashamed to call you my sister."

"Daddy?"

She saw the pain in his face. "I'm sorry, honey, but that's the way it is."

"Fine," she had said and immediately turned on her heel and walked out.

With each absorbed by personal problems, Richards and Jamison drove the rest of the way in silence, a silence underlined by the back-and-forth swish of their windshield wipers. Just before they reached the westernmost of the Harris Farms, they met a camera truck from one of the Raleigh stations. A long shot of the shed was all they could have gotten though because Major Bryant had posted a uniformed officer there to keep the site secured from gawkers. With rain still pouring from the charcoal gray sky, they passed the main house and went first to the white frame bungalow occupied by the farm manager. Richards stopped near the back door, and at the sound of their horn, Sid Lomax walked out on the porch and motioned for them to drive under the car shelter, a set of iron posts set in a concrete slab and topped by long sheets of corrugated tin.

"I was afraid you might be those reporters back," he said as Percy Denning pulled in right beside them with his field kit in the trunk.

"We need a list of everybody on the place," Richards told Lomax when the courtesies were out of the way. "And Deputy Denning's here to take everybody's fingerprints."

"He was dumb enough to leave prints on the axe handle?" Lomax asked.

"And on the padlock, too," Denning said with grim satisfaction.

"If you want to start with the names, come on in to my office," Lomax said and led the way back into the house.

The deep screened porch held a few straight wooden chairs. A couple of clean metal ashtrays sat on the ledges. No swing, no rockers, no cheery welcome mat by either of the two doors. The one on the left was half glass and no curtains blocked a view of a kitchen so spartan and uncluttered, so lacking in soft touches of color or superfluous knickknacks, that Richards instantly knew that no woman lived here.

The door on the right opened into a large and equally tidy office. More straight wooden chairs stood in front of a wide desk where an open laptop and some manila file folders lay. The top angled around to the side to hold a sleek combination printer, fax, and copier. A lamp sat on a low file cabinet beneath the side window to complete the office's furnishings. Both the desk and the worn leather chair behind it were positioned so that Lomax could work with his back to the rear wall and see someone at the door before they knocked.

He sat, pulled the laptop closer and tapped on the keys. "I'm assuming you're only interested in the people working here now? Not the ones who moved to the other farms?"

"Everybody here on that last Sunday you saw your boss," said Richards.

"Right."

More tapping, then the printer came to life with a twinkle of lights and an electronic hum as sheets of paper began to slide smoothly into the front tray.

"Two copies enough?"

"Could you make it three?" Richards asked.

"No problem."

They waited while Lomax aligned the pages and stapled each set.

"The first list, that's the names of everybody working here on the first of January. The ones with Xs in front of them are those we fired or who quit."

"Any of them leave mad?"

"Yeah, but Harris didn't have anything to do with them, if that's what you're asking. I was the one fired their sorry asses." His fingers touched the names in question. "These two were always drunk. This one was a troublemaker. Couldn't get along with anybody. This one went off his nut. Those five just quit. Said they were going back to Mexico."

Richards and Denning made notations of his remarks on the pages he'd given them. "And the rest?" she asked.

"They're the ones we moved over to one of the other farms the day after I last saw him. That was Monday, the twentieth of February. The last page is the people still here."

Again, they marked the pages and when they were finished, the farm manager held out his hands. "Want to take my prints first?"

"Why don't we go down to the camp and do them all at once?" Denning said.

"Fine. I don't know if everybody's there, though. Hard as it's raining, we couldn't get the tractors into the field so I gave everyone the morning off."

As migrant camps go, this one was almost luxurious compared to some the deputies had seen. It reminded Richards of motels from the fifties and sixties that sprouted along the old New York–to-Florida routes through the state before the interstates bypassed them—long cinder-block rectangles falling into disrepair.

Here, communal bathrooms with shower stalls and toilets, one for each sex, lay at opposite ends of each rectangle. The men's bunkhouse was a long room lined with metal cots. Most were topped by stained mattresses bare of any linens, but some still had their blankets and pillows and a man was asleep in one of them. At the far end was a bank of metal lockers. Most of the doors hung open, but a few were still secured by locks of various sizes and styles. At the near end was a battered refrigerator, cookstove, and sink. An open space in the center held a motley collection of tables and chairs where three more men were watching a Spanish-language program.

"*¿Dónde está Juan?*" Lomax asked.

Richards was pleased to realize that she could catch the gist of the reply, which was that the crew chief and his wife, along with another woman and two men, had gone into Dobbs to do laundry and buy groceries. And when Lomax could not seem to make them understand what the deputies wanted, she was able to explain with the generous use of hand gestures.

They knew, of course, that *el patrón* had been murdered in the shed over by the big house?

"*Sí, sí.*"

Whoever did such an awful thing had left fingerprints on the axe handle, she explained, so they were there to take everyone's prints.

At this, the men exchanged furtive looks and started to protest, but Richards tried to reassure them by promising that they were not there to check for green cards or work visas and the fingerprints would be destroyed as soon as they were compared with the killer's prints.

They were uneasy and highly suspicious, but Lomax went first and that helped convince them that they were not being singled out. As he wiped the ink from his fingers, the others came forward one by one and let Denning ink their fingertips and roll each one across the proper square on the white cards. Someone woke up the man in the cot. Reeking of alcohol, he, too, shuffled over to give his prints.

When Denning started to pack up their cards, Richards said, "No. I told them they'd be destroyed as soon as you did the comparison, so why don't you go ahead and do it now while we're questioning them, okay?"

Grumbling, Denning went out for a powerful magnifying glass and his field microscope and set to work. He had blown up the prints of the killer and marked the most prominent identifiers on each print—the forks, eyes, bridges, spurs, deltas, and island ridges that are easiest to spot. From the position of the killer's fingerprints on the bloody axe handle, he was able to say which were the three middle ones, which meant he could look for conspicuous markers on one of the workers' three right fingers and see if they matched one on the killer's.

While he squinted at the lines and ridges, Lomax unlocked a nearby door that opened onto quarters for a couple with children. It was marginally better than the bunkhouse: a good-sized eat-in kitchen that also functioned as a den with thrift store couch and chairs, two tiny bedrooms, a half-bath with sink and toilet.

"Mrs. Harris comes out a couple of times a season to check on things," Lomax told Jamison and Richards. "Makes sure the stoves and toilets and refrigerators work. Has the Goodwill store deliver a load of furniture every year or so. She's good about that."

"Even after their separation?" asked Jamison.

"Oh yeah. The big house isn't part of Harris Farms, but the camp and the sheds are. She was over here the day we moved the others to Farm Number Three to see what was going to need replacing or fixing."

"Was Harris around?"

"Like I told Major Bryant, ma'am. I didn't see him after Sunday dinner at the Cracker Barrel. I figured he knew she was going to be here, so he just stayed out of her way. She's got a right sharp tongue on her, if you know what I mean."

Despite their earlier friction, Jamison raised an eyebrow to Richards and she gave a half nod to indicate that Mrs. Harris's presence had registered. Someone else to check on.

In the meantime, she set her legal pad on the table before her, looked at the list, and asked Lomax to send in Jésus Vazquez.

An hour later, the two deputies had finished questioning all four men, who each swore that he knew nothing about the murder. They were all vague about that Sunday, although they remembered Monday very clearly since that was when their friends left on the trucks, the same day that *la señora* swept through the camp. No, they had not seen *el patrón* either day.

Who hated him?

Shrugs. Why would anybody hate him? He was the big boss—*el gran jefe*. He gave orders to Lomax, Lomax implemented them. Only one man admitted ever speaking to Harris and that had been months ago. The work was hard, but that's what they were there for. Their quarters were okay. They got paid on time. Lomax and Juan between them kept the camp pretty stable because Juan had children. So no open drug use. No drunken displays of violence or excessive profanity.

The sheds? Why would anyone go over there on Sunday? Sunday was a day off in the wintertime. Those who were leaving had spent most of the day packing up. Those who were staying had either played cards or gone into town or visited a club—El Toro Negro in Dobbs or La Cantina Rosa in Cotton Grove.

By midday, the deputies had finished with their questions and Denning had cleared all four men. Their relief was evident when Denning tore the fingerprint cards to shreds. Nevertheless one man held out his hand for the scraps and stuffed them into the half-empty mug of coffee on the table.

CHAPTER 24

A farmer's wife adds comfort which only a certain quality of feminine ingenuity can devise and execute.

—*Profitable Farming in the Southern States,* 1890

DWIGHT BRYANT
LATE TUESDAY MORNING, MARCH 7

Although Dwight would always prefer fieldwork to clearing his desk, paper had piled up that needed his attention and a rainy March day was as good a time as any to tackle it. After deploying his detectives, he spent the morning reading reports, filling out forms, updating the duty rosters, and earmarking things that Bo needed to see.

Time to get a little more aggressive about filling the empty slots in the department, too, he thought. Even if Dalton's provisional promotion were made permanent, they were still going to be short two detectives if Jamison really did leave. Three officers were needed in the patrol division and they could really stand to beef up Narcotics. Maybe he and Bo ought to go talk to the criminal justice classes out at Colleton Community. Hell, maybe they should even start trolling in the high schools.

By midday, the most pressing chores were behind him and when Deborah called around 12:30, he agreed to splash over and join her at a nearby soup and sandwich place where she was already having lunch.

This close to the courthouse, the café was always busy. The sky had begun to lighten, but there was still enough rain to make courthouse personnel reluctant to walk very far. The place was jammed today with every seat taken and a long line waiting at the counter. As soon as he reached the table where Deborah and another judge were seated, he sensed her barely concealed excitement.

"Here, Dwight," said Judge Parker, setting his dishes and utensils back on his tray. "Take my seat. I'm finished."

"You sure?"

"Just holding it for you, son."

"Thanks, Luther," said Deborah, as the older man rose. "And I really appreciate it."

He laughed and white teeth flashed in his chocolate brown face. "Just remember that you owe me one."

"Owe him one for what?" Dwight asked, sliding into the chair on the other side of the narrow table. She was wearing the cropped blue wool jacket that echoed her clear blue eyes. Around her neck, gleaming against her white sweater, was the thin gold chain with the outline of a small heart encrusted with diamond chips that she had worn almost every day since the night he gave it to her.

"He's going to ask Ellis Glover to assign Ally Mycroft to him for the rest of the week. Get her out of my courtroom."

Dwight grinned, knowing how that particular clerk irritated Deborah. "So what's up?"

"It's—" She paused, then gave an exasperated, "Look, something odd happened yesterday. I didn't give it a second thought at the time, but it must have registered on my subconscious and talking about the murder with Luther just now made me remember, which is why I called you. And I know we said I wouldn't stick my nose in your work and you wouldn't complicate mine, but— Oh God! Sorry. I'm babbling, aren't I? Here, have the rest of my soup."

"Why don't I just get my own?" he said, amused that she was taking their agreement so seriously.

"Because you might not want to wait on the line. Because maybe I'm seeing mountains where there's not even an anthill, but I had a migrant in court yesterday for a first appearance. Simple possession. He lives at the camp out there at the old Buckley place. One of the Harris Farms workers."

"And?"

"And I asked him through the interpreter if he knew Buck Harris. He said he did, but only by sight. Then he said, *'Es muerto, no?'* or something like that, but I didn't think twice about it because you'd just told me that the torso belonged to his boss, and besides, I got distracted by a screaming woman and a crying baby."

"Well, damn!" said Dwight, immediately recognizing the significance of what she was saying.

"Right. How did he know Harris was dead? He'd been in jail since Saturday night. Even you didn't know it was Harris till yesterday."

"Where's this guy now?"

"Still over there in your jail so far as I know. I set his bond, appointed him an attorney, but unless he made bail, he's still there. His name is Rafael Sanaugustin," she said and scribbled it on a napkin. "And for what it's worth, I got the impression that he wasn't really involved, that it was more like something he'd heard and wanted confirmed."

After reading the name, Dwight tucked the napkin in his shirt pocket. "Who'd you appoint?"

"Millard King."

He finished the rest of her vegetable soup in three spoonfuls and pushed back in the chair. "Thanks, shug. And I'm probably going to regret saying it, but any time your subconscious throws up something like this, nose away, okay?"

She cut her eyes at him as he stood. "Really?"

"Just don't abuse it," he warned, looking as stern as he could in the face of her sudden smile.

The rain was now a thin drizzle as Dwight took the courthouse steps two at a time and cut through the atrium to ring for the elevator that connected the third-floor courtrooms with the Sheriff's Department and the county jail down in the basement. To his bemusement, when the doors slid open, there was the same attorney Deborah had appointed to defend that migrant.

Millard King had the blond and beefy good looks of a second-string college football player. Courthouse gossip had him engaged to a Hillsborough debutante, the daughter of a well-connected appellate judge. King was said to be politically ambitious, but no one yet had a handle on whether that meant he wanted to run for governor, the North Carolina Assembly, or the US Senate. As he was only twenty-eight, it was thought that he was waiting for a case that would give him big-fish name recognition in Colleton County's small pond. Besides, said the cattier speculators, his sharp-tongued wife-to-be would probably have a thought or two on the subject.

He nodded to Dwight as the chief deputy stepped in beside him. "Bryant. How's it going?"

"Fine. Talk to you a minute?"

"Sure. I was just on my way down to the jail."

"To see"— Dwight pulled out the napkin Deborah had given him —"Rafael Sanaugustin?"

"How'd you know?"

"That's where I was headed myself. I need to have a talk with your client."

"About those two little rocks? That's hardly worth messing with, is it? Unless you think he's part of something bigger?"

"That's what I want to ask him. I'll call around and see if we can find someone to interpret."

"Oh, that won't be necessary," King said with an air of smug complacency. "I'm pretty fluent."

"Yeah?"

"I've studied Spanish since high school. My roommate in college was Cuban and we spent our junior year in Spain. The way things were going even back then, I figured it wouldn't hurt to be able to speak to voters directly if I ever got in the game."

Heretofore, Dwight had paid scant attention to rumors

that the debutante had cut King out of the pack to further her own aspirations. Having been there himself in his first marriage, he had felt a stab of sympathy for King, a sympathy that was now plummeting to the basement faster than the elevator.

If King had fixed his eyes on the prize as early as high school, maybe it was a match made in heaven after all, Dwight decided, and a spurt of happiness shot through him as he thought of his life with Deborah. He could almost feel sorry for the younger man. Would the satisfaction of reaching even the highest office in the land equal the pleasure of planting trees with a woman you loved?

They were almost too late. Three Latinos were there to bail Rafael Sanaugustin out—two women and a man—and they were just finishing up the paperwork when Dwight called over their shoulders that he was here with Sanaugustin's attorney to see the prisoner.

"Five minutes and y'all would've missed him," the officer said and explained why.

King stepped forward and introduced himself in Spanish that sounded to Dwight every bit as fluent as he had earlier bragged.

Wearing jeans and wool jackets, the three looked back at him impassively. The women were bareheaded and appeared to be in their early thirties; the man wore a brown Stetson and was at least ten years older. When he spoke, it was to Dwight. "Juan Santos, crew chief at Harris Farms."

"Sanaugustin is a member of your crew?" Dwight asked.

The man nodded.

"You were at the farm yesterday? On the tractor?"

Again he nodded.

"One of these women related to him?"

Santos nodded to the shorter woman. "His wife."

"Please tell her that I'm sorry, but she's going to have to wait a little longer. I need to question him first."

Both women immediately tugged on Santos's arms anxiously, speaking so rapidly that the only words Dwight caught were *los niños*.

He shook off their hands and before Millard King could translate, said, "They say we cannot wait long. The children come home at three-thirty."

Dwight glanced at his watch: 12:56. "We'll try to be brief."

"How long?" said Santos. "We'll go to the grocery store and come back."

"Fifteen or twenty minutes for me, if he cooperates," Dwight said. "What about you, King?"

"Fifteen minutes, tops."

"*Bueno*," Santos said.

Sanaugustin's wife protested sharply, but the crew chief herded them both out of the office and the jailer brought Sanaugustin down to the interview room.

When the migrant worker came strolling in, he was obviously surprised to see two Anglos instead of his friends. According to his booking sheet, Sanaugustin was five-eight and thirty-three years old. He had straight black hair, wary dark eyes, a prominent nose, and a small scar on his left cheek. His jeans, black sweatshirt, and the unbuttoned plaid wool lumberjack shirt that topped them were all a little worse for the wear after three nights in jail. He hesitated in the doorway, but the jailer nudged him inside and closed the door behind him.

Dwight gestured for him to take a seat and waited while Millard King explained that he was the attorney the judge had appointed to represent him yesterday and that he was here to discuss those charges, but first this officer, Major Bryant, had some questions for him.

Dwight had procured a tape recorder from the front desk and as he set it up, King frowned. "What's this about, Bryant?"

"Ask him to state his name and address, please," Dwight said pleasantly.

Both men complied and Dwight added the date and the names of those present.

"How long has he worked for Harris Farms?"

"Two years."

"How did he know that Buck Harris was dead?"

They had released the identity of the mutilated body last night, so it had been all over the morning news. Nevertheless, Millard King drew himself up and said, "*What?* Wait a minute, here, Bryant. You accusing my client of murder?"

"I have witnesses who can testify that he suspected that Harris was dead before it was public knowledge. All I'm asking is how did he know it before the rest of us?"

"Okay, but I'm going to warn him that he doesn't have to answer if it self-incriminates."

"Fine, but remind him that we now have his fingerprints on file."

"You have the killer's fingerprints?"

Dwight gave a pointed look to his watch. "Once his people come back, he's free to go, you know."

Annoyed, King translated Dwight's questions and it was soon apparent that the farmworker was denying knowledge of anything, anywhere, any time. But when King pressed him and rubbed his thumbs across his own fingerprints, Sanaugustin went mute.

Then, hesitantly, he framed a question and King looked at Dwight. "He wants to know if fingerprints show up on everything."

"Like what?"

King gave a hands-up gesture of futility. "He won't say."

Dwight considered for a long moment, his brown eyes fixed on the Mexican, who dropped his own eyes. Dwight had never thought of himself as intuitive. He put more faith in connecting the dots than in leaping over them. But Deborah had been a judge for four years. Hundreds of liars and con artists had stood before her. If it was her opinion that Sanaugustin's question was to get confirmation of something suspected but not positively known, surely that counted for something. But if that were the case, why was this guy worried about fingerprints? Unless—?

"Tell him that yes, we can lift fingerprints off of wooden doors," he said, hoping to God that Denning had indeed dusted the doors of that bloody abattoir. "And if he touched the car, his prints will be there as well."

When translated, his words unleashed such a torrent of Spanish that even King was taken aback. He motioned for his client to slow down. At least twice in the narrative, the man crossed himself.

Eventually, he ran out of words, crossed himself a final

time, and waited for King to turn to Dwight and repeat what had been said.

Everyone at the camp had heard about the body parts that were appearing along the length of their road, he had told King. They had even, may God forgive them, joked about it. But no one connected it with their farm. How should they? It was an Anglo thing, nothing to do with them. As for him, yes, he had once been a heavy user, but now he was trying to stay clean for the sake of the children. That's why he gave most of his money to his wife to save for them. But on Saturday Juan had sent him over to the sheds to get a tractor hitch and he went to the wrong shed by mistake. Inside was the big boss's car and that made him curious. Why was the car there? Then when he got closer, he heard the flies and smelled the stench of blood. Lots of blood. Bloody chains lay on the floor. Nearby, a bloody axe.

He had panicked, slammed the door shut, then found the tractor hitch he'd been sent for. As soon as he could get away, he had made his wife give him money and had come into town to buy something that would take away the sight and the smell. That was the truth. On his mother's grave he would swear it.

Ever since a killer had suckered him with a convincing show of grief and bewilderment over the death of a spouse, Dwight no longer trusted his instincts as to whether someone was lying or telling the truth, but there was something about the man's show of exaggerated wide-eyed innocence at the end that made him wonder if they were hearing the whole story.

"Who did he tell?"

"He says nobody."

"Ask him who hated his boss enough to do that?"

Again the negative shrug and a refusal to speculate.

"Juan Santos? Sid Lomax?"

But Rafael Sanaugustin continued to swear that this was the full extent of his knowledge and beyond that they could not budge him.

Dwight switched off the tape recorder and carried it back out to the desk, leaving Millard King to discuss the possession charges with his client.

When Juan Santos and the two women returned, he had them go around to his office with him. According to the jailer's log, no one had visited Sanaugustin since he was locked up Saturday night, so the likelihood of their having conferred was minimal but not wholly out of the question because he'd used his one phone call to tell Santos where he was. When Dwight first asked about Sanaugustin's movements on Saturday, Santos did not immediately mention sending him for a tractor hitch. That detail was sandwiched in between their problems with one of the tractors and how they were falling behind schedule with the spring plowing, and it seemed to come almost as an afterthought, as if it were something of little importance. Despite rigorous questioning, all three denied knowing what Sanaugustin had seen on Saturday and all declared that they had first learned of it and of Buck Harris's death when Dwight was out there on the farm yesterday.

Dwight stared at them in frustration. Impossible to know who really knew what, but he was willing to bet that Señora Sanaugustin knew more than she was willing to admit. Wives usually did. True to his word, though, he turned them all loose at two o'clock and reached for his phone to call Richards and bring her up to date on what he'd learned.

She sounded equally dispirited when she reported that they had come up pretty dry as well. "But we did learn that Mrs. Harris was out here on the farm that Monday," she said. "And at least it's stopped raining."

CHAPTER 25

The employer who treats his help fairly and reasonably in all respects is the one who will, as a general rule, secure the best results from their service.

—*Profitable Farming in the Southern States,* 1890

No sooner did Juan Santos and the two women leave, than Dwight's phone rang. It was Pete Taylor.

"Sorry, Bryant, but Mrs. Harris's daughter is flying in this afternoon and she can't make it up to Dobbs today. What about tomorrow morning?"

"Fine," said Dwight. "Nine o'clock?"

"That'll work for her. And . . . uh . . . this is a little gruesome, but she was asking me about funeral arrangements for Harris. The daughter's going to want to know. But his head's still missing, isn't it?"

"'Fraid so, Taylor," he said, seeing no need for the daughter to know what else was missing. "I know it's weird for her, but we may not find it for months. If ever. The ME's probably ready to release what we do have, though."

"I'll get back to you on that," said Taylor. "See you in the morning. Nine o'clock."

With his afternoon unexpectedly clear, Dwight called McLamb and got an update on the Mitchiner case. Because the two deputies would not be speaking to the old man's daughter till five, Dwight sent them to question some witnesses about a violent home invasion that had taken place in Black Creek over the weekend. "While you're in that neighborhood, try dropping the name of Mitchiner's daughter. See if she has any enemies who might have thought that they'd hurt her if they hurt him."

After attending to a few more administrative details, Dwight called Richards to say that he was coming out to the Buckley place. "Tell Mrs. Samuelson we want to speak to her again."

"Should I try questioning Sanaugustin's wife when she gets here?"

"Not if the men are around. If she's going to talk at all, it'll probably be when they're not there."

Despite the gory murder and the puzzle of Mitchiner's hand, Dwight felt almost lighthearted as he drove out along Ward Dairy Road. The sun was breaking through the clouds, trees were beginning to bud and more than one yard sported bright bursts of yellow forsythia bushes. The rains would have settled the dirt around the roots of the trees they had planted this weekend, and whatever the problems with Cal, Deborah seemed to be taking them in stride.

He was not particularly superstitious but he caught

himself checking the cab of the truck for some wood to touch.

Just to be on the safe side.

After years of wanting what he thought he could never have, these last few months had been so good that he was almost afraid he was going to jinx his luck by even acknowledging it. He told himself to concentrate instead on the cases at hand.

Start with Mitchiner. An old man with a fading grasp on reality. Had he wandered away on his own or had someone taken him? The hand proved that someone knew where his body was because it had been cut loose and carried from that isolated spot on Black Creek downstream to a more frequented place on Apple Creek. Why?

Because they wanted the hand to be found? Because they knew it would lead back to the body further upstream?

Deborah was fond of asking "Who profits?" but on the face of it, no one. Yes, Mitchiner's daughter was suing the rest home, but that was almost reflexive these days even though most such cases no longer generated large settlements. Besides, everyone said that she and her son were devoted to the old man. Before he got his driver's license, the kid rode his bicycle over there after school almost every afternoon to play checkers with him; after he turned sixteen, he came as regularly to take his grandfather out for a drive around town. The daughter was there a couple of nights a week and again on the weekends. On Saturdays, she had seen to his physical well-being, trimming his hair and toenails and seeing that he bathed properly. On Sundays, she had taken him to church for his spiritual well-being.

According to the statements given when Mitchiner first went missing, he liked to visit the graveyard where his wife and parents were buried and to walk the old neighborhood, so that's where their first search efforts had been concentrated. How had he wound up in the creek, miles from his childhood haunts?

And Buck Harris.

Everyone said he was a bull of a man, a physical man who still liked to climb on a tractor and stay hands-on with every aspect of his crops, yet always up for sex. Whose ox had *he* gored?

The possibilities were almost endless. One of the migrants at the camp? Someone he had done business with? Someone whose woman he'd taken? Certainly someone familiar with that empty shed. Mrs. Samuelson had said the killer must be "a hateful and hating man." He couldn't argue with that. To kill and butcher and then strew the parts around for the buzzards?

And yeah, spouses and lovers were usually their best suspects, but surely no woman would have done what was done to Harris? On the other hand, that missing part of his anatomy certainly did seem to suggest a sexual motive. But what in God's name could he have done to inspire such cruelty? Think of gaining consciousness to find yourself lying there in chains, naked and vulnerable as a killer lifts an axe and swings it down on your bone and flesh. The killer clearly meant for him to know it was coming, otherwise why the chains? Why not just go ahead and kill him quickly and cleanly?

If Harris was lucky, the first blow would have made him black out from the shock to his system. If he wasn't lucky—?

Dwight tried to cleanse the images from his mind.

Mayleen Richards and Jack Jamison were waiting for him near the rear of Buck Harris's homeplace. Two old-fashioned bench swings hung from the limbs of an enormous oak tree and the deputies seemed to be enjoying the warm afternoon sunshine, although Richards's dispirited greeting made Dwight think that Jamison must have told her about his resignation.

"Where's Denning?" he asked.

"He's back at the shed, going over the car with a fine-tooth comb," Jamison said.

"I thought he did that last night."

"He did, but you know Denning."

Dwight nodded. Attention to detail and a willingness to check and recheck were precisely why he'd promoted Percy Denning to the job.

He glanced inquiringly at the shabby, unfamiliar car parked at the edge of the yard.

"Mrs. Samuelson's got those two migrant women helping her give the place a good cleaning. They got here about ten minutes ago," Richards said. "She expects Mrs. Harris and her daughter to stay here tomorrow night. She also seems to think the daughter inherits this place."

"She's right," said Dwight as he rang the back doorbell. "At least, that's what his lawyer told me."

After a minute or two with no answer, he rang again.

There was another short wait, then Mrs. Samuelson opened the door with a visible annoyance that was only slightly tempered by seeing him there instead of the two deputies again. Today, her white bib apron covered a short-sleeved maroon dress and it was nowhere near as crisp as the first time she had talked to them. This apron had seen some serious action.

"I'm sorry, Major . . . Bryant, is it?"

"Yes, ma'am."

"Major Bryant, I'm real busy right now."

"I'm sure you are, ma'am, but we have a few more questions for you."

She started to protest, but then seemed to realize that it would save time in the long run to capitulate and get it over with. She held the door open wide for them, "But please wipe your feet on the mat. We already mopped the kitchen floor."

Feeling six years old again, they did as they were told and followed her into the large kitchen. She invited them to sit down at the old wooden table, but there was no offer of coffee or cinnamon rolls today.

"You know what we found out there in that equipment shed yesterday?" Dwight asked.

She nodded, her lips tight.

"That means he was killed by someone familiar with this place. So I ask you again, Mrs. Samuelson. Who on this farm thought they had a reason to kill Mr. Harris?"

"And I tell you again, Major Bryant, that I don't know. If it's something to do with the farm, you need to ask Sid Lomax. If it's something to do with his personal life, maybe you need to be asking that Smith woman. Maybe she had a boyfriend who didn't like her messing around with him."

"What about Mrs. Harris?"

"What about her? They split up, but that doesn't mean she hated him enough to do something like that."

"When did you last see her?"

"Maybe Christmas?" The housekeeper got up and used a paper towel to clean a smudge on the window glass over the sink. With her back to them, she said, "She brought some presents for the children here and she always remembers me at Christmas, too."

"She was the one who actually hired you here, wasn't she?"

"That's right." A fingerprint on the front of the stainless-steel refrigerator seemed to need her attention, too.

"Mrs. Samuelson."

"I'm listening. I can listen and work, too."

He got up and went over to look down into her face. "She was here the day he went missing, wasn't she?"

"I don't know what you're talking about."

"A bunch of people saw her."

She took a deep breath and came back to the table. "All right. Yes. She was here that Monday, but there is no way under God's blue sky that she could have done that awful thing."

"She came to the house?"

Mrs. Samuelson gave a reluctant nod.

"What time?"

"I don't know. He wasn't in the house when I came in that morning and I didn't see his car, so I thought he'd taken off. I figured she'd be coming over to bring some stuff for the camp when the trucks came to move most of the crew back to New Bern, and I reckon he did, too. For all his big talk, she could always get the best of him in an argument and anytime she was coming to check up on things, he'd clear out."

She gestured to a door off the kitchen. "There's a little room in there with a television and a lounge chair so I can take a rest without going out to my apartment. I fixed lunch and then I went in to put my feet up for a few minutes. Only I went to sleep. And when I woke up, she was upstairs taking a shower."

"She came all the way from New Bern to take a shower?"

Mrs. Samuelson gave an impatient shake of her head. "There was a mud puddle down by the camp. Had ice across it, but it wasn't solid and she backed into it accidentally and wound up sitting down in it. Got soaked to the skin, she said. Cut her leg and her hand, too, so she came over here and took a shower and changed into one of his shirts and an old pair of jeans."

"What did she do with her own clothes?"

"Took 'em home to wash, I reckon. They went out of here in a garbage bag. And before you ask me, it was her own shoes she went out in and they certainly weren't bloody."

Dwight raised a skeptical eyebrow at Mrs. Samuelson's assertions. "Anybody see her take this tumble?"

"I don't know. Maybe one of the women helping me?" She stood as if to go call them.

"In a minute," Dwight said. "Your apartment. It's over the garage, you said?"

She nodded.

"So you would hear the door open and Mr. Harris's car start up?"

"If it was in the garage. A lot of times he parked around by the side door."

"Where you could see it from your windows?"

"If I was looking. If he was gone and I didn't hear him come in during the night, then I'd look out the window first thing every morning to see whether I needed to come over and start breakfast. There's an intercom, too, and sometimes he'd buzz me and say he wanted breakfast earlier than usual."

"So when's the last time you heard or saw his car?"

She frowned in concentration, then shook her head. "I'm sorry, Major Bryant. He came and went at all hours and I just can't fix it in my mind. All I can say is that it wasn't there Monday morning and I really did put it down to Mrs. Harris coming. Now can I please get back to my work?"

Dwight nodded. "One thing more though. Who did you really work for, Mrs. Samuelson? Buck Harris or his ex-wife?"

"He signed my paycheck," she said promptly.

"But?"

She returned his gaze without answering.

"Is there a Mr. Samuelson? Or do you and Mrs. Harris have that in common as well?"

Tight-lipped, the housekeeper stood up. "Which one of those women you want to talk to first?"

Before he could answer, his pager went off and he immediately called in. "Yeah, Faye?"

"Aren't you out there at the Harris Farm?"

"Yes."

"There's a Sid Lomax screaming in my ear for you to come. He says he's out there in the field. They just found a head."

CHAPTER 26

Successful farmers do not break up a cart or so, and kill a mule or so during each year, and then curse their crops because the price is not high enough to pay for their extravagance.

—*Profitable Farming in the Southern States,* 1890

A clearly shaken Sid Lomax waited in his truck for them at a cut through some woods that separated one of the large fields from the other.

As Dwight stopped even with him, the farm manager pulled the bill of his cap lower on his forehead. His leathery face was pale beneath its tan and his only comment was a terse, "Follow me," as his tires dug off in the soft dirt to lead them up a lane at the edge of the field. Dwight put his truck in four-wheel drive and glanced in his mirror. Denning had caught up with him and Richards and Jamison were with him. She must have realized that a car might mire down out here after all the rain. They topped a small rise, then down a gentle slope to where two tractors with heavy turning plows blocked their initial view of a fence post at the far corner of the field.

The treated post was approximately five feet high and about half as thick as a telephone pole. Several men were clustered upwind from it. As Lomax and the deputies got out of their vehicles, the men edged back and they had a clear view. For a split second, looking at the thing rammed down on the top of the post, Dwight was reminded of a rotting jack-o'-lantern several days past Halloween when the pumpkin head verged on collapse. This head was worse—a thatch of graying hair, darkened skin, empty eye sockets, and a ghastly array of grinning teeth because most of the lips were gone as well.

Crows? Buzzards?

Blowflies buzzed and hummed in the warm afternoon sun and a few early yellow jackets were there as well. A thick rope of red ants snaked up one side of the post.

"Oh dear God in the morning!" Denning murmured as he moved in with his camera. With his eye on the viewfinder, he zoomed in on what was nailed to the post almost exactly halfway between the grisly head and the ground. "Was that his dick?"

If so, there was almost nothing left of it now except where a nail held a flaccid strip of skin that fluttered in the light spring breeze.

In the next hour, Dwight had called the sheriff in Jones County, then sent two detectives down to start interviewing the migrants who had been transferred over to Harris Farm #3 between Kinston and New Bern. He had pulled Raeford McLamb and Sam Dalton out of Black Creek and they were now helping Jamison and a interpreter question everyone who still worked here on the Buckley place. Sid Lomax had volunteered his office desk and his kitchen table for their use. He was under the impression that Juan Santos could be trusted to help translate accurately, "But hell, bo," he told Dwight wearily. "At this point, I don't know who's telling the truth and who's lying through his rotten teeth. It's gotta be one of 'em though, doesn't it?"

"Somebody familiar with the farm, for sure," Dwight agreed and led Lomax through a retelling of how they had discovered Buck Harris's head.

"Between the cold and then the rain, we're behind schedule on the plowing. This field's so sandy though, the rain drains right through it and I thought it'd be okay to finally get the tractors out here this afternoon. First pass they made, Vazquez spotted it. Santos had the walkie-talkie and as soon as he saw that post, he called me. Ten minutes later, I was on the horn to 911. I thought your people had already left. Man, was I glad to hear they were still here and you were, too."

Mayleen Richards had given Dwight the third set of names that Lomax had run off for them and he held them out to the farm manager now. "How 'bout you save us some time and put a check mark by every name that ever had words with Harris."

"I'm telling you. None of 'em had that much to do with him. Yeah, he'd come out in the fields once in a while, plow a few rounds on the tractor, haul a truckload of tomatoes to the warehouse, but he didn't speak a word of their lingo. Harris was one of those who think if people are going to come work in this country, it's up to them to learn English, not for him to have to speak Spanish. He'd talk real loud to them. If they didn't understand enough to answer, then he didn't bother with them. Not that he did much, even with those that could."

"Like Juan Santos?"

"Nothing more than to ask how the work was going, were the tomatoes ripening up on schedule, how bad were the worms? I'll be honest with you, Bryant. I don't think Harris thought of these people as fully human. More like work animals. Just a couple of notches up from horses or mules. If it hadn't been for Mrs. Harris and OSHA, I believe he'd have worked them like mules and stabled them like mules, too. The only time he really put his hand in for more than a day, though, was last spring when my parents were out in California and Dad had a heart attack so I had to fly out. I thought we ought to bring somebody over from Kinston, but he said he could handle it for a few days. My dad died, and it was over a week before I could get back. He wasn't too happy about that, but he did keep everything on schedule. God knows what actually went on. Santos never said much, just that Mrs. Harris was out here and they had a big fight about something. They were legally separated by then, though."

"You think he got on Santos's ass about something while you were gone?"

Lomax let out a long breath and settled his cap more firmly on his head. He met Dwight's eyes without blinking. "You're asking me if Santos could've done this. Ol' son, I don't know anybody that could've done it. Besides, that was almost a year ago. If Harris still had a beef with him, he'd've fired him. And if Juan Santos had a beef with him, I do believe he'd've quit or done something about it long before this, don't you? Who has a hate this big that waits a year to get even? Besides, I thought you had fingerprints."

"We do," Dwight conceded. "But we don't have comparison prints for everyone who ever walked across this land. So tell me about Mrs. Harris?"

"What about her?"

"She get along with everybody?"

"She's a hard-nosed businesswoman, if that's what you mean, but she treats her people fair. Sees that the housing's up to government standards, makes sure the kids go to school. Expects value for her dollar, but doesn't forget that these are human beings, not work animals. She used to work out in the fields when they were first married, so she knows what it takes to make a crop. Even better, she's from the 'trust 'em or bust 'em' school of thought. You show that you know your job and you're doing it and she leaves you alone."

"I hear she was out here that Monday when Harris went missing. You see her?"

"Sure. She came over with the trucks to move the workers to Farm Number Three. Trucks brought some new furniture. Two new refrigerators. Well, new to us. I think she buys everything at the Goodwill store. Claims it helps them and upgrades us and I reckon she's right."

"She ask about Harris, where he was?"

Lomax shook his head. "Ever since they separated, it's like he didn't exist. She never mentioned him if she could help it. She just took care of the things she wanted done and didn't worry if that's what he wanted or not."

"I heard she sat down in a mud puddle around lunch-time."

"Yeah?" For a moment he almost smiled. "Didn't see it."

"Hear about it?"

"No. Should I have?"

"The bosslady up to her butt in mud? I'd've thought so."

"We were pretty busy around then. Where'd it happen?"

"Somewhere around the camp's what I heard."

"Sorry. Maybe you should ask the women."

"Good idea," said Dwight, knowing that's where Mayleen Richards was at the moment, taking advantage of the men being tied up here for a while.

But when Richards rejoined them, she had nothing to confirm or deny the mud puddle story. "The women say they saw her in the morning when she came with new refrigerators for the married quarters and they had to empty the old ones, which were on their last legs. She asked about the children and about their health. She had picked up a couple of bilingual schoolbooks for the women, but after that they didn't see her again."

It was nearing four before they were finished with all the statements. Denning had bagged the head and what was left of Harris's penis. He stopped by the farm manager's place to tell them that he was taking the remains over to Chapel Hill. "Don't know if y'all noticed or not, but there was a knotted bloody rag around the fence post where it caught on the wire. Looks to me like it could've been a gag that slipped down when the crows got at him. Would explain why nobody heard him scream. But unless there's a bullet hole I'm not seeing in this head, I don't know that it'll tell the ME anything he didn't already know but I guess we ought to go through all the motions."

Dwight nodded. "I don't suppose you've heard anything back on those fingerprints yet?"

"Sorry, sir."

"What about Santos or Sanaugustin?"

"Yessir. I did a quick and dirty on the men. No match. Haven't had a chance to compare the prints on the axe with the women's prints yet. I can let you know by in the morning though."

"Good."

McLamb and Dalton volunteered to go back to Black Creek to interview Mrs. Stone and her son. "See if we can't pick up a lead from them."

"Fine," Dwight said. "I'll authorize the overtime."

Rather than go all the way back to Dobbs himself, he called Bo and brought the sheriff up to date, then headed off to pick up his son.

CHAPTER 27

When a young man gets married, and the little chaps come along according to nature, he ought to get on a farm to raise them.

—*Profitable Farming in the Southern States,* 1890

DEBORAH KNOTT
TUESDAY NIGHT, MARCH 7

That night was a bar association dinner in Makely, and Portland and I drove down together. Avery had opted to skip the dinner and stay home with his daughter, but we still left late because she had to nurse little Carolyn first.

Avery asked me about the rumors flying around the courthouse that they'd found Buck Harris's head stuck on a fence post, but I didn't get a chance to call Dwight till after I'd adjourned at five-fifteen and I was afraid I might interrupt the talk he planned to have with Cal. Satisfying my curiosity could wait. That head wasn't going anywhere.

Except maybe over to the ME's office in Chapel Hill.

"You're not making Dwight take sides, are you?" Portland asked when we were finally in the car and I had told her a little about the situation with Cal. She was totally thrilled when I married Dwight, and she worries that I'm going to mess up if I'm not careful.

"Of course not," I said.

"Because he may be crazy about you, but Cal's his son."

"Like I need a lecture on this? After four years of family court? After watching Kidd Chapin's daughter make him choose between her and me? Hell, Por! I may be dumb, but I'm not stupid. Cal and I got along just fine before Jonna died. I'm pretty sure he liked me back then and he'll probably like me again once he settles in. It's a rough time for him, a lot of adjustments, but I don't think he wants to split Dwight and me up. He's not a conniver like Amber. Besides, boys don't usually think like that. My brothers and their sons have always been pretty easy to read, even when they were getting ready to bend the rules or break the law. Unlike my nieces. Girls are out there plotting three moves ahead. Remember?"

"Oh, sugar!" she said with a grin, and I knew she was recalling some of the stuff we used to get into, the way we could manipulate teachers and boyfriends from kindergarten on.

She pulled out a pack of Life Savers, the latest weapon in her diet arsenal and offered me one. The clean smell of peppermint filled the car.

"Have you talked to your friend Flame since Buck Harris's body was identified?" I asked.

"Yeah, she stopped by for coffee this afternoon on her

way back to Wilmington. She said there was no reason for her to stay, that his ex-wife and daughter certainly wouldn't save her a seat at any memorial service and she didn't want to add to his daughter's grief."

"She okay herself?"

"Not right now, but she will be. I'm not going to say she didn't really love him, but I'm sure his bank account helped, so I doubt if her heart's completely broken. Besides, Flame's always known when to cut her losses."

"Not a total loss, though, is it?" I said as I dimmed my lights for an oncoming car.

"Reid told her she was in the will. She didn't say for how much though."

"Dwight kicked me out of his office before I could get Reid to tell me, but remember when he took your umbrella this morning?"

"And did *not* leave it at the office, the bastard."

"Well, just before you got there, when he was trying to borrow one from me, he said she was down for half a million."

"Interesting. We had lunch last week and she was worried about the mortgage on her B-and-B. A half-million sure makes a nice consolation prize."

"Also makes a motive for murder."

"No way!" Portland protested. But she mulled it over as I pulled out to pass a slow-moving pickup. "Dwight got her in his range finder?"

"Probably. Along with Mrs. Harris and everybody on the farm, I should think. Not that he tells me everything."

"Yeah, right," she jeered. "I don't suppose he's said anything about Karen Braswell's place getting shot up?"

"Nope. But I haven't really talked to him since this morning and that only happened last night, right?"

"Well, when you do, would you please stress that this guy's gone over the edge? Bo promised to tell his people to be on the lookout in her neighborhood and so did Lonnie Revell, for what that's worth."

Lonnie Revell is Dobbs's chief of police. Nice guy but not the brightest star in the town's constellation.

I repeated what Dwight had said about hurricanes and the need to head for high ground when you know one's on the way.

"Moving in with her mother's not really high ground, but with a little luck, he'll do something to get himself arrested again before he finds out that's where she is. I just hope you'll give him a couple of years next time."

"Hey, no *ex parte* talk here, okay?"

"What's *ex parte?* You've already heard his case and if there *is* a next time, there's not a judge in the district who could possibly be unaware of the situation unless it's Harrison Hobart and isn't that old dinosaur ever going to turn seventy-two?"

Seventy-two's the mandatory retirement age and it looked like he was going to hang on till the end. Hobart's a throwback to an earlier age when men were men and their women kept silent. Not only in church but everywhere else if he'd had his way. He had tried to keep female attorneys from wearing slacks in his courtroom, and whenever I had to argue a case before him, he never failed to lecture me that skirts were the only attire proper for the courtroom.

"If that's true," I had said sweetly, gesturing to our district attorney who sat at the prosecution's table and tried not to grin, "then the day Mr. Woodall comes to court in a skirt, I'll wear one, too."

Hobart had threatened me with contempt, but the next day every woman in the courthouse showed up in pants, even the clerks who didn't particularly like me but who liked being lectured on dress and decorum even less. He had been censured more than once and his last one came when he informed the jury that the defendant might not be sitting there if her husband had taken a strap to her backside once in a while.

"I think his birthday's this spring," Portland said as I parked in front of the restaurant on the north edge of Makely.

Because of our late start, most of the tables were filled by the time we paid our money and looked for seats. And wouldn't you know it? The only table with two empty chairs had Harrison Hobart at it. It was a no-brainer.

We split up.

Portland caught a ride back to Dobbs with Reid, so I headed straight home after the dinner and got there a little before ten. Both my guys were in bed, but only Cal was asleep. Dwight was watching the early news, but he turned it off and came out to the kitchen for a glass of milk and the last of the chocolate chip cookies while I reheated a cup of coffee left over from the morning.

I told him about the dinner and Portland's comments about Flame Smith. "Is she a suspect?"

"Probably not. She gave me the names of people who

saw her down in Wilmington during the three days after Harris was last seen. I've got a query in with the sheriff down there. He said he'd check her statement for me."

"I hear you finally found the head?"

"Yeah. Stuck on a fence post at the back of one of the fields out there, so it's definitely someone familiar with the place."

"Get anything out of that migrant who knew Harris was dead?" I asked.

"He says he stumbled into that empty shed by mistake, and seeing all that blood and gore's what made him go looking for a quick high on Saturday."

"But?" I asked, hearing something more in his voice.

"Oh hell, Deb'rah. I don't know. I got the feeling that he was holding something back, but if he ever had any real dealings with Harris, no one seems to know about it. The only other worker still there that had much to do with him is Sanaugustin's buddy Juan Santos. Both of 'em are married. Both have kids. The farm manager, Sid Lomax, thinks Santos and Harris might have had a run-in last spring when he had to fly out to California and Harris came in to run things. But that was almost a year ago. Besides, it sounds like Harris's real run-in was with his wife."

"Was he maybe trying to exercise his *droit de seigneur* with one of the migrant women?"

"What's that?"

"The privilege of ownership."

"Like a plantation owner with his female slaves?"

"Something like that."

"Well, his housekeeper did say he slept with the wife

of a different worker, but they moved to the farm below Kinston months ago. I suppose he could have tried it with one of the other women, although the housekeeper says he was pretty much saving it for Flame Smith these last few months." He broke a cookie in half, dunked it in his milk, then savored the soft sweetness. "You make a mean cookie, Mrs. Bryant."

"Why thank you, Major." Then, just to make sure, I said, "You really don't mind that I haven't changed my name professionally, do you?"

He smiled and glanced at my left hand. "Not as long as that ring stays on your finger."

"What about Mrs. Harris?" I asked since he was in a talkative mood. "Is she still wearing a ring?"

"Who knows? If we can't pin down the time of death, she may claim she's a widow and not an ex. She's scheduled to come in tomorrow morning." He told me about the tumble she supposedly took in a mud puddle the Monday after Harris was last seen. "Only nobody actually saw her do it and the housekeeper says she bundled her clothes up in a garbage bag and borrowed some of his things to wear back to New Bern."

"Whoa!" I said. "She came in the house and took a shower and no one saw if it really was mud on her clothes?"

"Mrs. Samuelson says there was no blood on her sneakers, just a little mud. If she was going to lie for the bosslady, why stop at sneakers?"

"Unless . . ." I said slowly.

"Unless what?"

"I keep a second pair of old shoes in the trunk of my

car," I reminded him. "To save my good ones if it's mucky or I have to walk on soft dirt."

"I'll keep that in mind when I talk to her tomorrow."

"Speaking of talks, how did it go with Cal tonight?"

He shook his head. "It didn't. First Haywood was here to drop off a load of firewood to get us through April. Then Mr. Kezzie came by for a few minutes with some extra cabbage plants for our garden—"

"We have a garden?" I teased.

"We do now. I mentioned to Seth that it'd be nice to grow tomatoes, so he plowed us a few short rows beside the blueberry bushes and somebody must've told Doris you were out tonight because she called up and insisted that Cal and I had to go over there and eat with her and Robert. That woman never takes no for an answer, does she?"

He sounded so exasperated, I had to laugh.

"Then coming home in the truck, I was just fixing to start and damned if McLamb didn't pick that time to call and report his conversation with Mitchiner's daughter and grandson. By the time we got back to the house, it was bedtime and when I went in to say good night, he had his head under his pillow, trying not to let me hear him crying."

"Over Jonna?" I said sympathetically.

Dwight nodded. "I just didn't have the heart to lay anything else on him right then."

"I'm glad you didn't." I ached for Cal. For Dwight, too, who has to watch his son grieve for something that can never be made right.

He drained his glass and carried it over to the dishwasher, along with my now-empty coffee cup. I switched off the kitchen light and followed him to our bedroom.

"I don't suppose McLamb got much out of the Mitchiner family?"

"Not really," he said as we undressed and got ready for bed. "One interesting thing though. He said that the daughter and the grandson sort of got into it for a minute about the lawsuit. The boy wants her to drop it."

"Really?"

"McLamb said he all but accused her of wanting to profit by his grandfather's death and that she got pretty defensive."

"Oh?"

"Yeah, he's going to check out her alibi tomorrow. She was supposed to be working and the kid had her car until it was time to pick her up after work, but since we don't know precisely when Mitchiner went missing, it's possible that she dropped the boy off somewhere and went on to the nursing home. Here, need some help with that?"

I had pulled my sweater over my head and a lock of hair was caught in the back zipper.

He gently worked it free and then one thing led to another.

As it usually does.

(Ping!)

CHAPTER 28

For us, it has truly seemed that each day dawned upon a change.

—*Profitable Farming in the Southern States,* 1890

Cal's emotional meltdown the night before must have cleared his system because he was in a cheerful mood the next morning and no longer seemed to be resentful about missing Monday night's game. He let Bandit out for his morning run without being asked and only had to be reminded once to take off his Canes cap at the table. He laid a pad and pencil beside his cereal bowl and asked me to tell him the names of all my brothers, beginning with Robert—"He said I could call them Uncle Robert and Aunt Doris"—so that he could write them down and start getting them straight.

"They could be a whole baseball team with two relief pitchers," he marveled and was intrigued to hear that one of the little twins—Adam—lived in California. "Is he near Disneyland? Could we go visit him sometime?"

It was sunshine after rain.

I was due for an oil change, so I left when he and Dwight

went to meet the schoolbus and drove over to leave my car at Jimmy White's. Jimmy's been my mechanic ever since I took the curve in front of his garage too fast shortly after getting my driver's license a million years ago. He pulled it out of the ditch, replaced the front fender, and let me pay him on time without telling my parents, although he did threaten to tell his uncle who was a state trooper if I didn't take my foot off the gas pedal once in a while. Gray-haired now and starting to slow down a little, he's turning more and more of the heavy work over to his son James. Back then, it was just Jimmy and one bay. Today it was Jimmy, James, and two employees and the one bay had become three. Instead of the old oil-stained denim coveralls they used to wear, all four of them sported crisp blue shirts that they put on fresh each morning and sent out to be laundered every week.

After so much rain, the air was washed clean and fluffy white clouds drifted across a clear blue sky. A soft spring breeze ruffled my hair as we stood in the sunlit yard waiting for Dwight to pick me up. I accepted their offer of a cup of coffee and we talked about the changes in the neighborhood and of all the new people that had moved in and wanted him to service their cars without trying to build a relationship. "Like, just because they got the cash money, they think they're gonna get moved to the front of the line ahead of people that's been here all along."

James, who had graduated from high school a couple of years behind me, said, "What gets me hot though's when they don't trust us. They'll want us to give the car a tune-up and if we say we had to replace one of the belts, they'll want to see it and half the time they act like they think we cut it so we could charge 'em for a new one."

Jimmy snorted. "That's when we tell them they need to go find theirselves a new mechanic."

I glanced at all the cars lined up around the yard and said, "Looks like you've got more work than you can handle anyhow."

He nodded with satisfaction. "I'm just glad I listened to you and bought them two acres next door and let you do all that paperwork about the zoning. We're gonna break ground next month, finally build that fancy new garage James here's been planning and we probably couldn't do it if we were starting fresh today. Not with all the big money houses going in on this road."

I had handled some of their legal matters before I ran for judge. Seven years ago, Jimmy hadn't seen the need to have his property legally zoned for business. He'd run a messy, sprawling garage out there in what used to be the middle of nowhere for twenty-five years and he'd expected to run it for twenty-five more. It was the typical rural land owner's mind-set: "It's my land and I can do what I want with it." But when the planning commission started getting serious about zoning, I had encouraged Jimmy to get a proper business permit so that he could expand if he wanted to without the limitations often imposed on businesses that have been grandfathered in. I'm not saying the planning commission takes race into consideration, but a lot of black-owned shops like this one have either been denied the right to expand or have been zoned out of existence in the last three or four years.

"We'll put a berm in front, plant it with trees and evergreen bushes so you can't see in from the road," said James. "There's a Mexican across the branch with a nursery that does landscaping. Diaz. We're gonna trade work. Make it look pretty. Enough folks know we're here that we don't need to put up but just a little teeny sign."

"Now don't y'all get so upscale you can't take care of my car," I said as Dwight turned into their drive.

Jimmy laughed. "Girl, anytime you need a new fender, I'll fix you up. 'Course, now that you went and married Dwight, I reckon you don't drive too fast no more."

"You think?" said Dwight who'd rolled down his window in time to hear Jimmy's last remark. "I'm gonna have to write her up myself to slow her down."

James opened the passenger door for me and as I stepped up to get in, his comment about the nursery finally registered. "Diaz," I said. "Miguel Diaz?"

"Mike Diaz, yes," James said. "You know him?"

"We've met. I just didn't realize his nursery was nearby."

"Just across the branch. They've made 'em a right nice place over there."

Jimmy promised that my car would be ready by midafternoon and as we headed for Dobbs, I said, "Mike Diaz, Dwight."

"Who's he?"

"Mayleen Richards's new boyfriend, according to Faye Myers."

"Yeah? How do you know him?"

"He came to court last week to speak for that guy that took a tractor and plowed up a stretch of yards, remember? Back in January?"

Dwight shook his head. With all the violent crimes he had to deal with, he misses a lot of the lesser ones that make it to my courtroom.

"I thought I told you about him. Palmez or Palmirez or something like that. One of my freaky Friday cases."

"You told me about the guy who tried to steal one of the old lampposts off the town commons and how Dr. Allred ticketed a man who parked at a handicap spot without a tag and then let a three-legged dog run free. I don't remember a tractor."

I briefly recapped. "Diaz took him on at the nursery after he got fired from wherever he stole the tractor and he promised to see that the damages were repaired. I forget if I gave the guy a fine or a suspended sentence. I'd have to look it up. Anyhow, when Faye was telling me about Mayleen's new boyfriend, she said I'd met him and that this Mike Diaz was the one."

"Diaz," Dwight said reflectively. "Why's that name seem familiar?"

"Faye said Mayleen met him when she was working a case back in January."

"That's right. I remember seeing his name on one of the reports she filed. He had some sort of connection to J.D. Rouse's wife." Rouse was a rounder whose freewheeling arrogance had gotten him shot. "So Richards is hooked up with him?"

"According to Faye she is. Remember?" I said smugly. "I told you she was looking different."

"Is this where I have to listen to you brag about feminine intuition?" he groaned.

I laughed.

"So what does your day look like?" he asked. "You gonna be able to cut out before five?"

"Unless something unexpected comes up, this could be a light day. Four of the cases I was supposed to hear today settled yesterday afternoon and I have good vibes about another one, so I may be ready to roll by four. You going to leave on time?"

"I sure hope so. Robert had some seed potatoes left over. It's getting a little late to plant them but—"

"Potatoes? And cabbages yesterday? I thought you were just going to tend a few tomato plants."

"Yeah, but I forgot how little kids love to scratch around and find potatoes."

I patted his arm. "Big kids, too, right?"

He gave a sheepish nod.

Faye Myers was coming on duty when we entered the basement lobby, so I said I'd catch up with him later and stopped to chat. There had been a bad wreck last night, she told me. Two highschool girls killed outright and another in serious condition at Dobbs Memorial Hospital. Alcohol and no seatbelts were thought to be factors.

They were from the eastern part of the county and unknown to me, but I could still imagine the grief their families were feeling today. That sort of news always gives me a catch in my throat until I hear the names and can breathe again, knowing it's not any of my nieces or nephews. Thank God, it'll be another eight years before we have to worry about Cal behind the wheel of a car. Dwight's already told me that Cal's first car's going to be a big heavy clunker, an old Grand Marquis or a Crown Victoria. He keeps saying that he wants a lot of steel between his son and another car until he's had four or five years of experience. "No way am I handing a sixteen-year-old the keys to a candy-red sports car," he says.

We'll see. I remember the T Bird I'd wheedled out of Mother and Daddy. The exhilaration of empowerment. Free to hang with my friends, to cruise the streets of Cotton Grove on the weekends, or sneak off to the lake with Portland. I guess my brothers had given them so much grief when they first got wheels that they didn't realize girls would take just as many chances. As long as we met their curfews, we were considered responsible drivers.

Faye leaned closer and I was suddenly awash with a feeling of déjà vu as she lowered her voice and said, "I might not ought to be telling this, but Flip said he almost got high himself from the smell of beer in that car when he pulled them out. He says all three could've blown a ten or twelve."

CHAPTER 29

With ideas of false economy, some farmers employ only about one-half the hired help that is necessary to perform the work in the proper time and manner and by working this force to the utmost, early and late, they endeavor to accomplish all the work for the season at a much less expense than would ordinarily be involved in accomplishing it.

—*Profitable Farming in the Southern States,* 1890

Dwight Bryant
Wednesday Morning, March 8

Wearing one of his trademark bow ties—today's had little American flags on a blue background—and a starched blue shirt, Pete Taylor appeared in Dwight's doorway promptly at nine and held it open for his client and a younger woman. "Major Bryant? Detective Richards? This is Mrs. Harris and her daughter, Mrs. Hochmann."

Dwight and Mayleen Richards immediately stood to welcome them.

Mrs. Harris was what kind-hearted people tactfully call a "right good-sized woman." She was easily five-ten, solidly built, with a broad and weathered face and a handshake as strong as most men's. She wore a maroon tailored suit that looked expensive but did little to flatter or hide the extra pounds on her frame. Her wavy hair was cut short and was jet black, except where the roots were showing a lot of salt and not much pepper. Her large hazel eyes were her best feature.

Shrewd eyes, too, thought Dwight as he watched her glance around his office, taking in his awards and commendations, appraising his deputy. Eyes that didn't miss a trick.

Her daughter appeared to be in her late twenties. She was equally tall and big-boned, but so thin as to almost appear gaunt. Unlike her mother, her eyes were an indeterminate color, set deep in their sockets, and her cheekbones stood out in relief. Her dark hair was pulled straight back from her face in a single braid that fell halfway down her back. No jewelry except for a loose gold band on her left hand. Her black pantsuit looked like something that had been bought at a thrift store. Not exactly the picture of a New York heiress now worth at least three million, he thought. More like a nun who had taken a vow of poverty. He remembered what Mrs. Samuelson had said about her concern for the less fortunate since her husband's death.

"Thank you for coming," Dwight said after they were all seated and had declined coffee or tea. He offered condolences to both women and set a mini-recorder on the desk.

"This is strictly informal," he told them, "and any time you want me to turn it off, just ask."

"Now," said Mrs. Harris.

The daughter started to say something, then shrugged and leaned back in her chair.

"As you wish," Dwight said. He switched it off and pulled out a legal pad instead. After noting the day's date, he addressed the younger woman.

"I don't want to upset you, Mrs. Hochmann, but do you know what was done to your father?"

"That he was dismembered and his parts dumped from one end of Ward Dairy Road to the other?" Her eyes filled, but her voice was steady. "Yes. Mr. Taylor says that everything's been found now?"

"All except one arm, I'm afraid."

"I've been in touch with the medical examiner's office," said Pete Taylor. "They'll release his body for burial this afternoon."

"But they won't tell us when he died," Mrs. Harris said. Frustration smoldered in her tone. "All they'll say is sometime between the afternoon of Sunday the nineteenth and Wednesday the twenty-second. That's not good enough, Major Bryant."

"What Mrs. Harris means," Pete Taylor interposed, "is that we don't know whether or not he died before their divorce was final."

"I know," Dwight said. "And I'm sorry you've been left hanging, ma'am. Despite all those forensic programs on television, unless we can find a witness or the killer confesses, there's no way to say with pinpoint accuracy when it happened. I understand you were out on the farm that Monday morning? The twentieth?"

"Yes."

"Did you see him that day?"

"No."

"When *did* you last see or speak to him?"

"I have no idea. If we needed to communicate, it was either through our attorneys or by e-mail. I don't think we spoke directly to each other in almost a year."

"Yet you went out to the farm where he was staying?"

"Until everything is divided, that farm is as much mine as his and it's my right to see that our workers are properly housed and treated."

"Does that mean Mr. Harris mistreated them?"

"I didn't say that."

"Didn't you?"

She glared at him and clamped her lips tight.

"Who hated him enough to kill him like that?"

"I have no idea."

"Any mistreatment of the workers?"

"Not that I heard anything about and I believe I would have. The crew chief, Juan Santos, knows their rights. Besides, we only keep a skeleton crew during the winter and they're free to hire out as day laborers when things are slow."

"I understand that Harris Farms was cited for an OSHA violation six years ago?"

Her hazel eyes narrowed.

"I believe you were fined a couple of thousand dollars?"

She gave a barely perceptible nod.

"Who was responsible for the violation? You or Mr. Harris?"

There was no answer and she met his steady gaze without blinking.

Pete Taylor stirred uneasily, but it was the daughter who caved.

"Oh for heaven's sake, Mother! Tell him." She turned to Dwight. "I loved my dad, Major Bryant, even though I hated the way he ran the farms. But OSHA and EPA and yes, law people like you not only let him get away with it, it's as if you almost encouraged him to break the laws."

"Susan!" her mother said sharply.

"No, Mother. I'm through biting my tongue. From now on I'm going to speak the truth. You think I don't know the real cost of growing a bushel of tomatoes? That I don't know how Harris Farms shows such a good profit year after year?"

"Harris Farms sent you to school, miss! Gave you an education that lets you look down on your own parents."

"Not you, Mother." She touched her mother's hand. "Never you. I know you did your best."

She turned back to Dwight. "Growers like my dad cut against the market every way they can. They ignore the warning labels on chemicals, they ignore phony social security numbers, they turn a blind eye to how labor contractors take advantage of their people, and they don't give a damn about a migrant's living conditions or whether or not the children are in school. My mother does. When Harris Farms finally got cited, Mother got involved. She checks the paperwork and makes sure everyone's documented, she doesn't let little kids work in the fields, and she made

Dad get rid of those squalid trailers he had down there in the back fields of the Buckley place. No decent plumbing and no place to wash off the pesticides. My mother—"

"Your mother's a bleeding-heart saint," Mrs. Harris said sarcastically.

"Well, you are, compared to Dad."

"Only because it's cheaper in the long run to do the right thing," her mother said gruffly. "It's all dollars and cents. I don't want us shut down or slapped with a big fine."

"Slapped is the right word," Susan Hochmann told Dwight. "There aren't enough inspectors to check out all the camps and farms and follow a case through the courts, so a slap on the wrist was all they got. A puny two-thousand-dollar fine. Nothing to really hurt."

"You don't know that's where it would stop next time," said Mrs. Harris, "and I don't want to find out. I don't want to wake up and see Harris Farms all over the newspapers and television like Ag-Mart. I don't want anybody making us an example. If playing by the rules or decent plumbing or stoves that work and refrigerators that actually keep food cold can keep us out of court, then it's worth the few extra dollars."

"But your husband felt differently?" Dwight asked.

"He grew up poor. We both did. And we both worked hard in the early days. Out there in the fields rain or shine, whether it was hot or cold, doing what had to be done to plant and plow and stake and harvest. Wouldn't you think he could've remembered what it was like to walk in those shoes? Instead, he griped that I was coddling them. I finally had enough and when that little redheaded bitch let him stick his—"

She caught herself before uttering the crude words that were on the tip of her tongue. "That's when I told him I was through, that I was getting my own lawyer. And damned if he didn't file papers first so that I've had to come to court in Dobbs instead of doing it down in New Bern."

She sat back in her chair and pursed her lips while Dwight made quick notes on the legal pad.

"What about you, Mrs. Hochmann?" he said. "When did you last speak to your father?"

"Valentine's Day," she said promptly. "He didn't like phones, but he always sent me roses and he called that evening."

"Was he worried about anything?"

"Worried that someone was going to . . . to—" She could not bring herself to say the words and sat there mutely, shaking her head.

"Mrs. Harris, are you absolutely certain you didn't see your husband on that Monday?"

"I'm certain."

"In fact, you tried to avoid all contact with him, right?"

"Right."

"Yet you went into his house that day and took a shower and left wearing some of his clothes."

"Yes," she said.

Susan Hochmann's head immediately swung around to look at her mother quizzically.

"Would you like to say why?"

Clearly she did not.

"Mother?"

"Oh, for pete's sake, Susan! Don't look at me like that. I did *not* kill Buck and then go sluice his blood off me. I fell in a stupid mud puddle and wrecked the clothes I was wearing. Of course I went in and took a shower. I knew he wouldn't be there. He was afraid to look me in the eye."

"Why?" asked Mayleen Richards.

Until now, the deputy had sat so quietly that the others had almost forgotten that she was in the room.

"I beg your pardon?" said Mrs. Harris.

"Everyone says he was a big man with a short fuse and a strong will. Why was he afraid of you?"

"I—I didn't mean it like that." For the first time, her voice faltered, but she made a quick recovery. "It was because I could always get the best of him when we argued. That's all."

"The last time you spoke to him was last spring, you said?" asked Dwight.

"That's right."

"People say you two had a huge fight then. What was that about?"

Mrs. Harris stood up and looked down at Pete Taylor. "Are we done here?"

Her daughter stood, too, a puzzled look on her face. "Mother?"

"It had nothing to do with why he was killed," she said.

"Was it over his girlfriend?"

"I don't want to talk about that here, Susan," she said and swept from the room.

Susan Hochmann turned to the two deputies with a helpless shrug. "We'll be staying at Dad's place for a couple of nights. Please call me if you learn anything else."

"I will," said Dwight. "And Mrs. Hochmann?"

"Yes?"

"I hope you'll call *me* if you learn anything we should know."

She nodded and hurried after her mother. Dwight looked at Richards. "What do you think?"

"I think I ought to go back to that migrant camp and see if I can't find out exactly what the Harrises fought about last spring."

"Not Flame Smith," Dwight agreed. "Take Jamison with you."

"Is he really going to resign?" Richards asked.

Dwight sighed. " 'Fraid so."

CHAPTER 30

It is only from the record of our mistakes in the past that wisdom can ever be derived to lead us to success in the future.

—*Profitable Farming in the Southern States,* 1890

Deborah Knott
Wednesday Afternoon, March 8

The stars were in alignment that day. It wasn't simply one more case that settled, it was two. I caught up with all my paperwork and even heard one of Luther Parker's cases—a couple of teenage boys drag racing after school—before wandering downstairs to meet Dwight around three-thirty.

Bo Poole was seated in Dwight's office and looked particularly sharp in a dark suit, white shirt, and somber tie.

"Hey, Bo," I said. "Whose funeral?"

He grinned and shook his head at Dwight. "You got my sympathy, son. She don't miss a thing, does she?"

"I better plead the fifth," Dwight said, smiling at me.

"So who died?" I asked again. "Anybody I know?"

"They buried poor ol' Fred Mitchiner this afternoon and I figured I ought to go and pay my respects. He's the one showed me how to skin a mink when I wasn't knee-high to a grasshopper and I feel real bad that we didn't find him before he drowned in the creek."

"Surely his family doesn't blame you for that?"

"Well, I think they do, a little. His daughter does, anyhow. I went by the house afterwards. Thought I'd give her a chance to vent on me. Figure this department owes her that much. McLamb and Dalton were out there yesterday, she said. They'd told her about how somebody cut his hand loose and moved it and she was still pretty hot and bothered about that, as well."

"Poor Bo," I said sympathetically. "I guess her son gave you an earful, too. I hear he was over there faithfully."

"Ennis? Naw. He's a good kid. I think he's just glad to have it over with. In fact, I think he's about talked Lessie out of suing the rest home."

"Yeah, that's what McLamb told me," said Dwight as he gathered up some papers and stuck them in a file folder. "That the staff had been good to his grandfather and he didn't think they ought to be penalized for the old man's death."

Bo said, "Even when Miz Stone told him that it was the insurance company that would pay, he said it wouldn't be right to take money when God had answered her prayers."

"God?" I asked.

"Evidently she was on her knees every night since he wandered off, praying to God to let her find out what happened to him, so that she could rest easy. If she turned around and asked for money, too, it'd be like spitting in God's eye, he told her. Not many teenage boys think like that these days."

"No," I said, remembering those boys I'd just had in my courtroom. Not bad kids, but kids. Kids with shiny new drivers' licenses who think they're going to live forever because they never think beyond the immediate and—

"Oh," I said.

"What?" said Dwight.

"The grandson."

"Huh?"

"He took his grandfather out that day," I said. "And everybody assumes he brought the old guy back because he always did. But did anyone actually see him?"

Bo frowned and leaned back in his chair.

"You saying he killed his own grandfather?" Dwight asked skeptically.

"No, I'm not saying that. But somebody did move that hand so y'all would backtrack on the creek and find his body, right? Somebody who wanted him found but didn't want to admit how he got there? Could it have been the boy?"

Bo thought about it a minute, then gave a slow nod. "You know something, Dwight? That makes as much sense as anything else we've heard. Could be he's feeling guilty and that's the real reason he doesn't want blood money." He hoisted himself out of the chair with a sigh. "Reckon I'd better go back and catch him while he's still strung out from the funeral. See if I can't find out what really happened."

CHAPTER 31

It is a maxim of the law, based upon common sense and experience, that for every wrong there is a remedy, but before the remedy can be applied, the cause from whence the evil springs must be definitely ascertained.

—*Profitable Farming in the Southern States,* 1890

Sheriff Bowman Poole
Wednesday Afternoon, March 8

Friends from Mrs. Stone's church were still at the house when Bo Poole returned and it was not difficult for him to cut young Ennis Stone out of the crowd. "I just want him to retrace the route that last day he took his granddaddy out," he told her. "Maybe it'll help him remember something we can use. We won't be gone long."

The boy looked apprehensive but got in the sheriff's van without protest.

"Let's see now," said Bo. "You picked him up after school, right?"

"Yessir. About three-thirty."

"And took him where?"

"To Sparky's. For a cheeseburger. He loved cheeseburgers."

"Where's this Sparky's?"

Ennis directed him to a fast-food joint on the south side of Black Creek. As Bo suspected, it was only a short distance from the footpath that led down to the creek.

He pulled into the parking lot and said, "Then what?"

The boy shrugged. "Then I took him back to Sunset Meadows."

"And helped him lie down for a rest?"

"Yessir." He pointed down the street. "That's the way we went."

But Bo did not move the car. Instead, he looked back at Sparky's. It seemed to be a popular hangout. There were video games at one end and teenagers came and went. A couple of girls waved to Ennis, but he barely acknowledged them.

"Friends of yours?"

He nodded.

After a minute, Bo shifted from neutral and drove down the street, but instead of turning left, back into town, he turned right and continued on till he reached the cable where the street dead-ended.

"Your granddaddy used to run a trapline along the creek down there. Did you know that?"

"Yessir." It was barely a whisper.

Bo switched off the engine and turned to look at the boy, who seemed to shrink against the door.

"You want to tell me what really happened, Ennis?"

"I told you. I got him a cheeseburger and then I took him back. I don't know what happened after that."

"Yes, you do," Bo said gently.

The boy's brown eyes dropped before that steady gaze and tears welled up in them.

"He liked to sit and watch the water," he said, his voice choked with grief. "He'd sit there for hours if I'd let him. Just sit and hum and watch the water. I'd get us a cheeseburger and walk down to where there was a log to sit on and we'd eat our burgers and he'd start humming. He loved it. Was like he was watching television or something. Once he started humming, he could sit all day. He'd even try to fight me when it was time to get up and go. That's why I thought it'd be okay. Every time we ever came, he never moved. Honest, Sheriff!"

Bo fumbled under the seat till he found a box of tissues.

Ennis blew his nose but tears continued to streak down his cheeks.

"I just ran back for some fries and I meant to come right back, but DeeDee— I mean, a friend of mine was there, you know? And we talked for a minute. I swear to God I wasn't gone fifteen minutes."

"And he wasn't here when you got back?"

"I couldn't believe it. I ran upstream first to where the underbrush clears out and I couldn't see him, so then I went downstream and . . . and . . . he was lying there in the cold water. Dead. I just about died, too. I didn't know what to do."

He broke down again and it was several minutes before he could continue. "I couldn't go home and tell my mom that I'd left him alone to let him go die like that. She'd have told it in church, had everybody praying for my sin like I was a stupid-ass creep. I know I should have gone for help, but he was dead and it wasn't going to bring him back. It was dumb. I *know* it was dumb! But I figured he'd be missed real quick and then everybody'd be out looking and I was sure he'd be found right away but then he wasn't and after that it was too late for me to say I'd lied."

Ennis pulled another handful of tissues from the box and Bo waited till his sobs quieted into sniffles, as he had waited out the sorrow and remorse of so many others over the years—

"I only left the baby for a minute."

"I didn't know it was loaded."

"I thought he could swim, but—"

"Better tell me the rest of it, son."

"Mom was crying every night and praying to just let him be found. I couldn't take it any longer. I heard some girls in my biology class say they were going to go look for ferns down at the fishing hole on Apple Creek the next day. I thought if I could move him down there . . . but I couldn't, so then I thought if they found his hand . . . like they found that other hand . . . but . . ." He broke off and took several long deep breaths. "I had to use my knife. I kept telling myself he couldn't feel anything . . . but . . ."

He looked at Bo helplessly. "You going to tell my mom?"

"Somebody needs to," Bo said. "Don't you think?"

Ennis nodded, misery etched in every line of his face. "Am I in trouble with the law, too?"

Bo thought about the man-hours spent searching. The helicopter. The dogs.

"We'll see," he said.

CHAPTER 32

A farmer's life is a pretty hard one in some respects, especially if he has a sorry farm and he is a sorry farmer, but the average farmer can be about as happy as anybody.

—*Profitable Farming in the Southern States,* 1890

DEBORAH KNOTT
WEDNESDAY EVENING, MARCH 8

We were a couple of miles out of Dobbs, each of us immersed in our own thoughts, when I suddenly remembered that I'd meant to pick up something for supper.

"Tonight's Wednesday," Dwight said. "How 'bout we go for barbecue?"

"Really?" As soon as he'd said it, my gloom started to lift. A Wednesday night at Paulie's Barbecue House was exactly what I needed. "You won't be bored?"

Dwight doesn't play an instrument although he has a good singing voice.

"Nope. You haven't been since Cal came and I bet he'd like it, too. Give him some more names to add to that list he started this morning."

I had to laugh. It was bad enough that I had eleven brothers. Wait till he realized exactly how many aunts and uncles and cousins there were, too.

"We have to plant the potatoes first," he warned.

"Deal," I said happily.

By the time we got to Jimmy's, I had heard about Dwight's interview with Mrs. Harris and her daughter, who seemed to disdain the money her parents had made.

"Not so disdainful that she's not going to take it," I said. "Reid told me she wants to turn the house into a migrant center or something. If Amy doesn't get her grant for the hospital, I'm thinking somebody ought to introduce them to each other."

"While Reid was talking, he happen to say what Buck Harris did to so seriously piss off his ex-wife last spring? Assuming she is his ex-wife and not his widow."

"Besides taking a younger mistress?" I asked.

"You're the one with the woman's intuition," he said. "But Richards and I both got the impression that she's using the mistress as a smoke screen to keep from talking about what really happened."

While I settled up with Jimmy, Dwight went on and picked up Cal so that the three of us got home at the same time. I called Daddy to see if he wanted to meet us later, then changed into jeans and sneakers. By the time I got outside, Dwight and Cal had cut the seed potatoes into chunks, making sure that each chunk had one or two eyes that would sprout into a plant. Seth had opened a furrow about eight inches deep when he was here with the plows, and Cal and I dropped the potatoes in the furrow, cut side down, about a foot apart. Dwight followed along behind with the hoe and covered them with three or four inches of dirt. In a week or so, after they'd sprouted, he would come back and pull another few inches of dirt over the stems until eventually they would be hilled up at least a foot deep in the sandy loam.

"Why so deep?" Cal asked when the process was described to him.

"Because the new potatoes form between the chunk we're planting and the surface of the soil," I explained.

"We have to give them enough room to grow or else they'll pop through the ground," said Dwight. "If they're exposed to light, they'll turn green and green potatoes are poison."

With less than five pounds of potatoes to plant, it didn't take us long to get them in the ground.

Then we washed up and I put my guitar in the back of the truck.

On the drive over, while telling Cal who he could expect to see, I said, "Steve Paulie owns the place, but I can never remember if he's my third cousin or a second cousin once removed."

Cal was puzzled. "How do you remove a cousin?"

"Removed just means a degree of separation," I said. "Look, R.W.'s your first cousin because his dad and your dad are brothers, okay?"

He nodded.

"Now if R.W. had a child, he would be your first cousin,

once removed. But if he had a child and you had a child, they would be second cousins. Got it?"

"And if they had children, they would be third cousins?"

"By George, 'e's got it!" I said with an exaggerated English accent.

"So what are Mary Pat and Jake to me?"

"Just good friends, I'm afraid, honey."

No way was I going to try to untangle Kate's relationship to her young ward. Enough to know they were cousins even though Mary Pat now called her Mom. Just as it was enough to know that the owner of Paulie's Barbecue House was related to me through one of Daddy's aunts.

Every Wednesday night, friends and relatives gather there to eat supper and then do a little picking and singing for an hour or so. It's very informal. Some Wednesdays, there aren't enough to bother. Other times, there'll be twelve or fourteen of us. Before I married Dwight, I would join them at least once a month for some good fellowshipping as Haywood calls it, but this would be the first time since New Year's.

We ordered plates of barbecue—that wonderful eastern Carolina smoked pork, coarsely chopped and seasoned with vinegar and hot sauce. It's always served with coleslaw and spiced apples and a bottomless basket of crispy hushpuppies, and everything gets washed down with pitchers of sweet iced tea.

"Want to split a side order of chicken livers?" I asked Dwight and Cal.

You'd've thought I had offered them anchovies the way they both turned up their noses, but Aunt Sister was seated at the end of the long table and she called down to say, "I could eat one or two if you're getting them."

Dwight always wants to tell me how unhealthful they are, but I just point to Aunt Sister, who's over eighty and still going strong. Daddy was there next to her and allowed as how he wouldn't mind a taste either, so I moved on down the table to be closer to them.

After supper, the instruments came out. Daddy and Haywood both play the fiddle, Isabel has a banjo and Aunt Sister plays a dulcimer. Zach's Emma and Andrew's Ruth spell each other on the piano and Herman's son Reese is good with the harmonica. The rest of us, including Steve Paulie, play guitar and those that don't play tap their toes and sing.

There were at least a dozen of us, and soon the place was rocking. From rousing gospel hymns to country ballads and back again. Mother used to say that she fell in love with Daddy for his fiddle-playing and he was in good form tonight, his fingers moving nimbly up and down the neck as he bowed the strings of his mellow old fiddle. Aunt Sister's daughter Beverly was there and she, Annie Sue, Emma, and Ruth blended their voices into such sweet cousinly harmony on one of the hymns that I got chill bumps.

Cal kept his eyes glued on Reese, fascinated by the way my nephew used his harmonica to counterpoint the melody line or make musical jokes. I glanced over at Dwight and he winked at me.

The music lifted me up and for a time, washed away both the sadness I had felt for Fred Mitchiner's grandson and the ugliness of Buck Harris's death. Shortly after nine though, I noticed that Cal was yawning. "Time we were calling it a night," I said.

Aunt Sister looked at Daddy and without a word, both began to play an old familiar tune. Annie Sue's clear soprano voice joined in softly before they'd played two bars and the rest of us picked it up until it floated over us in gentle benediction:

God be with you till we meet again
By his counsels guide, uphold you,
With his sheep securely fold you;
God be with you till we meet again.

CHAPTER 33

Success may be attained once by accident, but permanent results are found only attendant upon a practice based upon correct theory.

—*Profitable Farming in the Southern States,* 1890

I had just loaded the last breakfast plate in the dishwasher the next morning when the phone rang.

"Oh good," Dwight said. "You haven't left yet. I'm halfway to Dobbs and I just realized that I left some papers I'll need on the floor beside our bed. Could you bring them when you come?"

"Sure," I told him and immediately went to our room to find them. When I circled the bed to his side, I saw several sheets of paper on top of a manila file folder. I picked them up and straightened them, and saw that the top page was titled "Harris Farm #1: Workers on site as of 1 January." One name leaped out at me and I smiled as I read it, then tucked the pages neatly into the folder and placed it with my purse so I'd remember to take it with me.

On my drive in, though, that name began to gnaw at

me. January? I thought about the blowup Mrs. Harris had with her husband last spring, almost a year ago.

Why would someone wait nine or ten months to avenge a wrong if that's when Buck Harris had done anything worth avenging? And why chop off his arms and legs in such a rage?

Unless—?

Unbidden came the memory of how Will's wife, Amy, had vented last Saturday when I helped her write her grant proposal. Emma, too, when she and her cousins were arguing with Haywood. I coupled it with what Faye Myers had almost told me on Tuesday and a nebulous theory began to form.

At Bethel Baptist Church on Ward Dairy Road, I pulled into the churchyard to call my favorite clerk in Ellis Glover's office and ask her to pull a file for me.

When I got to the courthouse, I stopped there first.

It was as I thought. The original addresses were the same.

Downstairs, Faye Myers was on duty at the dispatch desk. I waited till she was off the phone and then asked her to finish telling me what she'd started to on Tuesday. "About what Flip told you when you were telling me about Mike Diaz and Mayleen Richards," I reminded her.

"Well, I probably shouldn't repeat it," she said. And of course, she did.

It was worse than I'd thought, but it clarified the whole situation and I walked on down to Dwight's office. He saw my face and his smile turned to concern.

"Deb'rah? What's wrong, shug?"

I closed his door. "Did Mayleen Richards learn much from those migrants yesterday?"

He shook his head. "She couldn't pry a thing out of them except that the two women did see Mrs. Harris take that tumble into the mud. They didn't tell before because they respect her and thought she would be humiliated if they did. Why?"

"I think I know who butchered Buck Harris," I told him bleakly. "Ernesto Palmeiro."

"Who?"

"The tractor guy that I had in court Friday." I opened his file and pointed to Palmeiro's name on the list of workers living on Harris Farm #1 in January. It was followed by a María Palmeiro. Neither name was on the current list the farm manager had given them.

Then I showed him the file I'd had the clerk pull for me. "When Palmeiro was arrested in January, his address was Ward Dairy Road. See? But that was before you knew it was Harris's body so it didn't really register. Everyone said he was loco for taking the tractor because his wife had left him after they lost their baby. But he was heading east, not south. I think he was trying to get to New Bern to find Buck Harris. If he had, Harris would have been chopped up at least a month and a half sooner."

"But why?"

"You said the blowup between the Harrises was last spring. That's when the tomato fields would have been sprayed with a pesticide. Eight or nine months later—in January—the Palmeiro baby was born. Stillborn. With no arms or legs." I couldn't keep my voice from shaking.

"No arms and no legs, Dwight. Just like that torso you found."

"Jesus H!" he murmured as he began to connect the dots. He opened his door and shouted, "All detectives! In my office. Now!"

Five or six deputies came hurrying in, including Mayleen Richards.

"Tell them," Dwight said.

While I repeated my conjectures, Dwight took Percy Denning aside and sent him to pull the fingerprint card on Palmeiro. A copy of the prints had been sent to the state's central crime lab, but like most crime labs around the country, ours is so underfunded and understaffed that the fingerprints connected to a misdemeanor theft would not have been entered into their computers yet.

As I went back upstairs to a courtroom where I was expected to dispense a little justice, an old rhyme that John Claude used to quote pounded through my head.

For want of a nail, a shoe was lost.
For want of a shoe, a horse was lost.
For want of a horse, a rider was lost.
For want of a rider, a battle was lost.

Or, as my no-nonsense mother used to say more succinctly, "Penny-wise, pound foolish."

With better funding, more crimes could be solved more quickly. In England, I hear they're using DNA to solve ordinary burglaries. Here in America we can't even afford to test for all the rapes and murders, much less enter the fingerprints of every convicted felon into a national database in a timely way.

. . . *All for the want of a nail.*

CHAPTER 34

Search ever after the truth—not the truth which justifies you or your pet theories to yourself, but seek truth for truth's sake, and when you have found it, follow its lead.

—*Profitable Farming in the Southern States,* 1890

Mayleen Richards
Thursday Morning, March 9

While two squad cars headed for the old Buckley place, three others peeled out for the Diaz nursery, blue lights flashing and sirens wailing, with Dwight Bryant bringing up the rear in his own truck.

Mayleen Richards was keenly aware of not being in on the kill.

"I think not," was all Major Bryant had said when she asked to go with them to arrest Ernesto Palmeiro instead of confronting the women of Harris Farm #1 again.

A cold lump still lodged in her chest from hearing Judge Knott say, "Miguel Diaz of Diaz y Garcia Landscaping came to court with him last Friday and spoke for him. It's my understanding that he works there now."

The judge had not once glanced in Mayleen's direction, but coupled with the long level look she got from Major Bryant when he denied her request, she was sure they were both aware of her relationship with Mike.

And what about Mike? He knew of Palmeiro's stillborn baby. Did he also know that Palmeiro had killed Buck Harris?

There was no doubt in anyone's mind now that he was the killer, and his desperate drive with the tractor had gone from being a funny story to something of grim seriousness in the brief minutes it had taken Percy Denning to look at Palmeiro's fingerprints and find the significant markers he had noted from the prints on the bloody axe.

Her own fingers itched to call Diaz, but she kept both hands on the steering wheel. Beside her, Jack Jamison seemed to be on an adrenaline high, a combination of wrapping up this homicide and the anticipation of leaving for Texas next week.

"If I pass the selection and training process, they'll ship me out immediately, so this could be my last weekend with Cindy and Jay for a year."

"I'm not going to say break a leg," she said tartly.

"How do you mean that?"

"Oh hell, Jack. I don't really know. Both ways, I guess. I still think you're crazy to put yourself in harm's way like this, but if it's what you want, then I really do hope you pass and that it works out for you."

It was after nine before the second team reached the nursery. The woman who came to the door seemed frightened by so many police cars. Dwight recognized her from a murder investigation back in January and the sight of him seemed to reassure her. In halting English, she told them that her cousin Miguel Diaz and his crew had left for a job nearly two hours ago.

"Ernesto Palmeiro," said Dwight. "Is he here or with your cousin?"

She shook her head. "No here. He leave *sábado*—Saturday. Go Mexico. You ask Miguel."

"Tell me about him," Dwight said. But she immediately lapsed into Spanish and claimed not to understand.

Fortunately, they had brought along a interpreter.

"She says he was from the village next to theirs back in Mexico, but they did not really know him until his wife gave birth to a badly deformed baby in January. A baby that died. After that, the wife left and Ernesto went crazy. He was arrested and from jail he sent word to her brother and her cousin that they must help him, as compatriots of the same valley. They didn't want to, but felt it was their duty. They gave him work, gave him blankets and let him sleep in the shed. They also helped him repair the damage he had done. Saturday, her cousin Miguel gave him his wages and told him to leave. More than that, she says she doesn't know."

She did give them the number for her cousin's cell phone though; and when Dwight called it, Miguel Diaz told them where they were working. The site was a new development off Ward Dairy Road near Bethel Baptist, less than fifteen minutes away.

He was waiting for them at the entrance of the new subdivision, and Dwight tried to take his measure as

Diaz got out of his truck to meet them. A clean-shaven man with light brown skin and straight black hair. Without that black Stetson and the workboots, he'd probably stand five-nine or five-ten, just a shade taller than Mayleen Richards. Regular features. Slim hips and a slender build that conveyed strength and confidence. Hard to read his face because he wore mirrored sunglasses this bright sunny morning.

Dwight introduced himself and they shook hands. In lightly accented English, Diaz asked how he might be of service.

"We're looking for Ernesto Palmeiro," Dwight said. "We're told you went to court for him last week and that he works for you now."

"Did work," Diaz said easily. "No more. He left for Mexico on Saturday. At least that's where he said he was going. Is there more trouble, Major Bryant?"

"Didn't you guarantee he'd repair the yards he plowed up?"

"They're finished. We put the last yard back with new bushes Friday night. I let him work for me during the day, then work on the damages in the evening, and I kept his pay till it was finished, just like I promised the judge."

He seemed puzzled by the three cars that still flashed their emergency lights. "All this for some flowers and bushes? I can show you, Major. It's all fixed."

"Not flowers and bushes," Dwight said. "You've heard about Buck Harris? Palmeiro's boss? Owner of the farm where he used to live and work, and where he stole that tractor?"

"He was killed, yes?" He shook his head. "A bad business. Very bad."

"Ernesto Palmeiro did it."

Impossible to gauge his reaction behind those reflective glasses. Diaz did not exclaim or protest, but he did let out the long indrawn breath he had taken.

"You don't seem surprised," Dwight said grimly.

"Did I know he was the butcher? No, Major. But you're right. I think I am not surprised. You heard about his son? His first child? Who died the same hour he was born, thanks be to God?" He crossed himself.

Dwight nodded. "Why did he blame Harris?"

"It was his farm. María was working there. Beyond that I don't know. I didn't want to know. I gave him work and a place to stay. I spoke for him in court and as soon as I had done all that I pledged, I paid him his money and told him to leave. He said he was going home. The honor of my village required me to help him when he asked for it. It did not require me to like him or take him to my bosom."

No, thought Dwight. Just my deputy. And how much did she know? She had flushed bright red when Deborah mentioned Diaz's name.

"How much money did he leave with?"

"Fifteen hundred dollars. I gave him the flowers and shrubs at our cost."

"We'll want to speak to your men who worked with him."

"Of course, Major, but they'll only tell you the same."

"I bet they will," Dwight said. He motioned to Raeford McLamb, who had stood nearby listening. "Separate those men and get a statement from each of them as to what they knew about Palmeiro."

"Want me to translate for you?" asked Diaz with a slight smile.

"No thanks," Dwight said. "We brought our own interpreter."

It took less than an hour. Each man was separately questioned, then allowed to go back to work.

Dwight did not wait to hear the predictable results. Instead, he got in his truck and drove over to the old Buckley place, Harris Farm #1, where Richards and Jamison were bearing down on Felicia Sanaugustin and Mercedes Santos, who swore separately and together that they knew nothing about the Palmeiros or their baby.

"I don't understand why they keep saying that," a frustrated Richards told Dwight. "They know we know that the baby was born here in the camp and that the EMS truck responded to an emergency call here in January. Why won't they admit that the baby was stillborn and had serious birth defects?"

"Maybe for the same reason they didn't tell you about Mrs. Harris falling in the mud puddle till they knew she had told you," Dwight said. "Let me go see if she's here."

He drove up to the house and found Mrs. Harris and her daughter having coffee in the bright sunny kitchen with Mrs. Samuelson. Even though the housekeeper immediately stood and busied herself over at the sink the moment he entered, it was clear from the plates and cups on the table that neither woman stood on ceremony with the other. No bosslady/servant protocol here.

More than ever, the Harris daughter looked like someone who had come straight from a soup kitchen. She wore loose-fitting black warm-up pants and an oversized Duke sweatshirt that hung on her thin frame.

"We know who killed your father, Mrs. Hochmann," he said when the formalities were done.

She looked at him, startled. "Who?"

"One of the migrant workers here, an Ernesto Palmeiro."

The name clearly meant nothing to her. Even Mrs. Samuelson looked blank. But not Mrs. Harris.

"He and his wife María worked in the tomato crop here," he said. "She got pregnant last spring and had a baby here in January. Either stillborn or it died soon after. We've heard conflicting stories."

Mrs. Hochmann looked concerned and murmured sympathetically. Her mother sat silently.

"It was born without arms or legs. It was only a torso with a head," he said.

"Oh my God!" said Susan Hochmann. "That's why he—? But why, Major?"

"Ask your mother," Dwight said harshly.

"My mother?" She turned in her chair. "Mother?"

"Has she told you what she and your father really fought about last spring when María Palmeiro was less than one month pregnant? When that baby was still forming in her womb?"

"Mother?"

"Be still, Susan! He doesn't know," her mother said. "He's only guessing."

"Am I? We'll subpoena the records for this farm. They'll show who was where when the tomatoes were sprayed that week. Too many people know."

"Records are sometimes spotty." She gave a dismissive shrug. "And these are my people. They won't talk."

Dwight looked at her, genuinely puzzled. "Why are you still protecting him?"

"He made the workers go into the field before it was safe?" asked her daughter.

"Sid Lomax described your father as somebody who couldn't bear to see workers standing around idly while the clock was running," Dwight said. "You yourself described the trailers he used to house them in, trailers that had no running water where they could wash off the pesticides. Why did they need to wash off the pesticides, Mrs. Harris? They would have been safe if they'd waited forty-eight hours to go back in the fields."

Susan Hochmann looked sick.

"Oh, Mother," she whispered.

At that moment the light finally broke for Dwight as he looked at the older woman's weathered face. "You're afraid of another fine, aren't you? Another OSHA investigation. Maybe a huge lawsuit. You don't want another scandal for Harris Farms. Did you give María Palmeiro money to go back to Mexico, Mrs. Harris?"

"She wanted to go home," Mrs. Harris said angrily. "She'd lost her baby. The marriage was a mess. She just wanted to leave and forget it all. So yes, I gave her money.

But that doesn't mean Harris Farms caused the baby's birth defects."

Susan Hochmann's shoulders slumped as if weighted down by a ton of guilt and she shook her head in disbelief.

"It all fits, doesn't it?" Dwight said wearily. "Buck Harris was killed in that empty shed, but it was a shed that held spraying equipment. He was dismembered to look like the baby. Then his head and his"—he hesitated over leaving that second grisly image in the daughter's mind—"his head was left in the field where his wife was contaminated. It *was* that back field, wasn't it?"

Mrs. Harris nodded. "She didn't go in too soon," she said dully. "She was there while they were spraying. When I got down there that day and saw what was happening, I screamed at them to come out of the field and I sent them back to the camp to take showers. They were all green with it. But it was the second day of spraying and she was at the most vulnerable stage of pregnancy. I didn't know she was pregnant. I don't think she even knew for sure at that point. Buck and I got into it hot and heavy then. Sid Lomax wouldn't have let it happen, but Sid was in California. His father had died. So Buck was in charge and by God he wasn't going to coddle anybody or pay a dime for people to stand around and wait till it was safe. 'You made me put in fancy hot and cold showers,' he said. 'Let 'em go wash off. Where's the harm?' After that, I stayed in New Bern and I didn't know about María till Mercedes Santos called me. I came immediately. And yes, I gave her the money to bury her baby and yes, I gave her money to fly home. Enough to buy a little house and a sewing machine and start a new life for herself. All her husband wanted to do was stay drunk. She's better off without him."

"He didn't think so," Dwight said and turned on his heel and walked out. He needed air. Long deep drafts of clean spring air.

Mayleen Richards was waiting beside his truck. "No luck, Major?"

He gave her a quick synopsis of what had passed in the kitchen but before they could confer on their next actions, Susan Hochmann called from the back porch and crossed the yard to them.

"You were right," she said, nodding to Richards. "Mother's terrified of a lawsuit. I'm not though. What can I do to help?"

"Do you speak Spanish?" Richards asked.

The woman nodded.

"Mrs. Sanaugustin let slip something that makes me think her husband might know more than he's told, but she's clammed up altogether now and won't say a word."

"Sanaugustin?"

Dwight told her about the worker who said he had seen the bloody slaughter scene in the shed on Saturday, two days before they discovered it.

"Sanaugustin," Mrs. Hochmann said again. "Felicia?"

"Sí," said Richards and immediately turned as red as the shoulder-length red hair that gleamed in the sunlight. "I mean, yes."

"Let me talk to her. I think she trusts me almost as much as she trusts Mother."

She got in the prowl car with Richards and Dwight

led the way back down to the camp. It took a few minutes, but at last Felicia Sanaugustin threw up her hands and told them everything. Yes, the baby was as they had said. Yes, María Palmeiro had been covered with pesticide. No, she did not know the name. Only that it was green and it made them break out in a rash even though they washed it off every day. And yes, she admitted, she and Rafael knew that Ernesto had killed *el patrón*. Early Monday morning, before it was really light, Rafael had walked up to the sheds to get a dolly to move the old refrigerator out in preparation for the new one *la señora* had promised to bring. As he approached the empty shed, he had felt a great need to relieve himself and so had stepped into the bushes there. A moment before he finished, he heard the rusty hinge squeak and saw the door open. Then Ernesto Palmeiro had put out his head and looked all around.

Rafael had stood motionless. Something about the man's stealthy movements frightened him so that he could not even pull up his zipper. The light was still so poor that it was hard to be sure that it even *was* Ernesto. Especially since he was not supposed to be there. He had been fired the month before.

Sanaugustin waited until he was sure the other was gone, then curiosity compelled him to look inside the shed.

"She says we know what he saw," said Mrs. Hochmann.

"Your father's remains?"

She put the question to Felicia Sanaugustin and the woman shook her head.

"*Sangre solamente,*" she whispered.

Only blood.

"But it was fresh blood. And it dripped from the back of the car," said Susan Hochmann, desperately trying not to let the horror of the woman's tale become personal. "He closed the door and immediately went back to the camp and said nothing of what he'd seen to anyone. Everyone said that Palmeiro was crazy and he was fearful for his own life if he accused him. He told himself that he didn't really know anything for certain at that point. He did not know for sure what man or animal it was that had been killed there."

The migrant woman continued and Mrs. Hochmann translated. Rafael had brooded all week as the body parts began to appear along the road, yet no one else connected them with their boss, even when word drifted down to the camp that people were starting to ask for him.

So last Saturday, Rafael had sneaked back to the shed. The smell! The flies! *Ai-yi-yi!*

This time he had taken some of the money that they were saving to get a place of their own and he had gone into town and bought drugs and got arrested. And what, she wailed, was to happen to them now?

Susan Hochmann spoke in soothing tones and when the woman had quieted, she said to Dwight, "I told her nothing was going to happen to them, Major. They've done nothing wrong. Have they?"

"Nothing illegal maybe," said Dwight, "but they may have just cut your inheritance pretty drastically. If he's willing to testify that he saw Palmeiro leave that bloody scene early that Monday morning, then your parents' divorce is invalid. The summary judgment wasn't signed until that afternoon. Depending on what your mother does, it could mean that you won't get half the business now."

A wry smile flickered across her broad plain face. "Want to bet?"

Dwight left the mopping up to Jamison and the other detectives and told Richards to ride back to Dobbs with him to start the reports and put out an APB on Ernesto Palmeiro, who had a five-day lead on them and was probably already back in Mexico by now.

Their talk was of the case and the ramifications of what they'd learned and the very real likelihood that they'd never get him extradited back to Colleton County. All very professional until they were about five miles from town and Dwight said, "Anything you need to tell me, Richards?"

"Sir?"

"You heard me."

"About what, Major?"

"About Miguel Diaz."

"On a personal level? Or about him speaking for Palmeiro and giving him work while he repaired the damage he'd done?"

"Your personal life's your own as long as it doesn't compromise your handling of the job." He kept his tone neutral.

Her eyes flashed indignantly. "You think I let our relationship get in the way of the investigation?"

"That's what I'm asking. Did you?"

She shook her head. "No, sir. I really don't think I did. I didn't know Mike had gone to court for Palmeiro till Friday. McLamb mentioned that he'd seen him at the courthouse and when I asked Mike, he was absolutely up front about it. He said he felt sorry for the guy because his baby had died and his wife had left him. He didn't describe the baby's condition, just that it was stillborn. We didn't know the body parts were Harris's yet and I certainly didn't know till this morning when your—when Judge Knott told us that Palmeiro had worked for Harris. That was the first time I'd heard it."

"It wasn't the first time Diaz had heard it, though," Dwight said.

Richards let the implications of his words sink in. "Did he know Palmeiro killed Harris?" she asked hesitantly.

"He says not."

"Do you believe him?"

Dwight shrugged. "*Know* is one of those slippery words. Did Palmeiro confess to him? Did he see the guy swing the axe? Probably not."

"But you think he knew," Richards said.

"Don't you?"

They rode in silence another mile or two, then Richards said, "My family. My dad and my brothers and my sister? They say that they'll never speak to me again if I marry him."

"What about your mother?"

"She'll go along with them, but she'd probably sneak and call me once in a while."

"Family's important," he observed as they reached the Dobbs city limits.

She sighed. "Yes."

Dwight pulled into the parking lot beside the courthouse and cut the engine. As she reached for the door handle, he said, "Look, Richards. Your personal life is none of my business as long as you can keep it separate from the job. But I'm going to say this even though I probably shouldn't. If you're going to break up with him because you don't love him, that's one thing. But don't use the job or what he knew or didn't know as an excuse if it's really because of your family. You owe it to yourself to tell him the truth."

CHAPTER 35

The retention of the old family homestead and farm by a long line of ancestry for successive generations is, in many respects a desideratum, whether we regard it in the practical light of an investment or of a pardonable pride, as the basis of the sentiment of family honor and respectability that is to be associated with the name and the inheritance.

—*Profitable Farming in the Southern States,* 1890

DEBORAH KNOTT
THURSDAY EVENING, MARCH 9

By the time I adjourned for the day, the news had gone all around the courthouse that Buck Harris had been murdered by one of his field hands because his wanton carelessness with pesticides had caused the stillbirth of that field hand's baby.

The news media had swarmed around the courthouse and out to the Buckley place as well, not that they got much joy there. None of the workers wanted to talk, and Mrs. Harris refused to meet with them; but her daughter, while sidestepping any statements that would admit culpability, was ready to use the situation as a soapbox to propose a more socially responsible program for "guest workers." Reporters came away with an earful of statistics about the appalling conditions most growers imposed on their laborers, all for the saving of a few pennies a pound on the fruits and vegetables they harvested. While it was interesting that the "tomato heiress," as they were calling her, planned to move down from New York and turn the family homeplace into a center for bettering the lives of migrants, Susan Hochmann was not photogenic enough to hold their attention for long.

Here in the courthouse, sympathies seemed to take a slight shift from the dead man to his killer as more and more details came out about the baby and about Harris's deliberate violations of OSHA and EPA regulations, not to mention simple human decency.

"You hate to blame the victim," said a records clerk who had just come back from maternity leave with a CD full of baby pictures as her new screen saver, "but damned if he wasn't asking for it."

"I'm not saying it's ever right to kill," one of the attorneys told me, "but I'd take his case in a heartbeat. Bet I could get him off with a suspended sentence, too."

All cameras focused on the sensational gory murder. It would be the lead story of the day. Not much attention would be paid to the shooting death of a young woman by her abusive ex-husband who then turned the gun on himself. Nothing particularly newsworthy about that. Happens all the time, doesn't it?

As soon as I heard, I adjourned court an hour early and went around to Portland's house.

"She's upstairs," Avery said when he let me in. "Dwight was here before. It was good of him to come tell her himself."

I found her standing by a window in the nursery. Her eyes were red and swollen when she turned to me. "She couldn't make it to high ground, Deborah."

"I know, honey," I said and opened my arms to her as she burst into tears.

The baby awoke as we were talking and she sat down with little Carolyn and opened her shirt to nurse her. "If it weren't for you," she told her daughter, "I'd be killing a bottle of bourbon about now."

Her eyes filled up with tears again. "I guess I'll call Linda Allred tonight. Tell her to add another statistic to her list."

When I got home that evening, Daddy was sitting on the porch to watch Dwight and Cal finish cleaning out the interior of the truck before carefully smoothing a Hurricanes sticker to the back bumper. Cal wanted to clamp our flag on the window, but Dwight vetoed that idea.

"Save it for Deborah's car," he said. "My truck's not a moving billboard."

Bandit was frisking around the yard in an unsuccessful attempt to get Blue and Ladybell to romp with him, but those two hounds were too old and dignified for such frivolity.

Dwight followed me into our bedroom while I changed out of heels and panty hose into jeans and sneakers. "You hear about Karen Braswell?"

I nodded. "Thanks for going over there yourself."

"She gonna be okay?"

"The baby helps."

"God, Deb'rah. What's it gonna take? This is the second one in three months. We took his damn guns. Where'd he get that one?"

"Don't beat up on yourself, Dwight. You said it yourself. There's no stopping somebody who's determined to kill and doesn't care about the consequences. If it hadn't been a gun, it would have been a knife or even his bare hands."

We went back outdoors and the blessed mundane flowed back over us. Cal was antsy to leave because they planned to pick up a new pair of sneakers for him on the way in. The lower the sun sank, the cooler the air became and my sweater was suddenly not thick enough.

"Come on in," I told Daddy, "and I'll fix us something to eat."

"Naw, Maidie's making supper. Why don't you come eat with us? You know there's always extra."

"Okay," I said, but he didn't get up.

"Are we expecting somebody?" I asked.

"Some of the children said they was gonna stop by, show us what they plan to grow on that land we give 'em last week."

Even as he spoke, a couple of pickups drove up and several of my nieces and nephews tumbled out—Zach's Lee and Emma, Seth's Jessie, Haywood's Jane Ann, and

Robert's Bobby, who carried a large sunflower that he handed to me with a flourish.

"Sunflowers?" I laughed. "You're going to grow sunflowers?"

"Hey, they're real trendy now," he told me.

"The short ones make great cut flowers," said Jane Ann, "but those that we don't sell fresh, we can wire the dried heads and sell as organic sunflower seeds to hang from a bird feeder. Cardinals go crazy over them."

"But this is going to be our real moneymaker." Jessie set a bud vase with a single stem of pure white flowers on the table and an incredibly sweet fragrance met me even before I leaned forward to smell. "*Polianthes tuberosa.* Almost no pests, doesn't need a lot of fertilizer, and we can market them for fifty cents to a dollar a stem depending on whether we sell them retail or wholesale. This one cost me two-fifty at the florist shop in Cotton Grove and he said he'd much rather buy locally than getting them shipped in from Mexico."

"Yeah," said Lee. "Judy Johnson, Mother's cousin up near Richmond, has an acre that she and her husband tend pretty much by themselves. She says we'll probably be able to cut ours from the end of July till frost. Up there, they cut anywhere from a hundred and fifty to six hundred stems a day."

"That's a gross of close to nine thousand dollars an acre," said Emma, who seemed to be channeling the soul of an accountant these days.

"What about fertilizer?" Daddy asked. "I hear that organic stuff's right expensive."

"Chicken manure," said Bobby. "You know that poultry place over on Old Forty-eight? He raises the biddies from hatching to six weeks and he's got a mountain of it out back. Says we can have it for the hauling. We'll compost the new stuff and go ahead and spread the old soon as we can afford a spreader."

Daddy laughed. "Y'all ever take a good look at some of them things a-setting under the shelters back of those old stick barns?"

Lee's face lit up. "You've got a manure spreader?"

"Parked it there twenty-five years ago when we got rid of the last of the mules and cows. It probably needs new tires and some WD-40, but y'all can have it if you want."

Jane Ann jumped up and gave him a big hug that almost knocked his hat off. "You just saved us four hundred dollars and trucking one down from Burlington, Granddaddy!"

They all rushed off to check it out before dark, as excited as if Daddy had told them he had an old spaceship they could use to fly to the moon.

He straightened his hat and stood to go. "What you reckon Robert's gonna say when they drag that old thing out?"

I laughed. "Myself, I can't wait to hear what Haywood and Isabel have to say about growing flowers for a crop."

"Beats ostriches," he said slyly.

"What about you?" I asked as we walked out to his truck. The hounds jumped up in back and I put Bandit in the cab between us. "What do you think about growing flowers?"

He smiled. "Tell you what, shug. Flowers or mushrooms or even ostriches—it don't matter one little bit. Anything that keeps 'em here on the farm another generation's just fine with me."

ABOUT THE AUTHOR

Margaret Maron grew up on a farm near Raleigh, North Carolina, but for many years lived in Brooklyn, New York. When she returned to her North Carolina roots with her artist-husband, Joe, she began a series based on her own background. The first book, *Bootlegger's Daughter*, became a *Washington Post* bestseller that swept the top mystery awards for its year and is among the 100 Favorite Mysteries of the Century as selected by the Independent Mystery Booksellers Association. Later Deborah Knott novels *Up Jumps the Devil* and *Storm Track* won the Agatha Award for Best Novel. To find out more about the author, you can visit www.margaretmaron.com.

When unchecked urbanization
and political corruption lead to murder,
Deborah Knott must confront some dark realities ...

Please turn this page
for a preview of

DEATH'S HALF ACRE

by Margaret Maron

Available in hardcover

CHAPTER 1

Tuesday morning's light mist lay over the field of young tobacco. It softened the air and turned the tall pines beyond into gray shadows of themselves. The recently-turned earth gave off an honest aroma that was sweet to the old man who stood motionless to take it all in. Another year, another spring. Here in late April, the plants were only knee high with no hint of the pink blossoms to come, their leaves still small and crisp and deep green. Everything fresh and young.

Everything but me, the old man told himself.

One of two dogs beside him nudged his hand with a muzzle that had, in the last year, become almost as white as his master's hair. The man looked down with a rueful smile. "Yeah and you, too, poor ol' Blue."

He scratched the dog's soft as velvet ears, then the three of them ambled slowly on down the lane that circled the perimeter of this field. Cool early mornings used to mean the beginning of another day of hard sweaty work—fields to plow, animals to tend, the hundred and one back-breaking chores that make up a farmer's daily life.

Back at the house, Sue and Essie would be fixing breakfast, rousting the boys out of bed, asking the older ones to fill the woodbox and feed the chickens, sending the younger ones off to school . . .

The whole farm would buzz with meaningful work and raucous laughter.

He almost never thought about his first wife, but Annie Ruth had always liked mornings best, too. More times than he could count, she would be up before him. She scorned mirrors and plaited her hair by touch alone into a long thick braid as she looked out their window to watch the first light define the trees and fields beyond.

"Time to get moving," she would say briskly if he lay in bed too long to watch her.

Now his house was silent and empty every morning until Maidie came over to make breakfast; and even though he only piddled at working this last year or two, he still felt driven to walk the back lanes each day, to see his fields and woods as fresh and new as the dawn of creation, to make sure that everything was well within the borders of his land. Annie Ruth had usually been too busy to come walking, but Sue used to say, "Now don't you look all the pretty off the morning till I can come, too," and she would often slip away from the demands of the boys and the house to join him out here.

Together they would pause to enjoy the dogwoods that bloomed among the tall pines, to smell the sweet scent of wild crabapples on the ditchbanks or note that the corn could use a little side-dressing of soda to green it up. Away from the house and the boys, they could talk about the larger issues in their life together, the needs of someone in their extended families, or the help they might could give the proud man who was having a hard time of it. They could discuss what to do about Andrew or Frank and whether a good talking to would be enough to keep those two out of trouble or if it was going to take a trip to the woodshed to get the point across.

Yet they had all turned out well, he thought, as he ran their faces through his mind, taking stock of his sons as he took stock of his land. The Navy had straightened Frank out; and Sue's patience and April's love had straightened Andrew. There were problems with some of the grandchildren, but they would come out right in the end, too. Of this he had no doubt.

A few feet ahead of him, the younger dog suddenly went on alert. He followed the direction of her point and saw a doe emerge from the woods at the far edge of the field. Behind her, two young fawns hesitated, half hidden by the grape vines that hung down from the trees. Ladybelle gave an almost inaudible whine and Blue strained to see what had alerted her. Both of them looked back at him, but he gave the hand signal to stay and they obeyed. Nevertheless, the doe had caught his slight movement and she and the fawns melted back into the trees.

As the sun rose behind the pines and began to burn off the mist, he heard the sound of a motor and turned to see a small black truck slowly easing through the sandy ruts. He stood quietly until the truck pulled even with him and the driver cut its engine. The white man behind the wheel appeared to be in his mid-thirties and wore a gray work shirt with the name Ennis embroidered in red on the breast pocket. His short brown hair had thinned across the crown and but he had not yet begun to go gray.

"Sorry to bother you, Mr. Kezzie, but Miz Holt said you were out here and might not mind."

"Not a bit," Kezzie Knott said politely and waited for the man to identify himself.

"You probably don't remember me, but I'm James Ennis, Frances Pritchard's grandson."

The Pritchard land touched some that he owned over in the next township and Kezzie nodded at that familiar name. "You must be one of Mary's boys."

"Yessir." The younger man got out of the truck and extended his hand.

"What can I do for you, son?"

"It's about my grandmother, Mr. Kezzie. She's about to give away more of our land. Grandy might've left it in her name, but you know good as me he wanted her to pass it on down to my mother. It's been in our family over two hundred years and yeah, nobody wants to farm it any more, but it don't seem right for her to let somebody have for free what the whole family's sweated and bled for all these years. She says she's giving it back to the Lord, but it's not the Lord's name that's gonna be on that deed."

Kezzie Knott lit a cigarette from the hard pack that was always in his shirt pocket and leaned against the truck to listen to a story whose outline had become all too familiar in the last few years. Land you could hardly give away thirty years ago was now so dear that the income it brought in barely paid the rising taxes. The details might be different but the results were always the same—old folks talked out of their land for peanuts on the dollar value while some slick developer made a bundle. The only difference here was that the slick operator was a preacher and not a developer.

"She's always talked about you with respect, Mr. Kezzie. I was thinking that maybe if you could speak to her? It's not just for me and mine neither, but you remember Nancy, Mama's only sister?"

Kezzie Knott nodded. Frances Pritchard's older daughter must be close to sixty now and still had the mind of a sweet-natured three-year-old.

"He's promised Granny he'll take care of Nancy till she dies but you know how much a promise is worth."

"No more'n the air it's written on," the old man agreed. "Now I can't make you no promises myself, son, but I'll look into it for you and see what I can do."

If nothing else, he thought, there was someone in the deeds office that he might could get to lose the papers and snarl up the transaction with red tape for a few weeks.

Mid-afternoon and Cameron Bradshaw firmed the dirt around the last of the purple petunias, then sat back on his padded kneeling stool to admire his handiwork.

It might not be the English gardens he remembered from the tours he had taken with his grandparents before they lost their money, nor the showpiece he had tended before he and Candace split up, nevertheless, its beauty pleased him.

"A poor thing, but mine own," he murmured to himself. He pushed himself up off the stool, straightened his protesting joints, and tried again to remember who it was that said, "What every gardener needs is a cast iron back with a hinge in it."

The sun was not quite over the yardarm, but he decided he would pour himself a drink, take down his *Bartlett's*, and bring them both out here to the terrace. Nail down that quote once and for all.

He knew from happy experience that one quotation would lead to another, yet what better way to spend an April afternoon than to sit here in his garden and sip good scotch, to turn the pages at random and let his mind wander through the words of history's great thinkers?

He crossed the flagstone terrace and paused to savor again the beauty of purple petunias, red geraniums, and silver-gray dusty miller. More geraniums and petunias trailed from hanging baskets. White Lady Banks roses were beginning to bud amid the purple wisteria blossoms that hung like clusters of grapes from the trellis that shaded his back door, and terra-cotta tubs of shasta daisies, basil and dill stood on either side of the gate that opened onto a passageway to the street.

To his dismay, he heard the clip-clop of backless sandals hurrying up that same passageway.

He reached for the doorknob and wondered if there was time to get inside and pretend not to be at home.

As he suspected, it was Deanna.

Other men bragged about their children, he thought wearily—how bright they were, how industrious, how motivated to succeed, how thoughtful of their parents.

He had Dee.

Twenty-two years old. Bright? Yes. But motivated? Thoughtful of her parents?

Ha!

Yet, as he stood motionless under the wisteria vines that grew over the small trellis above his door and watched his daughter fumble with the gate latch, he could not suppress the enduring wonder that he and Candace had produced such beauty.

Today she was dressed in white clam-diggers that sat low on her slender hips, a bright green shirt, gold loop earrings and gold sandals. He gloomily noted that she had a black duffle bag slung over one shoulder.

Small-boned and deceptively delicate-looking, Dee had the wide deep-set eyes of his family. Their intense green came from her mother, though, as did her long reddish brown hair. From the genetic pool, she had drawn his thin Bradshaw nose and strong chin. The dimple in her right cheek had skipped a generation and came straight from his late mother-in-law, one of those trashy Seymours from east of Dobbs.

Or so he had been told by white-haired colleagues who sometimes, when in their cups, waxed nostalgic about that dimple and, behind his back, wondered aloud if they had sired his wife.

He himself could not put a face to Candace's mother. Before they lost their money, the Bradshaws had sent their children to private schools, so he had no direct memory of Alice Seymour Wells or her husband Macon even though the three of them were native to the county and must have been about the same age.

As the gate finally clicked open, Dee spotted him in the shaded doorway.

"Mom's kicked me out again," she said, her full red

lips poked out in a childish pout. She dropped her duffle bag on the white iron patio table where her father had planned to spend a peaceful afternoon. "Like it's my fault George puked on her fuckin' couch."

"You let him in the house?" asked Bradshaw, who still winced at the crudities young women so carelessly voiced today. "I thought she told you to quit seeing him."

"And I told *her* I'll see whoever I damn well please."

"Then she said, 'Not in *my* house you won't,' right?"

"Been there, done that, haven't you, Dad?"

"When are you going to quit yanking her chain, honey? If you're really going to drop out of college this near graduation, then don't just threaten to get a job. Do it. Stand on your own two feet."

"Like you do? Taking an allowance from her every month?"

His thin lips tightened. "It's not an allowance, Dee. And it comes out of the company, not from your mother."

"A company you started long before you met her."

"A company I still own," he reminded her. "And one that she helped build up to what it is today,

"So what? She couldn't have gotten her foot in half those doors without the Bradshaw name. And then you just gave it all to her and walked away."

It was an old complaint and one he was tired of hearing, especially since it was not strictly true. Yes, he had handed control of the company over to Candace when they separated, but it was with the stipulation that he would receive a certain percentage of the profits in perpetuity.

"I was ready to retire and it's an equitable arrangement."

He brushed away a spent blossom that had dropped onto his white hair from the wisteria vine above his head.

"You sure?"

"What do you mean?"

"She could be cooking the books, couldn't she?"

"Not with my accountant going over them twice a year."

"And how do you know she's not screwing him twice a year just to screw you?"

In spite of her language, Cameron Bradshaw was amused to picture nerdy little Roger Flackman in bed with Candace. She would eat him alive. On the other hand, that last check had been smaller than usual. He had put it down to Candace's preoccupation with her new position on the board of commissioners, but what if she and Roger really were—?

"So anyhow," said Dee, interrupting his thoughts as she picked up her duffle bag, "can I crash with you for a few days till Mom gets over being mad about the damn couch?"

"Only if you start looking for a job," he said firmly.

"Believe it or not, I think I've already found one," his daughter said.

Some forty-odd miles away, in Durham, Victor Talbert, VP of Talbert Pharmaceuticals, opened the door of the board room not really expecting to see anything except the long polished table and a dozen empty chairs. Instead, he found his father poring over a sheaf of surveyor's maps spread across the table.

"There you are," he said. "I've been looking all over for you. What's that? Plans for the new plant in China?"

"Hardly," his father said.

At fifty-five, Grayson Hooks Talbert wore his years lightly. His dark hair was going classically gray at the temples, his five-eleven frame carried no extra pounds, and his charcoal gray spring suit fit nicely without calling too much attention to its perfect tailoring.

He started to order his son away from the maps. Victor might be curious, but he would obey. Unlike his older son who would have looked, sneered, and promptly forgotten, assuming he was sober enough to bring the print into focus in the first place. A grasshopper and an ant. That's what he had for sons. One clever and inventive, but mercurial and dedicated to hedonistic self-destruction. The other a dutiful plodder who ran the New York office. Reliable and utterly trustworthy and totally incapable of the flights of imagination and ambition that had built this company into one of the state's major players and its president into a power broker who had the ear of senators and governors.

Victor Talbert looked at the identifying labels and frowned. "Colleton County?"

His father nodded.

"Our subsidiaries are screaming for a decision about our eastern markets and you keep coming back to this? Why, Dad? I thought you were finished out there. You made your point with that bootlegger when you built Grayson Village. You've got a good manager in place and it's peanuts anyhow. Why keep bothering with it? There's nothing for us out there."

"You think not?" Talbert said. He rolled up the maps, gave his son explicit instructions about the subsidiaries and said, "You going back to New York tonight?"

Victor nodded. "We have tickets to a play. Unless there's something else you want me to stay for?"

"No, I'll be up next week."

They walked down to his office together and once Victor was gone, Talbert told his assistant to order him a car and driver. "And tell him we'll be spending the night at the Grayson Village Inn."

From the windows of her corner office on the second floor of Adams Advertising, the company she had started with her husband, Jamie Jacobson could look out across Main Street and see the courthouse square where pansies blossomed extravagantly in the planters on either side of the wide low steps that led down to the sidewalk.

Another perfect spring day and this was the closest she had come to enjoying it since arriving at the office early that morning. Her own pansies needed attention and she had hoped to take off an hour in midday to enjoy the task. Instead, she had eaten a sandwich at her desk and tried to keep her mind focused on work.

A slender woman with sandy blond hair that had begun to sprout a few gray hairs now that she had passed forty, Jamie glanced at her watch and sighed. Five o'clock already and it would take at least another three hours to finish the presentation needed for a client first thing tomorrow morning.

She would have to skip supper and for a moment, she considered skipping tonight's board meeting as well. As one of only two Democrats on Colleton County's board of commissioners, she wondered why she kept bothering.

Unfortunately, a vote on the planning board's recommendations for slowing growth was scheduled for tonight and she could not pass up one last attempt to accept it, even though she knew Candace Bradshaw would use every trick in her bottomless bag to vote it down.

Much as Jamie Jacobson hated to admit it, the county's power brokers had planned well when they picked the newest chair of the board. Candace Bradshaw was as cute as a puppy and just as tail-waggingly eager to please the men who had put her in office and who now profited from the five-to-two decisions the board usually made under her chairmanship. A giggling, cuddly woman, she loved being chair. As long as the men pretended she held real power, she would do everything she could to make them happy, and if they wanted a controversial measure passed, she could be as tenacious as a little pit bull on their behalf.

For over three hundred years, Colleton County farmers had wrested a modest living from its mellow soil. Now, economists predicted that in another thirty years, the farms might all be gone, bulldozed under and covered with houses and big box chain stores as farmers took the quick and easy money. Housing bubbles might be bursting all over the rest of the country, but the red-hot market here showed few signs of cooling.

With its temperate climate, low unemployment rate, and even lower taxes, North Carolina was regularly touted as one of the country's most liveable places and people were streaming in from the old rustbelt states. They moved into the cheaply built houses before the paint was dry and immediately looked around for a nearby strip mall and an all-night pizzeria. Happily for the newcomers, local entrepreneurs were right there to service their needs with almost no interference from the local planning boards. Most of the commissioners believed whole-heartedly in laissez faire, and why not? Most of them were connected either directly or indirectly to the building trades and much of the new money flowed straight into their pockets.

As a battered old red Chevy pickup parked in front of the courthouse, Jamie sighed again and turned away from the window. Tonight's meeting would probably be another exercise in futility, a big waste of time; but for the sake of the people who had voted for her, she would be there even if it meant coming back to the office afterwards. Maybe after the presentation tomorrow she could take the afternoon off to smell the flowers in her own garden.

Candace Bradshaw's house was so recently built and furnished that carpets, drapes and sofas still had that new car smell. Although it was one of the more modest models in this upscale development—only three bedrooms with two and a half baths—the master bathroom had been custom-designed to her specifications.

To reach it, one walked through a hallway lined on both sides with closets that had sliding mirrored doors. More mirrors paneled all the bathroom walls, including the walls of the walk-in shower. They even fronted the cabinets. The only touches of color were the pink-flowered lavatory, the dark rose commode, and matching floor tiles.

And Candace Bradshaw herself, of course, wrapped in a rose bath sheet.

She turned on the shower, dropped the towel to the floor, and smiled at the multiple images of her naked body. Overall, she was entitled to that smile. Poverty and hard work had kept the pounds off when she was a girl; rigorous dieting and three miles a day on her treadmill kept them off as she approached her forty-second birthday. Yes, she saw the slight drooping of her full breasts, and yes, her waist was a bit thicker than the day she traded her cherry for a gold bracelet to a dirtbag who went off to Duke and came back with his nose in the air, till she won a seat on the board of commissioners and he needed some favors.

Well, that cost him more than a gold bracelet, a bracelet that was long gone anyhow, stolen by her own pa and hocked for a gallon of Kezzie Knott's white lightning, and how Deborah Knott ever got appointed to be a judge by a Republican governor with a bootlegging Democrat for a father she would never understand. Bound to be some dirt there somewhere, Candace thought for the hundredth time, and one of these days she was going to pick up a shovel and start digging. They still had the cleaning contract for Lee and Stephenson, Deborah Knott's old law firm, and—

A small bruise on her thigh distracted Candace Bradshaw's attention. Now how did she get that? she wondered as she went back to evaluating her body. Her legs had always been too short in proportion to the rest of her body and she used to envy girls with longer legs until it dawned on her that men of power were often short and short men did not take kindly to women who towered over them. Much better to be small and cuddly. Besides, her short thighs were fairly free of cellulite and her calves were still shapely, her ankles still trim. She had been good to her body, and in turn her body had been good to her.

Very good to her.

It had given her a free and clear title to this house. It had helped make her a power in her own right. It would help her take care of that bastard who—

Her head turned alertly. Was that the sound of a door latch?

She quickly stooped for the towel and covered herself even though she was supposed to be alone in the house.

"Deanna?" she called. She had taken Dee's house key, but locked doors and drawers had never stopped her daughter. Slowed her down, maybe, but never stopped her. Exasperation tinged her voice. "Is that you?"

Silence.

She walked past the mirrored closets, through her bedroom and out into the hall.

"Dee?"

No answer and a quick look through a front window did not show Dee's car parked on the circular drive outside.

She shrugged and returned to the bathroom. Hot water from three shower heads had begun to steam up the mirrors. She stepped into the stall, lifted her oval face to the needle-fine spray like a sunflower lifting to the sun, and sighed with happiness as water sluiced down her body, pulsating to the rhythm of her heartbeats.

This was her favorite place in the house and it was not unusual for her to shower twice a day. In periods of stress, three times.

Thank god there aren't any calories in water, she thought.

She could win the lottery tomorrow, the party could nominate her to run for governor, and nothing—*nothing!—would give her the same satisfaction as knowing she could have hot water at the turn of a tap, day or night.*

Growing up in a dilapidated trailer with a broken water heater that was never replaced, the only way to get hot water was if she heated it on the kitchen stove. Even then, she would often come back with a final kettle to find her mother sitting in the chipped and rust-stained bathtub she had so laboriously filled. "Well, hell, Miss Prissy-pants. What's your problem? When I was your age, the only thing we had was an old tin washtub and five or six of us would have to use the same water. It'd be pure black by the time it was my turn. You're lucky you got a tub big enough to wallow around in, Candy, and it ain't like I'm all that dirty or gonna pee in the water like my brothers did."

For a moment, she almost wished her parents could see her now. That she could show them how far she had come on her own with no help from them. Admittedly, it was only a fleeting wish. The happiest day of her life was when word came that Macon and Alice Wells had died in a fiery car crash, and she was suddenly free to reinvent herself, to legally change her name to Candace and call herself that instead of the Candy on her birth certificate. Not that she could ever pretend that she came from something more than the trashiest trailer park in Colleton County. The communal memory was too long to forget that her mother was a whore and her father a shiftless drunk. All the same, their ashes were now scattered to the four winds and they could never again embarrass her by showing up at her work or by calling her to come bail them out of jail.

She reached for the bar of soap.

Cake of soap, not bar, she reminded herself as she lathered her body in rose-scented suds. Handmade from organic goat milk. And what would Ma have made of paying five dollars for goat soap?

Or twenty dollars for a bottle of herbal shampoo?

She rinsed her hair, worked a handful of fragrant conditioner into each long chestnut tress that was artfully streaked with gold every five weeks at the best hairdresser in Dobbs, then rinsed again. Even when every trace of soap, shampoo and conditioner was gone, she continued to stand under the pulsing water. She cupped her hands beneath her breasts and lifted them up to the water till the nipples hardened. It was as if they were caressed by a lover's gentle hands, an undemanding lover whose only desire was to pleasure her and not himself. Unlike the brutish pawings she had endured to get where she was today, each pulse was a soft pat that calmed her nerves and suffused her senses with a feeling of well-being.

At last, she reluctantly turned off the taps and toweled her body and hair dry. She smoothed scented lotion on her skin; and when she had finished making up her face, she styled her hair with a hand dryer and a brush until it hung sleek and shining halfway down her back.

It vaguely worried her that women were advised to cut their hair shorter as they grew older, but she figured she had at least another six or eight years before she had to make that decision. Men liked long sexy hair and salesclerks still thought that she and Dee were sisters. Indeed, someone had recently taken a quick look at Dee's hungover pasty face and baggy eyes and mistakenly assumed that Dee was the mother and she the daughter.

Candace smiled at the memory of Dee's reaction to that.

Satisfied with her looks, she strolled over to the closet and pulled out a favorite spring dress. The white top was a respectable short-sleeved shirt with tiny pearl buttons and a boat collar cut low enough that when she leaned forward to share a confidential aside with one of her fellow board members, he could get a nice glimpse of cleavage. The skirt was green with white polka dots and cut on the bias so that it made a flirty flare at the hemline, a hemline so short that it added an illusion of length to her legs.

The dress made her feel flirty herself and would probably tempt old Harvey Underwood into patting her knees at the board meeting tonight.

As long as his hand stops at my knees and doesn't try to slide on up under my skirt, she thought. If it got her his vote against the planning board's recommendations, what did she care?

Let Jamie Jacobson fume and make sarcastic highfaluting remarks that half the time nobody could understand. She'd teach that long-legged bitch a few lessons about trying to take on Candace Bradshaw.

She carried the dress on into her bedroom and laid it on the bed. As she turned to a dresser for lingerie, a voice said, "Very nice, Candy."

"Don't call me Candy," she snapped as she reached for

a robe to cover her nakedness. "And what the hell are you doing here?"

"I came to see you. Although I didn't expect to see quite this much of you.

"How did you get in?"

"You must have left the door unlocked."

Candace gave an unladylike snort of derision. "Not hardly likely. What do you want?"

"Nothing that's not well within your abilities."

Candace flushed, knowing this was a dig at her lack of education. Okay, so she didn't go to college. Big damn deal. Most of the county commissioners had degrees from State or Carolina and who was their chair? And who ran Colleton County's largest managerial service?

"What's that?" she asked as the other handed her a sheet of paper.

"What do you care? It's a little late to go reading what you're told to sign. Just copy it on your pretty notepaper, okay?"

Candace Bradshaw's eyes widened as she read the few short sentences typed on the paper. "'I take full responsibility for my greediness'? 'I apologize to everybody in the county who trusted me'? You're crazy if you think I'll write anything like this. Get the hell out of my house and stay out or I'll—"

Her voice broke off at the sudden appearance of a small pistol. "You wouldn't dare!"

"No?" A pull of the trigger, a soft *pfft*, and a bullet buried itself in the pile rug next to her bare feet.

Candace's eyes widened in fear. "My God! You *are* crazy."

"Not crazy enough to go to jail because you messed up."

"*Me?* You're the one who said nobody would ever find out."

"And they wouldn't have if you hadn't been so greedy that they've started noticing."

Appalled, Candace listened as the facts were laid out—the questions that were starting to be asked, the people who were doing the asking.

Her real desk and computer were in the third bedroom that she had furnished as a home office, but a jerk of the pistol directed her over to the dainty desk where she wrote personal notes and cards.

It took only a moment or two to copy the typescript she had been handed.

To whom it may concern:

I have used my position to enrich myself and some of my friends. I acted alone though and I take full responsibility for my greediness. I am sincerely ashamed and I apologize to everyone in Colleton County who trusted me with their well-being.

When she finished, she signed it Candace Bradshaw with an angry flourish. "There! Satisfied?"

"Not quite. Not till it's safely locked away."

"I'll tell them you made me write it," she spat out.

"Won't matter. It'll be your word against mine, Candy."

"Don't call me Candy. And put down my robe!"

"Relax, *Candace*. I could ask you to give me your word that you wouldn't call Sheriff Poole and have me arrested before I can put your copy in a safe place and destroy the original, but we both know how much your word's worth.

I think I'd rather tie you up for a while, give you time to think things over and realize that anything you say about me will only make people believe it was all your doing."

With that pistol aimed at her chest, Candace stood up as instructed and draped the second robe over her shoulders backwards so that her arms were pinned to her sides and held almost immobile when the sash and the empty sleeves were tied in back.

All the while, her mind was racing furiously, weighing her options. The sash wasn't too tight and there was a little slack inside the second robe. It wouldn't be too hard to wriggle free. And then? If things really were coming unraveled, there had to be a way out of this mess. She'd call Cam. He'd help her find a way to throw all the blame on—

Abruptly, something looped her throat. There was a sudden tightening, a constriction that left her unable to breathe. Frantically, she struggled to jerk away, but the pressure increased inexorably.

No way to use her arms or hands to yank it away from her neck. In fear and rage, she sank to her knees and butted backwards with her head, her body arching and twisting to free herself, to take one deep life-saving breath. A quick lunge forward and she felt the cord loosen. For one second, she could almost breathe again.

Oh please oh please oh please—

And then the pressure was back. A frantic twist and something tore in her throat. Searing pain lanced across her dying brain and sparked a last incoherent thought of water...hot water ...

If you or someone you know
wants to improve their reading skills,
call the Literacy Help Line.
Reading...
WORDS ARE YOUR WHEELS
1-800-228-8813